"How many men you gonna kill tonight, Red?" the young outlaw asked as Colter walked back into the jailhouse.

"As many as it takes, I reckon."

"Hey, your name ain't Billy the Kid, is it? I never heard of the Kid sportin' a nasty scar on his face, though, less'n he ran into a brandin' iron of late."

Colter pulled one of the sandwiches out of his coat pocket and thrust it through the bar. Billy looked at it, surprised. "Pete Simon's free lunch, eh?" He chuckled and took the sandwich like a hungry though vaguely suspicious dog. "Thanks, Red. I thought I was gonna have to stomp a rat."

Colter began stoking the wood stove. Sitting back on his cot and devouring the sandwich hungrily, Billy said, "I could hear the pops o' them pistols way over here. You get all of 'em?"

"Yep."

"Christ!" Billy tried to whistle, but he only spat bread and meat. "Who taught you to shoot, anyways, Red?"

"Men like them."

continued . . .

MORE PRAISE FOR THE
NOVELS OF FRANK LESLIE

BAD JUSTICE

Frank Leslie

A SIGNET BOOK

SIGNET
Published by the Penguin Group
Penguin Group (USA) Inc., 375 Hudson Street,
New York, New York 10014, USA

USA | Canada | UK | Ireland | Australia
New Zealand | India | South Africa | China

Penguin Books Ltd., Registered Offices:
80 Strand, London WC2R 0RL, England
For more information about the Penguin Group visit penguin.com.

First published by Signet, an imprint of New American Library,
a division of Penguin Group (USA) Inc.

First Printing, April 2003

ISBN 978-0-451-41622-3

Printed in the United States of America
10 9 8 7 6 5 4 3 2 1

PUBLISHER'S NOTE
This is a work of fiction. Names, characters, places, and incidents either are the
product of the author's imagination or are used fictitiously, and any resemblance
to actual persons, living or dead, business establishments, events, or locales is
entirely coincidental.

The publisher does not have any control over and does not assume any
responsibility for author or third-party Web sites or their content.

ALWAYS LEARNING   **PEARSON**

In memory of my second mother, LaVerne

Chapter 1

"That was wonderful, Bill," said the girl, Chloe, flushed and breathless, as she lay back against her pillow.

"Shut up."

"Yes, Bill," the girl said, wincing beneath the stinging verbal lash, though Rondo had only muttered it under his breath.

Bill Rondo, Sheriff of Sapinero, Colorado Territory, hauled himself up on his elbows and dragged his near-useless legs to the edge of the bed. He rolled onto his right side and with his left hand grabbed an uncorked bottle off a table.

He himself was breathless and sweaty. He'd given the girl a hell of a workout. If only he'd gained more satisfaction from the union.

And caused her to . . .

It used to be he could please a woman.

Not that he really cared that he hadn't pleased

this one. He knew that Chloe had only pretended to enjoy the coupling, fearing Rondo's notorious temper. What whore ever enjoyed a tumble? It was business for them.

But Rondo had paid Jimmy Kearns, the girl's pimp and sole proprietor of the Dancing Tiger, Sapinero's most prominent bagnio, a pretty penny for some satisfaction, and what he had gotten instead was frustration and a vague ache in his loins.

Not that it was the whore's fault. She was a young, well set-up girl with frizzy blond hair and a plump, waifish face with china blue eyes and fine white teeth. A complete set, too. She had just enough flesh on her so a man knew he'd mounted a real girl and not a rag doll but not so much he felt he was hammering away at a slab of warm lard.

Rondo tipped the bottle back, letting the warm liquid roll down his throat, skid across his tonsils like hot chili peppers, and then plunge into his belly. It started a warm fire down there that spread up into his brain, soothing the shame and frustration he felt for being only half a man anymore—one whose loins worked only half again as well as his crippled legs. Half again as well as nothing was just enough to make him desire it but not quite enough to attain full pleasure from it.

"We can rest awhile, Bill," said the girl in her simpering voice, placing a gentle hand on his arm. "We can go again when you're ready. I just hate it that—"

Rondo looked at her over his shoulder. The girl brought her lips together. Her pale, plump, doll-like face turned white as porcelain.

Slowly, she removed her hand from Rondo's arm. Trepidation glazed her eyes, and she swallowed, probably remembering what had happened to another whore in this same bagnio only two months ago, when in a drunken rage Rondo had broken a whiskey bottle over the edge of a marble washstand and swiped it across the poor girl's neck, nearly cutting her head clean off her shoulders.

Yep, that's what this girl was remembering, all right. Rondo could see that dark recollection in little Chloe's eyes. The crib had looked like a butcher shop. Blood had splattered as high as the ceiling and as far away as the door.

"Nothing to be proud of, Bill," Rondo silently admonished himself. "Killing an innocent doxy just because your pecker worked little better than your legs . . ." But he still couldn't suppress the evil grin that stretched his mouth, lifting the nasty scar on his face to just beneath his left eye.

He might not have given himself or Chloe any carnal satisfaction, but he had put the fear of God into her, and that was something, anyway. As she rested her head back against her pillow once more, Rondo took another deep pull from the bottle before setting it back on the table. Then he reached down with his left hand and swung his near-useless legs off the side of the bed, dropping his bare feet to the floor.

He couldn't feel the thick rug beneath his feet. He could feel a very slight sensation down there, like a feather duster brushed against his soles, but that was all. In his legs he could occasionally feel a dull ache, and he could put some weight on them, but for all intents and purposes, the kid who had shot him up, turned his bones to gravel—one Colter Farrow— had pretty much rendered him half a man in many more ways than one.

After he'd shot him, the kid had burned into Rondo's face the same S brand that Rondo had burned into his . . . .

Just deserts, some would say. For Rondo it was the final insult and a loan that was now overdue—one that would one day be paid off most handsomely when a bounty man hunting the two-thousand-dollar reward that Rondo had placed on the kid's head brought that head back to Sapinero atop the redhead's shoulders.

So that Rondo could remove it in his own special way himself.

Only after he'd had his fill of the younker's screams, that is.

That thought caused the S to climb up higher on the sheriff's craggy face again, and for his thick, brushy, salt-and-pepper mustache to run up hard against his long, wedge-shaped nose. He chuckled.

Behind him, young Chloe said in her high, nasal voice that betrayed a note of relief, "Feelin' better about things, hon?"

"Yeah," Rondo said, preoccupying himself with the image of a broken bottle cleaving the young saddle tramp's head off in front of the entire town and half the county of Sapinero. "Yeah, I'm feelin' better, Chloe. But only marginally so."

"You want another tumble?"

Rondo was looking around the room at his scattered clothes and his wheelchair sitting in a corner. The anger returned now, as though he'd sat on a pair of bricks overheated in a snapping fire. What a fool he always made of himself, getting dressed in front of these whores whom he frequented because he had no other way besides whiskey of trying to make himself feel better until he got the chance to avenge his once-handsome face and his broken body.

"No, I reckon not," he said feebly, brushing his fingers across the knotted scar that always made the whores look askance when he was staring down at them from inches away. "But I reckon you can help me climb back into my duds and into that damned chariot."

"Of course I will, hon," Chloe said, throwing the covers back.

"And you can stop callin' me *hon*!"

"Of course, Mr. Rondo . . . *Sheriff*!"

When Rondo had endured the humiliation of having the whore dress him while he sat like a withered old man at the edge of the bed, nursing the bottle, and help him into his chair, he took some satisfaction in ordering Chloe to roll him a quirley and watching her perform the chore with fear-painted cheeks and shaking fingers.

"There!" she intoned, relieved, when she'd licked it closed and stuck it between Rondo's waiting lips. "Just how you like it, Sheriff!"

She scratched a match to life on the arm of his wheelchair, and touched the flame to the quirley. He drew the smoke into his lungs and blew it out into the neatly kept whore's room papered and carpeted in red and smelling like the incense she perfumed the air with.

"Shall I help you downstairs?"

"I'll call Rodney." Rondo adjusted the brown Stetson on his head, ran a hand down his string tie, and brushed a hand across the Colt he kept holstered on his right hip. He was still the sheriff of Sapinero, by God, and while his three deputies did most of the heavy lifting, he wasn't about to go around unarmed.

Sucking the quirley, he jerked his chin at the door.

Chloe rushed to open it, almost tripping over her own bare feet as she stepped back out of his way, and he wheeled himself out into the hall.

"Bye, Sheriff!"

"Till next time, Chloe," he growled, the quirley smoldering between his lips as he turned the chair hard right and began rolling himself along the hall toward the stairs, his corked bottle propped between him and the chair arm.

He rolled past doors behind which women moaned and men grunted or stumbled around, dressing or undressing. Ahead, the raucous sounds of Friday night revelry—the Box-Bar-B boys were in town— rose up the stairs on wings of churning tobacco smoke. Rondo could feel the vibration through his chair—with the parts of him that could still feel any-thing.

At the top of the broad, carpeted stairs, he swung the chair to face down into the bustling drinking hall. Because of the heavy smoke fog aglow from lanterns and bracket lamps and the large fire roaring in the fieldstone hearth, Rondo couldn't see much but jos-tling figures. The roar of conversations and laughter was continuous, stitched with the clicks of Jimmy Kearns's roulette wheels and punctuated by the rib-ald laughter and shrill, lusty shrieks of Kearns's comely whores—the best in southern Colorado.

Olden Boneswag, who doubled as a barber, was playing his piano in his usual loud, off-key way.

Rondo couldn't see Kearns's half-wit swamper,

Rodney Charles, the kid whose duty it was—in addition to sweeping, mopping, clearing tables, and cleaning spittoons—to help Rondo up and down the stairs in his chariot.

Rondo called the kid's name several times, but his scratchy voice, as weak as everything else about him, couldn't penetrate the cacophony swelling up from below. It was like screaming at a train roaring by only ten feet away.

The crippled sheriff of Sapinero puffed the quirley and scowled down into that broiling maelstrom, a fury building in him, swelling his eyes and puffing his red cheeks. He felt ignored, left out, forgotten about.

He felt not only impotent but weak and feeble.

Why wasn't that cork-headed kid waiting near the bottom of the stairs, damn his hide?

Never mind. Rondo could wheel himself down the stairs. His arms were strong enough for that. He wasn't entirely useless.

He took another pull from the bottle, corked it, returned the quirley to his teeth, and wheeled himself forward, watching that first step slide toward him, the others dropping off steeply below it, descending into the smoky haze. Gritting his teeth and mangling the quirley, Rondo eased himself over the top of the stairs and down to the first step with a jolt and a thud cushioned by the thick purple carpet trimmed with wine-red roses.

A whole damn field of red roses flowed down the stairs away from him and into that smoky perdition below. They were a maze, confusing him, seeming to rise out of that purple dirt to impede his way.

Rondo gritted his teeth again as he dropped

down to the next step with a jolting thud that was barely audible above the crowd's roar and the deafening, tinny patter of Olden Boneswag's piano.

His large brown hands wrapped tight around the top of the chariot's wheels, Rondo eased the chair down another step.

Another.

And another.

Thump. Thump. Thump. Thump.

And then his gradually weakening arms gave out.

"Hellfire!"

Gravity gave the chariot a savage push from behind.

Thump! Thump! Thump! Thump!

To Rondo's ears, the wheels sounded like the triggering of a Gatling gun as they struck the next four steps before that capricious bitch, Providence, swung the chair sharply left and turned it over, spilling Rondo, his quirley, and his corked bottle of whiskey into the roses sprouting up from the purple carpet peppered with cigarette burns and holes gouged by boot spurs.

Rondo cried out weakly as he rolled, turned a forward somersault, and then continued rolling, the bottle and his hat bouncing right along with him, the chair batting him brutally about the head, back, and shoulders. When he struck the saloon floor, the chair gave him one more parting whack as it bounced over him and flew up against a table.

Rondo lay still for a moment, staring at the purple carpeting with its infernal red roses. Gradually, the bells tolling in his head eased enough that he could hear the hush that had suddenly dropped over the room.

Then a girl slapped a hand to her near-naked bosoms and cried, *"Sheriff Rondo!"*

Boots thumped. Rondo felt the vibration of half a dozen men stomping toward him. He ground an elbow into the floor and used it to roll himself onto his back.

"Sheriff, you all right?" asked a man whom Rondo recognized as one of the Box-Bar-B boys bending over to scrutinize the crippled lawman, who lay sprawled like a landed fish at the bottom of the stairs.

Rondo cursed loudly and profusely. Several men swarmed around him, grabbing at his arms to lift him. But when he saw the string-bean moron, Rodney, push through the crowd to stare at him goggle-eyed, Rondo jerked his arms away and sank back against the stairs.

"Sheriff," the kid cried, his thick, curly blond hair tumbling down from his shabby bowler hat, "why didn't you tell me you was ready to come down? I'd have come and fetched ya!"

Rondo drew his Colt .45 from the holster on his right hip and shot the kid four times through his heart.

Chapter 2

Rodney blew straight back onto a table that had been recently vacated by four poker players. Bottles, shot glasses, scrip, specie, and playing cards flew in all directions.

The kid jerked several times, blood pumping from the four holes in his chest, and lay still.

A silence like that over a graveyard at midnight hung over the saloon. All eyes were on Rondo, who still held his Colt .45 straight out from his chest, smoke curling from the barrel. He lay back against the stairs, lips stretched back from his teeth, eyes nearly bulging from their sockets.

"Teach you to be a damn fool," the sheriff growled in the heavy, smoky silence.

"Holy shit!" someone whispered somewhere to Rondo's right.

Jimmy Kearns walked out from behind his

horseshoe-shaped bar on Rondo's left. He was a big, large-gutted man in a long green apron, with a thick bush of curly red hair and muttonchop whiskers of the same color. He looked at the blond-headed kid staring wide-eyed at the ceiling. Rodney's mouth was still wide from his final death scream.

"Christalmighty, Bill," Kearns said in his heavy Irish accent. "What's the bloody meanin' of this— shootin' the *idiot?*"

Rondo slid his Colt toward Kearns and clicked the hammer back loudly in the heavy silence. He narrowed one eye as he planted a bead on the saloon owner's forehead. Kearns's fat, ruddy face blanched, and he took one step back. His lips parted. Fear sharpened his eyes.

No one said anything. It was so quiet now that, beneath the crackling of the flames in the great stone hearth, Rondo could hear a single horseback rider pass in the street fronting the saloon. The horse blew and shook its head; Rondo could hear the bridle rattling against its teeth.

He kept his eyes on the fear-sharp eyes of Kearns, whose face was drawn taut, awaiting the bullet.

Finally, Rondo smiled, pleased with the fear he'd stirred in his old friend. He lifted the Colt's barrel, depressed the hammer, and laughed as though it had all been a joke. "Just foolin' with ya, Jimmy. I couldn't shoot you—now, could I? After all we been through? Who'd sell me whiskey and provide me with girls?"

The look on Kearns's face said the barman wasn't so sure the sheriff wouldn't shoot him. Maybe not a few years ago, before Rondo's run-in with the red-headed kid from the Lunatic Mountains. But not now. There'd been too much whiskey since that fateful day when Rondo had nearly died, and maybe it would have been best for the entire county if he had.

After what Rondo had done to little Patty, Kearns knew the sheriff was capable of anything.

Rondo holstered the weapon and looked at two men standing nearby, both of whom appeared to be holding their breath.

"Weaver, Finlay—give me a hand back into the ole chariot, will you?"

Ralph Weaver and Mort Finlay, shop owners in Sapinero, hurried forward and helped the sheriff into his wheelchair. Most of Kearns's clientele were still standing around, looking at the dead kid on the table, when a man's voice yelled from the front of the saloon, "What the hell's all the shootin' about?"

Rondo had just set his hat on his head when, looking toward the front of the room, he saw one of his deputies, Albert Price, walk slowly toward the table on which Rodney Charles lay. Price was a big, potbellied man in ragged cowpuncher's garb, because that's what he'd been when Rondo had given him the job as deputy. Price was mulish and downright belligerent, and that's just how Rondo liked the men who worked for him.

Price also kissed Rondo's ass every chance he got, and that was another requirement of the job.

Rondo yelled, "Albert, wheel me home. I've had my fill of this overpriced sud shop for one evening!"

Rondo was wheeling through the crowd, which parted for him quickly, and made his way toward the front of the room. His neck ached and one arm had been wrenched, but he thought he'd weathered the tumble he'd taken without serious injury.

"Didn't know you was here, boss." Price had stopped when he'd seen Rondo coming. The big, unshaven deputy was rising on his boot toes to stare over the crowd at the table on which the kid lay. "Say, isn't that . . . ?"

"Rodney Charles is deadern' last year's Christmas goose," Rondo growled, still sore about the kid's leaving him to make his way down the stairs alone. Rondo might have been killed! "My gift to McGinty. I'm tired, Albert. Dead-dog tired!"

McGinty was the local undertaker.

"You got it, boss!" Price slung his shotgun back behind his shoulder to let it dangle down his back by its leather lanyard, and hurried to grab the handles extending off the back of Rondo's chair.

When they were outside and Price was easing Rondo's chair down the saloon's front porch steps, the deputy said, "Two deputy U.S. marshals was here to see you earlier, boss."

"Oh? What about?"

Price pushed the sheriff out past the horses tied to the hitch racks fronting the saloon and then angled him toward the far side of the street, en route to Rondo's shack on the northern edge of Sapinero. Rondo buttoned his black frock coat against the October chill. Wood smoke spiced the air. His and Price's breaths frosted in the dark air before them.

"They said they'd gotten word that that kid who did you so wrong a couple years ago—you know, that scrawny redhead from up in the Lunies—was seen in the territory early last week. He was stayin' at some roadhouse over near Walsenburg. Leastways, that's what the roadhouse owner told the constable, who then told it to the federal boys when they rode through town a couple days later."

"Well, I'll be goddamned!" Rondo's voice quavered as Price wheeled him over the ruts, parallel to the boardwalks running along the main street's north side. "They got any idea where he is now?"

"They said they was gonna follow up a lead over at Skunk Creek and then ride back here, hopefully before sunset, but that was several hours ago now. They said it prob'ly wasn't him at all. You know how everybody's been watchin' for him around here, since you put that big reward on his head. They figure it's just another roadhouse owner's blarney. Just the same, they said for me to tell you to watch your back."

As Price steered him down a cross street, heading north, Rondo thought about the information. A lot of folks had said they'd seen Colter Farrow in the area over the past few years. But all those "Colter Farrows" had been mere saddle tramps or raggedy-heeled cowpunchers—one had even been a stagecoach shotgun rider—with hair that *might possibly* be called red in a pinch, though most had been brown-haired or even dark blond. Some had been marked with scars of a kind, though two or three had merely been marked by large pimples or moles, and one had no scar at all but an eye patch, though he was riding a coyote dun, like the one Farrow was known to straddle.

None whom Rondo had investigated had anything like the S that Rondo's quarry wore and that, ironically, Rondo wore himself. (Don't anyone say God didn't have a sense of humor. . . .)

The last scrap of information that had made its way to Bill Rondo had entailed a sighting of the kid in Mexico a good hundred or so miles south of the border in Sonora. That had made sense to Rondo. He'd heard that Farrow, no doubt out of necessity, had become a gunman of some repute over the years since he'd scarred and crippled the sheriff of Sapinero. He was wisely keeping his distance not only from Sapinero and his home ranch in the Lunatic Mountains, which Rondo had kept a close eye on for several months just after the dustup that had maimed and scarred him, but from the entire territory.

The kid returning here wouldn't make sense. That'd be like a jackrabbit burrowing with rattlesnakes, a cow heading for the slaughterhouse.

No, the roadhouse owner in Walsenburg was probably seeing Jesse James in every steely-eyed drifter who rode through town. Just another cock-and-bull story, wasting the federal boys' time.

Price wheeled Rondo into the shaggy outskirts of Sapinero and into the yard of his run-down, story-and-a-half, slant-roofed house that badly needed fresh paint. Rondo had bought the place from an old prospector who'd once worked a claim on the Cimarron River that flowed behind it, and added an extra room though he'd never gotten around to painting it or the rest of the tumbledown shack. An old chicken coop stood beside it, but Rondo had knocked out three walls and used it for a stable and a hay crib until he'd no longer been able to straddle a horse and thus had sold his steeldust to a local livery barn.

The place was dark and quiet, its gray walls hunched, pale as bones, in the chill, moonless night. Bald hills rose beyond it and the stream, crowned with stars.

It was a lonely damn place for a crippled man to live without benefit of female company. But Rondo had never gotten around to getting married before the redheaded demon from the Lunatic Mountains had scarred and crippled him. It was a safe bet he never would now.

No woman wanted an ugly cripple.

Likely till the end of his days, Rondo would lie with whores and hope to gain some satisfaction maybe once or twice a month, if he was lucky, spilling his sickly seed at Jimmy Kearns's place for two dollars a romp.

Pathetic damn life.

But that kid's note was coming due. Sooner or later, a bounty hunter would haul his scrawny, carrot-topped countenance into Sapinero, and Rondo would get his self-respect back if not the full use of his legs and pecker.

Price wheeled the sheriff across the barren yard—barren, that is, except for trash, tumbleweeds, and several patches of prickly pear—and up the ramp he'd had Price build over his steps. Rondo didn't have a lock for his plank door, so Price merely tripped the steel latch, gave the door a kick, and backed over the threshold and inside, pulling the chair over the jamb.

He turned Rondo around. The place was dark. It smelled of mouse shit, of the split pine logs piled on the floor beside the range, and old potatoes, though Rondo didn't do much cooking. The range lay to the right and against the opposite wall. A crude wooden table fronted it. There was a water barrel in the corner near the table, and a curtained doorway beyond which Rondo slept now that he could no longer get upstairs by himself.

"Pretty damn dark in here," Price said behind Rondo. "You want I should check it out?"

Rondo knew the deputy was thinking of Colter

Farrow. Under normal circumstances, Rondo wouldn't have given the kid a second thought. But in his vulnerable state, a vague apprehension dragged cold fingers across the back of his neck.

"Take a look upstairs," Rondo said, feeling foolish but not letting that leach into his voice.

When he lost the respect of the town and the men who worked for him, he'd be like an old wolf at the mercy of the pack.

Price lit the hurricane lantern on the table and walked into the shadows beyond the kitchen, the lamp flickering before him and casting far more shadows than light. He headed up the back stairs to the cramped second story, and the lamp's wan glow edged up the wall as he went. In the meantime, Rondo lit a candle and, holding the candle in his teeth, wheeled himself past the table.

He brushed the curtain away from the door and peered into his small bedroom outfitted with a cot and two chairs, a rifle leaning in a corner. One of the chairs had no back; this he used for a table near the cot. There were two boxes of cartridges on it, a pocket watch, a bottle, and a water glass.

An oval tintype of his late mother hung from a nail over the cot.

The room was empty.

Rondo wheeled himself around and over to the range just as Price's footsteps thumped on the creaky stairs angling up over the range. Presently, as Rondo began building a fire in the range, Price appeared and set the lamp on the table.

"Nothin'."

"Figured as much," Rondo said, tossing some kindling through the open stove door. "Get on back to your rounds, Albert. Who else is on duty tonight?"

"Creighton."

"Well, you an' Creighton stay on your toes. Don't let me hear you was caught catnappin' at your desks or playin' grabby-pants in one of the cells, hear?"

Price chuckled. "You got it, Sheriff. Anything else I can do for you before I go?"

"Get back to work, Albert. Make sure Halk Avery locked the door to his haberdashery. He's been forgettin' lately, since that seizure he had out in his privy a few weeks ago. Some damn half-breed's liable to rob him blind, and he'll be blamin' us."

"I done got the note to do that in my pocket right here, Sheriff." Price touched his vest. "Good night, then."

The deputy went out.

Rondo wheeled himself back a few feet to the box where he kept old newspapers. He plucked one off the pile, balled it up, and shoved it through the open stove door. He shoved in a couple more feather sticks and then he ripped a strip from another newspaper and lit it with a stove match. He let the flame build, chewing the paper down toward his hand, before thrusting it through the door with a soft *whoosh*.

There was another hollow *whoosh* as the kindling took. When a sizeable fire was burning in the firebox, he added a couple of small piñon logs. Leaving the door open, he backed toward the table, then stopped and, enjoying the fire's warmth, plucked the cork from his bottle.

The hair under his shirt collar pricked.

A cold hand was pressed to the small of his back. He felt a ghostly presence. In the corner of his left eye loomed a slender black shadow—one capped with the silhouette of a hat.

He froze, swung toward the table.

"Christ!"

A cold fist clutched his heart, making it kick like a branded calf. He leaned back in his chair, away from the black, hatted visage sitting on the far side of the table, near the door.

Sitting there as though it had been sitting there the whole damn time.

"Long time no see, Sheriff Rondo," said Colter Farrow.

Chapter 3

Rondo stared at the shadowy figure sitting across the table. Long hair fell from beneath the tobacco brown Stetson—copper red hair touched by the wan lamplight and the fire dancing in the stove behind Rondo.

The face beneath the hat was long and pale, with a straight nose, a flame-shaped chin. A dark S shone on the left cheek. It was a lightly freckled face, touched by the sun and wind. Still young but older than the one Rondo remembered searing the iron into, as though the scar itself had leached into the rest of the skin, crinkling it faintly at the eye corners and across the forehead.

Not a boy anymore was Colter Farrow. A young man. Maybe not so young, judging by the hard, shrewd eyes riveted on Rondo. The kid's mouth was a knife slash across the bottom of his clean-shaven face.

Rondo sucked a sharp breath, trying to calm himself against the fear-acid churning through his veins. "How in the hell did you get in here?" He knew, but in his exasperation it was the only thing he could think of to say.

"You're a right trusting man, Sheriff. Door's open." The redhead's voice was irritatingly mild, though the light brown eyes remained hard. He had a revolver on the table before him, near his left hand. Yes, he was left-handed. For some reason, Rondo remembered that. The kid was not touching the old Remington, and it was not aimed at Rondo, but it seemed all the more menacing for both those things.

Rondo's own hand fluttered up near the grips of his Colt, but the kid's revolver and the kid's hard, expressionless eyes kept him from drawing the weapon.

Rondo had felt damn vulnerable over the past few years, being confined to the old wooden chariot, but this was a new one even on him. He felt like an insect skewered on a child's needle. Fear raged in him. He was going to die. This was it. Oh, Christ— this was the end of the road.

He couldn't even call up any fury despite the presence of the person who'd shattered his legs and ruined his body and his life sitting right across from him, not ten feet away. The raw, animal fear was an all-powerful thing inside him.

"What the hell you want, kid?" The sheriff hated the quiver he heard in his voice, the tight knot he felt in his throat, the wash of tears threatening to ooze from his eyes. "H-haven't . . . haven't you done enough to me? *Look at me!*"

His voice cracked on that last, and he sniffed back a tear.

"You damn coward," the kid said tonelessly.

"What?"

"Look at you. Why don't you pull that hog leg? Go ahead, jerk iron." The kid's voice was so mild that he could have been giving confession. "Here— I'll make it easy for you."

Farrow removed his pistol from the table. As he sat back in his chair, he slid his left hand across his belly, and there was the soft snick of the Remington sliding into its scabbard on his right hip.

"There. Now we're startin' even."

Rondo just stared at him, frozen. His heart jerked and quivered until he thought it would tear free of its moorings.

"You were brave enough a few years ago," Colter said, his voice acquiring a faint, brittle edge now. "Brave enough when you were sided by your deputies, that is, to kill Trace Cassidy and nail him to the box of his own supply wagon and send him home to us, his family, in the Loonies. Half eaten by crows."

The kid's nostrils flared. His jaw drew taut.

"Brave enough with your deputies to bushwhack me, pin me down, and put this tattoo on my face, the same one I gave you later, you rotten bastard. Brave enough to put a two-thousand-dollar bounty on my head so I can't never go home again!

"Go ahead!" the kid shouted suddenly, bounding up out of his chair, the chair flying back behind him to bounce off the wall. "Pull iron or die with your hands empty, you old bastard!"

"Haven't you done enough?" Rondo bellowed, burying his scarred face in his hands. "You *crippled* me!"

He leaned forward in his chair and bawled into

his hands as loudly as a young child with a full load in its drawers.

Colter Farrow stared across the table at the pathetic creature slumped forward in his chair, weeping into his hands.

Colter felt no sympathy for the old killer. True, Colter had scarred him and crippled him, but only after Rondo had tortured and murdered Colter's foster father, Trace Cassidy, and burned the S into Colter's left cheek before he'd tried to finish Colter with a double-barreled shotgun.

Colter had shot the man through his arms and legs. Obviously, the shots to the legs had done the most damage. And then he'd given Rondo the same brand that the lunatic lawman had burned into Colter's face—the mark of "Sapinero." It had been Rondo's infamously savage way of marking his enemies—the men he didn't want to see in the town he considered his own.

Well, now Rondo had one, too. And two shattered legs. Colter regretted none of what he'd done to Rondo. His only mistake had been in not killing the man but allowing him to live to place that two-thousand-dollar bounty on Colter's head. That had haunted the rangy, redheaded ex-cowpuncher and horse-breaker for the past three years.

In that time, he'd been forced to become a gunman of some repute.

The bounty had kept him from returning to the ranch up in the Lunatic Mountains where his foster family lived—Ruth and the kids, Colter's half brother and half sister, David and Little May. The children were probably not so little anymore. He wanted to see Marianna Claymore again, too. Marianna had been his girl and they'd intended to be married before Rondo had killed Trace and sent him home crucified to the bed of his own freight wagon, and Ruth had sent Colter to avenge her husband.

That was the way things were done in the Lunatic Mountains. Men fought and died for their kin in much the same way they'd done in the Appalachians, which was where most of the Lunatic Mountain settlers hailed from.

Colter had heard rumors that in the three years since he'd been gone, his girl, Marianna, had married another, which was understandable. Marianna would be a woman now. Still, he'd like to see her again. For old times' sake, if nothing else, and to satisfy his bittersweet, masochistic urge to see what all he'd missed. All that Bill Rondo had stolen from him.

Marianna probably had a child or two by now. Children who could have been Colter's . . .

"How 'bout if I just finish you?" Colter asked Rondo now. "Put you out of your misery."

"Go ahead!" Rondo cried, lifting his head and flashing his wet eyes at Colter. "You've taken everything else from me. Might as well take my life, too!"

"No." Colter shook his head. "I didn't take half of what you took from me. And I didn't make you a hunted man, either . . . till now. But I'm not gonna kill you, Rondo. I didn't before because I wanted you to live as half a man, and I don't see any reason to put an end to your misery now. Not when I see what a good job I did."

Rondo blinked. "If you ain't here to kill me, Red, then what in hell do you want?"

Colter dug into a pocket of his hickory shirt and

slapped a folded sheet of paper onto the table. Rondo looked at it, then wheeled forward and plucked it off the table. He unfolded it, read it, and scowled curiously up at Colter.

"One of my 'wanted' circulars. So what?"

Colter reached into a pocket of his denim jacket and tossed a pencil stub onto the table. It rolled around and came to rest against an edge of one of the table's uneven planks.

"I want you to write a note on the back of that circular. Address it to the managing editor of the *Rocky Mountain News* in Denver. Tell him how you're rescinding the bounty on my head."

"You're loco," Rondo said. "You think bounty hunters read the paper?"

"No, but them folks who do will spread the word."

"You're still loco. Or a prime fool. I could easily put another one . . ." Rondo let his voice trail off and frowned at the sly half grin Colter stretched his lips with, lifting the S brand on his cheek up snug against his eye.

"And if you do, I'll come back here and kill you. No number of bodyguards you could hire will save you, either. I'll hunt you down and finish you off. I'll drill a round in your guts. And you don't want to die, Rondo. If you did, in your wretched state, you'd have put a bullet in your own brain by now. A man like you's gonna keep snarlin' and spreadin' your wretched meanness for as long as you can."

Rondo glared at Colter.

Colter nodded at the pencil stub and the wanted dodger on the table. "Go ahead. Write the note and sign it. I'll do you the favor of posting it for you. Keep in mind that if I see any bounty hunters on my trail after today, I'm gonna come back and drill that bullet in your liver, as promised." He grinned again. "Better hope word spreads fast."

Rondo ground his jaws. He wheeled himself forward until his knees were under the table. Then he turned the wanted circular over, picked up the pencil, touched the lead to his tongue, and began scribbling hastily. The pencil scratched over the paper. He signed the one-sentence missive with an angry flourish and tossed the pencil down on top of it.

"There you go. The bounty's rescinded. Now get the hell out . . ."

Again, Rondo let his voice trail off. He looked out the window flanking Colter. Colter heard what the sheriff had obviously heard—the thud of oncoming riders. The redhead glanced over his shoulder through the glass-paned window to see the silhouettes of two men on horses approaching from the direction of Sapinero's business district. One rode a white horse, the other appeared to be forking a dun, and they were coming on slowly.

Something shiny shone on each man's coat—up around where a badge would be pinned.

Colter had heard Rondo give a soft grunt. Now the kid turned his head back forward, and already he had his Remington out and cocked and aimed at the Sapinero sheriff's forehead. Rondo had his own Peacemaker only half out of its holster.

Colter stared at him. Rondo made a face, shoved the revolver back down in its holster, and cast his gaze once more past Colter and out the window. The thud of the horses' hooves grew gradually louder on the hard, cold ground outside Rondo's shack.

One of the mounts snorted. The men were talking in lazy, conversational tones.

"Now you're neck-deep in it, kid." Rondo laughed and slapped his arms down on the arms of his wheelchair. "Them two fellas out there are both deputy United States marshals, and they're comin' to visit with me about *you!*"

Chapter 4

"Damn," Colter said wistfully, glancing out the window once more but keeping his Remington aimed at Rondo. "This is turning out better than I expected."

"How's that?" Rondo was indignant. "Them two's marshals, you firebrand. You best get your skinny ass the hell out of my house and my town pronto!"

Pressing his back to the wall beside the window, Colter glared at Rondo. "You raise your voice like that again, you're gonna get that bullet in your guts sooner than you thought. I want you to invite those men in here. But if they have any idea you already got company before I can politely introduce myself, you'd best brace yourself for a mighty sore liver."

Colter doffed his hat, tossed it on the chair he'd vacated, and glanced out the window once more. The two riders had dismounted and, still talking, were tying their horses to Rondo's porch rail.

Colter walked around the table and pulled Rondo's Peacemaker from his holster. Wedging the pistol behind his own cartridge belt, he walked back around the table and pressed his back to the wall right of the door.

"You warn 'em," Colter told the sheriff, who sat in his wheelchair, glowering, nostrils flaring, "they'll die and you'll get that bullet in your belly."

He hadn't gotten the last word out before boots thumped on the creaky porch. A knock sounded twice. "Sheriff Rondo?"

Rondo's voice was taut, grim. "Come on in, fellas."

The door opened. It swung back toward Colter, but he'd positioned himself so that he could keep one eye on Rondo sitting in his chair in front of the range. The sheriff's face was stony, but his eyes were nervous, and he slid them toward Colter. The redhead could tell by the way both men hesitated that the sheriff had alerted them to trouble, which, being law dogs, they were doubtless accustomed to.

Colter stepped out from behind the door and rammed the barrel of his Remington into the lower back of the lawman nearest him—a slender gent in a long tan duster. "Come on in, fellas. More the merrier. Gotta warn you, though, one move toward your weapons and you'll die hard."

The man in front of Colter raised his hands to his shoulders. Colter stepped around him, confronting both men standing just inside the open doorway now.

"Sorry, boys," Rondo growled.

"Shit," muttered the lawman nearest Colter.

They were both relatively young men. The one nearest Colter wore a mustache drooping down both sides of his mouth. The second man had long dark brown hair and a full beard.

The one with the beard narrowed his eyes at Colter. "Farrow?"

"Come on in and close the door," Colter said, taking two steps back and keeping his revolver aimed from his belly. He clicked the hammer back loudly. "You born in a barn?"

They just glared at him, lips compressed, eyes wide and shiny with anger.

Colter said, "You know how many men I've killed because of this man here?" He canted his head at Rondo. "You think I have any qualms at all about shootin' two more? Hell, if you're friends of his, I'd just as *soon*!"

Apparently deciding they had a tiger by the tail, both men shuffled inside, gloved hands raised to their shoulders. The second lawman kicked the door closed.

"Unbuckle your gun belts, let 'em drop to the floor."

They complied, keeping their angry, indignant eyes on Colter, cheeks flushed with the embarrassment of having walked into his trap. When both men's gun rigs were on the floor at their feet, Colter wagged his Remington toward the far end of the table, near the curtained doorway to Rondo's sleeping quarters. "Back there. Keep your hands where I can see 'em."

"What do you hope to gain from this, Farrow?" said the first marshal. Dark freckles shone on his red weathered cheeks above his drooping mustache.

"Now that you boys are here, a little more than I expected. Go on, Rondo. Tell 'em why I'm so mad."

Rondo glowered, puzzled and incredulous.

"Go on!" Colter yelled. "Tell these two federal boys how it really played out. Tell about how you killed Trace and how I got this brand burned into my cheek and why I did the same to you!"

Rondo's cheeks turned red. His S brand turned white. He shifted his gaze uneasily between Colter and his two latest guests. The marshals beetled their brows and shifted their own puzzled looks between Colter and the sheriff of Sapinero.

"Start from the beginning, Rondo. With Trace havin' that affair with the Spurlock woman, about how the woman's father didn't like it, and since he was a big man in the county, he caused you not to like it, either."

It was a grim story and one that was hard for Colter to hear again because it recounted Trace Cassidy's betrayal of his wife, Ruth, and his two children, David and Little May, and Colter, as well. With a little more prodding, Rondo told it all to the two federal lawmen, who held their gazes on the crippled man, rapt.

He told about how Trace would visit Sapinero alone several times a year for supplies and about how he'd also secretly visit the daughter of one of the wealthiest ranchers in the county—Jacinta Spurlock. About how Trace had fathered a child with Miss Spurlock, and about how that had shamed and enraged her father, who, when he'd learned of his daughter's pregnancy, had sicced the two corrupt local law dogs, Bill Rondo and Rondo's deputy, Chico Bannon, on Trace.

And about how Colter had ridden down out of the Lunatic Mountains with orders from Ruth to avenge Trace's murder and had ended up with the brand of Sapinero on his face, though, eventually, he'd managed to return Rondo's favor in kind.

And had left the man in the state he was in now.

Oddly, Rondo told the entire story in a low monotone, staring out the window on the far side of the table, into the dark, cold night. Once he'd gotten going, he'd needed no further prodding. He told the entire thing without leaving anything out, even the crimes that incriminated him the most, like his and Bannon's torturing of Trace and their crucifying the rancher in the bed of his own supply wagon.

He'd spelled the whole thing out as though to a priest in a confessional box—even his sadistic branding of Colter Farrow.

When he'd finished, silence fell over the room. The dying fire in the open range snapped and crackled softly. Those were the only sounds until the first deputy sighed raggedly and said to his partner, "I reckon that changes things, don't it, Ed?"

Pop! Pop!

The unmistakable reports of a small-caliber pistol were so unexpected that Colter jerked with a start. Confusion was like a tree branch thrust into the spinning wheel of his mind.

His ears rang. For a second, the room was a blur.

Then he saw smoke puffing in the air in front of Rondo and what looked like a five-shot .36-caliber pocket pistol that the sheriff was extending in his right hand. At the same time, the two marshals grunted loudly and staggered back, clawing at their chests, the dark-bearded lawman falling through the curtained doorway behind him and hitting the floor with a loud thud.

Rondo turned to Colter, his mouth open as he laughed raucously, insanely, squinting and clicking his hideout gun's hammer back as he slid it toward the redhead. Colter's Remington spoke twice. The

Remy was twice as loud as Rondo's gun. Smoke and flames stabbed like silver-orange bayonets toward the Sapinero sheriff, knocking him back in his chair.

Rondo howled and tried to lift the little popper once more, and Colter shot him again. Rondo triggered the little pistol into the table as he flopped back in the chair, mewling and convulsing and holding his hands to his belly from which his blood and guts were oozing.

"You bastard!" the long-mustached lawman bellowed, leaning against the wall and glaring at Rondo. Then he dropped straight down to his butt. His arms fell to his sides, and he slid along the wall sideways to the floor.

Keeping his cocked Remy aimed at Rondo, whose convulsions were slowly dwindling as he lay back in his chair, Colter stared in shock at the nearest lawman, who lay unmoving in the corner. Colter's ears rang as much from his own leaping nerves as from the blasts of his and Rondo's guns. He glanced at Rondo, who sat unmoving now, holding his hands over his belly, and then he moved slowly around the table and stood over the marshal.

Blood bibbed the front of the man's shirt and the wool vest he wore beneath his duster. His chest was still. Colter slid the curtain aside from Rondo's sleeping quarters. The other marshal lay on his side, also unmoving, a pool of blood growing on the floor under his chest.

Colter stepped over to Rondo. The sheriff's eyes were open. He was staring up at Colter. At first, Colter thought he was dead. Then a slight smile tugged at the corners of the savage man's lips, beneath his pewter mustache. His chest rose and fell slowly, almost imperceptibly, and then it stopped moving.

Rondo's lids closed halfway over his eyes, and his hands fell away from his belly to rest palm up on the seat of his chair, beside his withered legs.

"You bastard," Colter muttered, glaring down at the dead man with the grisly S on his cheek. He couldn't help feeling that while Rondo was dead, the man had beaten him. Rondo had suffered, but in the end, he'd won his war with Colter Farrow. He would be wanted for not only Rondo's killing but the killings of the U.S. deputy marshals, as well.

Now there would be no end to Colter's running.

Colter glanced at the dead marshal in the corner. Bile churned in his guts. Apprehension raked his back like claws. Outside, hoof thuds rose—a horseback rider coming fast.

Colter cursed, wheeled, strode out of the kitchen to Rondo's back door near the stairs. He went out quickly and walked across the yard and past Rondo's privy and dilapidated stable. Colter had left the blaze-faced coyote dun he called Northwest tied in the shrubs behind the privy. Colter found the horse there, nickering, tugging on the reins Colter had tied to a wild currant branch. The horse sensed trouble and was ready to get moving.

Colter could still hear the hooves of a single horse galloping on the other side of Rondo's shack growing steadily louder.

"Easy," Colter said, patting the mustang's fine neck. "Easy, boy." He took the reins, swung into the saddle, and paused to reload his Remington. When he'd finished the chore and spun the cylinder, he realized that the hoof thuds had died.

He shoved the revolver into the soft leather

holster positioned for the cross draw on his right hip, touched the stock of his Winchester carbine jutting up from its scabbard beneath Colter's right thigh, and then reined the horse out of the shrubs.

He pushed through more shrubs, angling toward the hills humping up on the other side of the Cimarron River. Branches cracked beneath Northwest's hooves. Behind Colter, a man yelled, "*Hey!* You there—*stop!*"

A gun popped.

Colter ground his heels against Northwest's sides, and horse and rider bounded out of the brush and across a low wash. Ahead, the river shone in the starlight. This time of the year the stream was intermittently frozen. Fortunately, it wasn't frozen now. The air around it owned a steely chill. The water lifted a low, steady roar as it rushed over and around rocks, occasionally chugging over a snag.

It was broad and flat here, probably not overly deep.

Colter put the horse into the stream. At first, Northwest balked and shook his head at the icy water pushing against his hocks. Colter touched spurs to the horse's flanks and whipped his rein ends against the mustang's left hip.

"Come on, boy—this ain't no time to be squeamish about a little cold water!"

At the same time that thuds of galloping hooves again rose from the direction of Rondo's cabin, Northwest lurched forward. The surefooted horse made short work of the stream that never rose past his knees. He bounded up the low opposite bank and Colter steered him into a crease in the bald hills. Soon, he'd wended his way onto a horse trail angling northwest through the hills and rising toward the

Lunatic Mountains that he could not see in the night but knew they were there because that range was where he'd been born and raised.

His biggest mistake had been in ever leaving to avenge a man who'd betrayed his family, though of course Colter hadn't found that out until later. Along with all of Trace's other nasty secrets . . .

Behind him, galloping hooves tattooed a desperate rhythm. Colter reined Northwest to a halt and looked back down the trail.

A murky figure was galloping hard behind him—a shadow flitting across the pale, rocky hills. The rider had just crossed the river, which was a silver streak in the darkness, and he was following Colter's trail.

Chapter 5

Colter looked around. A thumb of rock jutted beside the trail. He swung down from the saddle and led Northwest up the slope on the trail's east side and into a slight notch between bluffs.

Sliding his Winchester from his saddle scabbard, Colter hurried up the shoulder of a steep, haystack-shaped butte around the base of which the trail angled.

He found a perch overlooking the trail and dropped to his butt. He didn't have to look along his back trail to know that the rider was still coming. The hoof thumps were growing louder. Colter could hear the man's horse taking raspy breaths.

When, judging by the sounds, he figured the man was within thirty yards, climbing the slope on the other side of the bluff, Colter swung around, loudly racked a cartridge into his Winchester's breech, and aimed the rifle down the backside of the butte.

Starlight flashed off the carbine's barrel.

Instantly, the rider stopped his horse, which whinnied indignantly and rose a few inches off its front hooves. Starlight shone in the whites of its eyes. The man was only about fifteen yards away from Colter. He stared up the butte, holding his reins in one hand and what appeared to be a shotgun in the other. A badge shone on his coat.

As he started to raise the heavy weapon, Colter said, "You wanna die tonight, mister?"

The man lowered the shotgun. "No, I sure don't." He paused and then said in a low, strained voice, "It's you, ain't it?"

"Depends on who 'you' is."

"Farrow."

Colter had had the uneasy feeling that knowledge of his presence in this country he'd fled three years ago had gotten around. That's why the marshals had been here—they'd been following up leads based on sightings. That's why they'd been visiting Rondo—because they'd rightly suspected that Colter was back to tie up loose strings.

Frustration weighed heavy on the redhead. He hated the desperation he heard in his voice when he said, "I didn't kill them marshals. I killed Rondo, but only after he shot those two federals."

He waited. The man was a dark silhouette staring up at him on his nervous horse.

"Okay," the man said. "Sure. You got it . . . Farrow." He tapped a finger against his hat and tried to sound sincere, but Colter heard the lie in it. "Got it right here in my thinker box. Rondo shot them marshals."

The man's saying it caused Colter to realize how ludicrous it sounded. How unbelievable.

"Well, then," the deputy said tensely, starting to rein his horse around, "I'll just head back and let everybody know."

"Yeah, you do that," Colter said, lowering his rifle barrel as the man leaned forward in his saddle and batted his heels against his horse's sides, barreling back down the trail in the direction of the river and Sapinero beyond it. He glanced once over his shoulder and then leaned forward again, galloping hard.

The rataplan of the horse's hooves dwindled quickly.

Silence.

In the direction of the Lunatic Mountains to the north, a coyote yodeled. Nearer, an owl hooted. Colter tapped his thumb against his Winchester's hammer, trying to absorb all that had just happened.

His plan to return home again had failed. The question loomed larger than ever: What would he do? Where would he go next?

His mind swirled. There was still a ringing in his ears, a dull ache in his temples that was the thudding of his heart.

Why had his life turned out so wrong? Had Trace's sins in Sapinero somehow leached into the young man he'd adopted, befouling his fate?

Was there some curse on his life?

He rubbed his cheek as though to remove the scar. But there was no removing it. There would never be any removing it. Wherever he went, whatever he did, it would always be with him. It would be the first thing all others would see.

And now it would probably decorate more wanted dodgers than ever. He'd be held responsible for killing more lawmen, *federal* lawmen, and the reward would likely be even higher.

World-weary, feeling the physical as well as mental fatigue deep in his bones, as well as a pounding loneliness and feeling of groundlessness, he walked back down the bluff. As he approached his horse, Northwest turned to him, gazed at him searchingly, flicking his ears. Colter was certain that he and the horse had been together long enough, even before they'd lit out from home to find out who'd killed Trace, that the horse not only sensed his moods but absorbed them.

The horse's eyes dropped. Northwest brushed his snout against Colter's arm in understanding and rippled his lips as he gave a long, doleful snort.

"Won't be headin' home any time soon, boy." The redhead felt his throat grow thick. Only right after he'd been branded had he felt this miserable, this close to feeling his knees buckle and for mournful wails to go ripping out of his chest.

But what good would that do? He had no choice but to keep going. To keep riding. He might as well do it like a man instead of some howling brat who'd lost his rock candy down the privy.

He slid his carbine into his saddle scabbard. He patted Northwest's snout, ran a hand down the horse's blaze. The dun nudged him, tossed his tail.

"We'll make it, hoss," Colter said, turning a stirrup out, poking his toe into it, and pulling himself into the leather. The tack creaked as he settled his weight and then reined the horse out of the notch and back down the slope to the trail.

Colter rode up and over a low divide in the darkness.

Knowing he couldn't ride far, as he and his horse

were both blown, he left the trail he'd been following, covering his tracks as best he could, and lit out
cross-country. He headed straight north, toward the
black line that hovered just above the northern horizon and that marked the mountains he called home.

For some reason, heading toward those mountains
even though he knew he couldn't actually ride into
them without leading the law or, worse, bounty hunters to Ruth's doorstep gave him a modicum of comfort. Also, if a posse lit out for him from Sapinero,
they'd expect him to head in that direction. So he'd
head north for a few miles, just to give his trackers
something to think about, and then he'd swing either
east or west and do his best to cover his trail.

That should thoroughly confuse anyone shadow-
ing him.

He doubted the hunters would actually head into
the mountains unless they had solid evidence in the
form of clear sign that he'd gone that way. Most
folks around knew that the Lunatic Mountain folks
were Southern by origin and clannish. They were
quick to protect their own, and they were also well
armed.

No, they'd have to have good reason to ride very
far into those formidable heights.

Colter's cross-country trek was a dangerous way
to travel even by day, much less by night, and he
soon began looking around for a sheltered place in
which to camp. He found a suitable one amongst
boulders scattered across the top of a hogback ridge.
It was a high perch with a clear view in three directions.

It was a cold night, but he couldn't risk a fire. For
supper, he washed some strips of old jerky down
with water. Then he sat back against a rock wall and

hunkered down in his wool coat, crossing his arms against the chill that seeped up out of the ground and out of the rock behind him to penetrate his bones.

Nearby, tied to an old root poking out of a crack in the rocks, Northwest ate oats from the feed sack that Colter had draped over his ears. Colter welcomed the hollow munching sounds. Familiar sounds. Comforting sounds on such a dark, silent, lonely night.

When the horse had finished its supper, Colter removed the sack, evacuated his bladder, sat down again, and stared for a long time toward Sapinero, mentally licking his wounds. After a time, he raised his knees and folded his arms over them. He rested his head forward atop his arms and tried to doze.

He'd need as much rest as he could get for the long pull ahead.

At the first pearl wash in the east, he rose stiffly and gathered his gear. He saddled Northwest and continued heading north.

Midmorning, he swung west. He wasn't sure why he picked west. He just as easily could have picked east, but he'd likely find more places to hide in the western mountains than he would out on the eastern plains.

Around noon, he was traveling along an ancient river bottom, at the base of a wall of sandstone cliffs, when a rumbling sounded from behind and above. Quickly, he pulled Northwest behind some rocks, on the southwest side of the dry river, and peeked out from around the rocks at the cliff rising on the river's north side.

The cliff sloped like a table missing a leg. Men were riding up the slope, pushing their horses hard. They were moving from southeast to northwest.

Colter caught a brief glimpse of the bunch as they passed a gap in the boulders lining the crest of the ridge. It was hard to say, but he guessed the posse numbered a good twenty, maybe thirty men.

As they clambered up the steep slope, they loosed several rocks down the cliff in their wake. The rocks clattered onto the bed of the ancient river. And then the men were gone, their dust drifting like smoke straight up above the cliff toward the cool blue autumn sky.

Colter had little doubt they were after him. They'd wisely decided he hadn't headed into the Lunatics, though they'd obviously spent valuable time trying to cut his sign when they'd realized they were riding north without reason.

What they were following now was the false trail he'd directed them to with a few tricks he'd picked up over his past three years of running. But soon they'd discover he'd led them astray. They would backtrack to pick up his sign and be more careful from then on.

"Let's go, Northwest," Colter said, touching spurs to the coyote dun's flanks and moving off down the bed of the ancient river whose origin, he knew from having hunted this country years ago with Trace, was high up in the San Juans. It filled with snowmelt every spring and became a powerful stream until around the Fourth of July, when the water receded to reveal the ancient, bone-colored rocks marked with ancient Indian signs and flecks of dinosaur bones.

The redhead had a mind to follow the cut up into the mountains and build a cabin in the high timber, where no one would ever find him. He'd live like a mountain man, shoot his own food, make his own clothes, keep his own council till the end of his days.

Such a life would be peaceful and uncomplicated. But the winters could be savage that high in the Sangre de Cristos, even tougher than in the Lunatics farther north and east. A man could get socked in by snow for weeks, sometimes months at a time.

Could he handle that kind of isolation—just him and his horse?

He'd known men who'd lived like that. Some of them had stopped at the Cassidy Ranch for water, and Trace, being the generous sort despite his other flaws, had invited them to a meal. Aside from a few, most had been strange, silent men. The lack of human contact had put folly in their eyes, grown their beards to nearly their belt buckles, and caused them to speak in riddles or plain nonsense, when they spoke at all. After such a visit, it sometimes took days to get the wild, sweet stench, like that of a fox den, out of the cabin.

Was that the kind of man Colter wanted to be? The kind of man who spent his old age laughing at the voices in his head?

The thought made him turn to the mountains and grimace.

When the old, rocky riverbed began to swing south toward the misty blue-green mountains looming steep and large in the southwest, Colter swung out of it and headed northwest, toward Monarch Pass, which would take him over a shoulder of the Lunatics and across the Sawatch to Gunnison and beyond.

He'd leave Colorado. This wasn't his home anymore. In fact, there was nothing for him here but trouble. He'd head into Utah, maybe winter there and in the spring continue east to the Pacific coast. Surely, no one would have heard of him in those distant parts. There, he could find regular work that paid wages and maybe settle down and live a normal life.

Was that possible for a young man with a grisly S burned into his face?

Could he find a woman and raise a family? Would any girl marry a man so hideously scarred or would he be forced to look to whores for companionship and carnal satisfaction? Not that they were so bad. Some he'd found right hospitable and even fun . . . for an hour or two at a time.

Two days later, having seen no sign of the posse, he rode to the bottom of Monarch Pass. Ahead on the right side of the stage trail he'd been following, in a clearing in the tall firs and pines, sat a long, low-slung cabin with a front porch propped on stone pylons.

A barn and corral sat to the left of the shack. Smoke curled from the large stone chimney abutting the end of the cabin nearest Colter, scenting the air with the smell of pine smoke and food.

A sign along the trail, at the edge of the yard, announced PINE CREEK STATION. A stage station, Colter thought. A stagecoach had passed him about an hour ago, when he'd stopped to rest Northwest at the top of the pass where a light snow had dusted the ground beneath the pines. The Concord had arrived at the station and left, heading on toward Gunnison and Montrose. Colter could see the fresh wheel ruts swinging into the yard, which was vacant now except for a dog digging for a mouse or a gopher in the yellow grass and mountain sage between the cabin and the barn.

The dog, a lemon and white setter, had its head stuffed into the hole, butt in the air, shaggy tail wagging like a flag.

Colter studied the layout. There were likely only a few people around, though he couldn't see or hear anyone. None could have heard about the shootings in Sapinero yet, this far away—not unless the posse had passed this way, and Colter didn't think it had, as he'd spied no sign. He didn't want to get trapped here in case the posse should show up.

But he sure could use a hot meal and a cup of coffee, the warmth of a fire. The sun was high, but the air was crisp, frosting the tip of his nose and his toes inside his boots.

He looked around warily, studied the trail that climbed the pass behind him, sheathed in towering, sun-dappled pines. His breath fogged the air around his head. He looked at the cabin, the gray smoke rising from its chimney. It was likely warm inside that cabin, and he'd been so cold for three days now that he doubted he'd ever get the chill entirely out of his bones.

What the hell? If the posse trapped him here, they'd likely shoot him, that's all. Put him out of his misery.

At least he'd go out warm.

Chapter 6

As Colter gigged Northwest into the yard, the dog
pulled its head out of the hole. The dog's eyes bright-
ened. It leaped to its feet, giving its body a delighted
twist, and came running toward the visitors, barking.
He wasn't a vicious dog. It was a friendly greeting
complete with wagging tail and a smile on the setter's
long white-spotted snout.

Colter put Northwest up to the hitch rack out in
front of the place, dismounted, and called the dog to
him. The dog instantly stopped barking, walked to
Colter yipping softly, eagerly, and groaned luxuriously at the pat and ear scratch that Colter gave him.
Northwest eyed the dog with a jealous cast to his
copper-eyed gaze.

When the dog had picked up an old, well-chewed
bone out of the dirt fronting the stock trough
and tried to lead Colter off to play, Colter chuckled
and tied Northwest to the hitch rack. He loosened

the horse's saddle cinch and then went on inside to
find the cluttered place—a combination post office,
saloon, and café—to be as homey and as warm as
he'd imagined.

The warm, smoky air was rife with the smell of
pine and fir and the succulent aromas of stew, fresh
bread, and boiled coffee. It was pleasantly dark in
the cabin, with gold mountain sunshine angling
through a few small, sashed windows and painting
glowing prisms on the floor and shelves stocked
with dry goods.

The friendly woman who ran the place served
Colter at the plank counter in the café section of the
cabin, and he ate hungrily, hunkered over his plate,
his hat pushed back off his forehead. He'd left his
rifle in his saddle boot, so as not to draw attention to
himself, and the food and coffee and the warmth of
the ticking range and crackling hearth were so
soothing that he didn't feel insecure without it.

For a few precious minutes, he forgot his trou-
bles.

Then he heard the thumps of an approaching
horse. He turned toward the small window left of
the front door and was relieved to see a horse and
a small buggy with a leather canopy pull into the
yard and stop in front of the shack. A man and a
woman were seated side by side in the buggy, the
woman holding a small child in a bonnet and a
bulky brown wool coat.

The woman who ran the place had been spong-
ing off tables when the buggy had rattled into the
yard. Now she dropped the sponge into her bucket
of soapy water, pressed a loose lock of gray hair into
the bun atop her head, and looked out a window.

"Well, I declare!" she said in delight.

She hurried outside, leaving the door open behind her, and exclaimed, "Well, look who we got here. Why, if it ain't Jason and Marianna Lang! And look who they brung along to see her old godmother!"

Colter had resumed forking stew into his mouth when he'd seen that it was not the posse who'd come calling, but now, hearing the name Marianna, he whipped his head to look out the open door and into the cool, bright yard.

Marianna? Surely not *his* Marianna—Marianna Claymore!

Heart thudding, he watched as the young man set the buggy's brake and then walked around the two-horse team to the near side of the buggy. He took the hand of the young woman and helped her down to the ground before reaching up and pulling the little girl off the seat and into his arms.

The old woman walked down the steps, chattering away in delight at seeing the young family and taking the child into her arms and jostling her and kissing the little girl's rosy cheeks. Colter didn't pay close attention to what was being said. His gaze was riveted on the young woman—a slender, sturdily built young woman who, from Colter's distance, appeared to be quite beautiful in a long fur coat and a red scarf wrapped around her neck.

She wore her rich dark brown hair in a French braid secured with a comb. Her eyes appeared brown. They sparkled in the sunshine with an earthy, wry intelligence. Her smile was open, holding nothing back.

Colter's heart thudded harder when the young woman glanced toward the coyote dun tied to the hitch rack. The young woman glanced away from the horse to the dog prancing around the newcomers, barking happily, and then, chuckling at the dog and reaching down to pet him, she looked at the horse again.

As she petted the dog, Colter could see her eyes held on the horse. She frowned curiously. And then she straightened and turned her pretty, tanned face—the tan, open face with the frank, vaguely ironic eyes of a mountain girl—toward the open door. The eyes seemed to widen slightly as she probed the cabin's inner depths.

Colter returned her stare, though he didn't think she could see him in here amongst the shadows. But he could see her. And it was almost as though she knew he was here even though she probably couldn't see more than a silhouette sitting at the plank-board counter, staring back at her.

Colter dropped his fork back onto his nearly empty tin plate. He dropped the small remaining chunk of dark bread he'd been mopping the gravy with.

Marianna . . . *Lang.* . . .

He almost said the words aloud as he worked them through the fog ensconcing his brain. His throat ached as he stared back at this beautiful young woman whom he'd last seen three years ago, when she was still just a girl, as he was just a boy.

A boy and a girl stealing away together, cavorting in streams, making love in a remote line shack . . . intending to be married soon and to raise their own family on their own small ranch.

Well, she likely had that ranch now if she'd married one of the Lang boys, whose father had an even larger spread than Marianna's old man, a prosperous cattleman in his own right.

She turned to her husband and the woman who ran the café, muttering something in a pleasant voice, though Colter couldn't hear what she'd said from this distance. And then, swiping breeze-jostled strands of hair from her eyes with her black-gloved hands, she mounted the porch steps in her black boots that showed below her fur coat and the hem of her wool skirt. She crossed the porch, boots pounding resolutely on the floorboards, and came inside.

Colter rose from his stool as she walked toward him, taking unhurried but long, purposeful strides. The door backlighted her now, casting her in silhouette. He couldn't see the expression on her face, but she could likely see his, which was probably grave. Bitter. At least, that's how he felt.

His heart was as heavy as ore.

He just stood there by the counter, feeling as though he'd been carved from granite as she walked up to him, stood before him. She was only an inch shorter than he was. His heart twisted as he drank her in—the oval face with long, delicate nose, a light spray of freckles across her cheeks, a firm jaw, and bold brown eyes that danced with the passion and easy humor of a warm, open heart.

Marianna Claymore had become a beautiful woman.

She didn't say anything for a full half a minute. Then she swallowed, and her full lips parted. She whispered, "Colter."

Her mouth quirked in a slight smile. At the same time, a watery sheen dropped over her eyes. She lifted her right hand and touched her first two fingers to the scar on his cheek.

She sucked a breath. "Oh . . . Colter."

He lifted his own hand, closed it around hers. "Marianna."

Her husband's voice said behind her, "Honey?"

He was looking in from the yard, holding the baby in his arms, the lady proprietor standing beside him, looking in, too. He was smiling curiously. The baby in his arms was reaching for an end of Lang's mustache.

Colter released Marianna's hand. He glanced at her, tried to say something else, but no words could make it past the hard knot in his throat. The S on his cheek burned nearly as hot as Rondo's iron had.

Looking self-consciously away, Colter stepped around Marianna and began walking toward the open front door, then stopped when he remembered his meal. He went back, not looking at her now, though she was looking at him, and he dropped some coins on the counter.

And then he strode to the front of the room and through the door.

Behind him, Marianna said, "Colter!"

His chest heaved, but he did not turn to her. There was nothing to say. He pinched his hat brim to the man—the Lang boy whom Colter had never known but he recognized the Lang features from the brothers he'd met in passing during spring and fall roundups—and thanked the woman for the meal.

They both regarded him with pleasant curiosity, the baby gooing and gurgling and waving an arm, as Colter walked over to the hitch rack and untied Northwest's reins. He was buckling the latigo strap beneath the horse's belly when he heard a low rumble. He looked up over his saddle toward the pass and saw riders galloping down the trail shaded by the towering pines and firs.

He cursed under his breath and swung into the saddle. He saw Marianna standing in the cabin's open doorway. She was staring toward Colter, as were her husband and the woman who ran the place. As the hooves continued to drum and make the ground vibrate, she and they turned toward where the riders were just now hammering out of the trees.

Colter shouted, "You all get inside!" and reined his horse away from the hitch rack.

He swung around to face the break in the forest where the trail spilled down from the pass. The riders were just now trotting their horses out of the forest and approaching the stage station, looking around warily. Most held rifles in one hand, reins in the other.

Colter slid his Winchester from his saddle scabbard and levered a round into the chamber.

The riders had been turning into the yard, but now, seeing him, they were checking their horses down. There were six men in the group before Colter, which meant that some might have gone back to Sapinero or that the group had split up to scour the mountains for him. They regarded him curiously, suspiciously, unable to see him clearly from that distance but instinctively knowing that they'd found the man they were after.

Colter glanced toward Marianna and the others in front of the cabin, all shunting their glances between him and the posse, their expressions quickly moving from puzzled to apprehensive to full of dread. . . .

The riders stared at Colter. He heard Marianna whisper fervently to her husband and then footsteps sounded on the porch as the man and the lady and the child moved into the shack. In the periphery of his vision, Colter saw that Marianna remained in the open doorway until someone pulled her back and closed the door.

Colter kept his eyes on the posse, who were spread out before him, most bearded, all dressed in heavy coats, some with scarves either over or beneath their hats and tied under their chins. The sunlight blazed in their breath frosting like smoke around their heads.

"Ride away," Colter said. "Just ride away."

The lead rider around whom the other five riders had gathered leaned slightly forward in his saddle, his rifle held sideways before him in his gloved hands. He wore a star on his chest—probably one of Rondo's deputies.

He stared at Colter, his small eyes partly concealed by the heavy brown flesh of his face and jutting brow. Colter could tell that the man wasn't considering taking his advice. The others must have known it, too, because the rider on the far right suddenly raised his Henry rifle, pressing the stock against his shoulder.

Colter's rifle came up automatically, and roared. The man with the Henry rifle grunted and triggered his rifle into the air as he rolled off the butt of his suddenly jolting paint horse.

"*Hold on!*" the deputy shouted, but two others did not heed his advice and also went tumbling from their jerking mounts as the roar of Colter's Winchester rocketed around the clearing.

Inside the cabin, the baby started crying.

The three others including the deputy scrambled off their mounts, the deputy getting his foot caught in a stirrup, falling heavily to the ground and losing his rifle. As the horses scattered, leaving the deputy in the center of the trail while the other two posse members took cover on either side of the trace, the deputy shouted, "*Hold fire!*"

Colter kept his smoking Winchester aimed at the man, silently warning the others.

Sitting up and propped on his arms, one leg bent beneath his heavy body, the deputy glanced at the men to either side of him and shouted again, "Hold your fire! Hold your fire!" His hat lay on the ground beside him, its crown having been pancaked by one of the horses. He glanced around at the men lying nearby, one groaning but the others lying still.

He turned to Colter once more.

"All right," he said, peevish. "We're goin' back."

Colter glanced toward the cabin. A face stared out at him from the window right of the door. He could see the thick brown hair framing the light tan oval of Marianna's face. Meanwhile, the baby continued crying, likely in its father's arms.

Colter backed Northwest slowly toward the gap in the trees that marked the mouth of the stage trail on the trail's west side. *Clomp, clomp, clomp* went the horse's hooves on the cold ground. Colter heard a mewling sound and turned to see the setter looking toward him from the cabin's rear, ears up, tail down, fear in the dog's innocent eyes.

Colter looked toward the downed deputy again. The other two men were hunkered one behind a rock, one behind a tree. None had their guns aimed at him.

As he entered the pine-fragrant shade of the forest on the west side of the yard, he glanced once more toward the cabin. If Marianna was still in the window, he couldn't see her behind the dark, uneven glass, which only reflected the lemon sunlight.

A tight fist had a hold of his heart. The fist's grip tightened as he realized he'd seen Marianna for the last time. And that this was the last time he'd ever be this close to his home.

He could never return here.

He glanced at the deputy staring at him in silent

fury from the ground. Then he swung the horse around quickly, touched steel to its flanks, and took off at a hard gallop, heading west through the pines.

He gritted his teeth against the emotion heaving inside him. He was on the verge of bawling like a damn baby, and what good was that going to do?

She was gone. She'd married a Lang, and the baby was theirs.

They'd live happily ever goddamn after.

Chapter 7

Colter rode hard for most of the rest of that day.

He camped in the forest, far from any trail. The next day he resumed his westward trek, skirting Gunnison and a day later heading along the rim of the Black Canyon of the Gunnison River. He continued avoiding main trails and all towns of any size except a few little mining camps where he stopped only to stock up on trail supplies, including oats or parched corn for Northwest.

Slowly, in no real hurry, though knowing winter was on the way by the growing cold and frequent snow dustings, he continued on to Utah. He only realized that he had crossed the territorial line when he passed a stage swing station whose rotting shingle announced its location as being that of the Utah Territory.

How long had it been since he'd crossed the line?

Running low on money, he was laid up for a week

in a little Mormon mountain settlement that, judging by the blank stares he received, did not cotton to
strangers. Especially a well-armed, obviously trail-
worn stranger with what they probably took to be the
mark of Satan on his cheek.

Nevertheless, he found work splitting wood for
a hotel run by an old Gentile who got roaring drunk
every night, played the banjo, and rancorously re-
called his time in the War Between the States and
those "dirty Rebs" who tried to kill him and all his
pards at the prison at Blackshear, Georgia, "and
were, for the most part, successful, damn their yellow hides!"

The old man, Murphy McKenzie, didn't seem to
mind Colter's scar and neither did he inquire about
it. Something told Colter that McKenzie was an old
outlaw himself, and most of his transient patrons
had the look of long-coulee riders themselves. They
got nearly as drunk as McKenzie himself did as
they sang along to the old man's banjo in front of the
snapping potbelly stove in the hotel's small, seedy
tavern, long after most of the town's pious citizens
had gone to bed.

If word had yet spread this far about Rondo and
the two dead marshals, Colter had no indication of
it. Under McKenzie's roof, he doubted it would
much matter.

He rode out of the settlement simply called Stop
Nine, as it was on a prominent stage line, eight days
after he'd entered it, with twelve dollars in his pocket
and a hell of a pounding ache in his head. McKenzie
had offered to shelter him over the winter, but Colter
had politely said no, because McKenzie had expected
him to drink with him. And Colter, who wanted to fit

in as much as any young man still trying to earn his stripes amongst more life-seasoned men, had tried.

He'd paid dearly for accepting sips from McKenzie's "snake jug," however. Colter was not accustomed to hard liquor of any kind, and McKenzie's own potent "snake brew," in addition to his "tomato wine," could only be called liquor in a pinch—if there was no other within a thousand square miles. Whatever the snake brew had been concocted from— Colter suspected grain, actual snake venom, gunpowder, and strychnine—had hammered dull spikes through both temples and both eyes and tied his guts in wire-tight knots. The tomato wine had been even worse.

The cigarettes he'd also smoked while singing along with the other outlaws and McKenzie and McKenzie's banjo had only aggravated his misery. For three days he felt as though a scorpion had crawled down his throat, wrapped itself around his tonsils, and died.

But his physical maladies were nothing compared to his mental anguish, for at the fringes of his mind he kept seeing Marianna and her husband and child.

Theirs was the life he should have had. He should have been raising a family in the Lunatic Mountains with the woman he loved. With Marianna.

But Bill Rondo had stolen that life from him. And now Marianna belonged to another man. Probably a good man—the Langs were known as good people. Still, Colter couldn't help feeling a nagging resentment no less poignant for being totally unreasonable and selfish.

He was just starting to feel better physically when

he got caught in a snowstorm in the Uinta Mountains. He'd been looking for a quiet mining camp to settle down in for the winter, before heading back down to Mexico in the spring, which was where he'd spent the previous year, but he hadn't found what he'd been looking for before the storm hit.

It was a light squall by mountain standards, but he had to hunker down in a cave at the side of a thickly wooded valley for one afternoon and night and watch the thick, wet snowflakes driven down at a slant through the slash of timber he'd sheltered in. The wind howled like wolves on the blood scent.

The next day he was saddling Northwest down below his cave from the dark maw of which the gray smoke of his cook fire curled when he heard the muffled thumps and crunches of approaching riders.

He quickly slid his Winchester from his saddle boot and stepped out away from his horse, cocking the rifle one-handed and staring through the trees to which only a few autumn leaves still clung. The trunks of oaks and birches were tufted with wet snow clumps, and they caused the pines and spruces to sag. Occasionally, snow would whisper down from the branches and drop to the ground with pillowy thumps.

Birds yacked in the trees, though they grew quiet as the riders approached—four men moving toward Colter through the snow and the timber. They were spaced about twenty feet apart, coming slowly now, dressed in fur or wool or thick canvas coats against the post-storm, mountain chill. One of the horses handily leaped a deadfall, and Northwest lifted a nervous whinny.

The horse that had just leaped the deadfall returned the greeting in kind.

The riders came on, canting their heads this way and that, staring toward Colter through the trees between them. None of them had a gun out. Their expressions were faintly puzzled.

Finally, one of the riders stopped. The other three stopped then, too. The rider who'd stopped first, riding a sleek, blaze-faced sorrel, canted his head to the left and said, "Billy?"

Colter replied with "You got the wrong hombre, friend. I ain't Billy. Don't even know a Billy."

He hoped that would be the end of it and these men would ride on. Instead, they kept staring at him as though they wanted him to be Billy so badly that they were going to stare at him until he *became* Billy, by God!

The men glanced around at each other and then gigged their horses forward, spreading out until they'd formed a semicircle around Colter and Northwest. Colter, owly to begin with after all he'd been through, was getting piss-burned.

"I told you fellas, I ain't Billy."

The one who'd spoken before stopped his horse thirty yards away and nearly directly in front of Colter. The other three were at Colter's ten o'clock and two o'clock positions.

"Where's Billy?" said the man who was doing the talking for the group. He'd said it with a skeptical, accusatory tone.

"Couldn't tell ya."

"Where's the others?"

"They must be with Billy."

The man at Colter's two o'clock position spoke up angrily. "You're from the posse, ain't ya?"

Posse?

The only posse Colter could think of was the one

that had been after him back in Colorado. But surely they wouldn't still be on his trail. No, they'd leave stalking him up to U.S. marshals and bounty hunters now. This man must have meant another posse, totally unrelated to him.

They were all looking cautiously around now. The one in the black hat reached for the rifle jutting from his saddle scabbard, and Colter said, "Leave that long gun where it's at, amigo."

The man in the black hat froze, his hand on the rifle's stock. He looked at Colter, hard-eyed, as did the others. A heavy silence descended over the forest, pregnant with danger.

"Look, I don't know who you fellas are, or who Billy is, or who the others are. I'm just passin' through. I holed up in this cave here to weather the storm. Now, if you were supposed to meet Billy and the others here, they'll no doubt be along shortly. If you want to stay, you're welcome. There's a fire in yonder and a small pile of dry wood. Help yourselves. Me? I'll be movin' on."

A sharp *crack* rose behind the strangers. To a man, they all flinched.

The one to Colter's right bellowed, "I knew it!" and reached for the two pistols belted around his waist, on the outside of his buffalo coat.

They'd thought the crack was a triggered rifle. Colter glimpsed a deer leaping through a snowy brush snag about forty yards behind them, in the direction of the stream running along the valley floor, just as he blew the man at two o'clock off his horse. He lowered his rifle to cock it as the other three brought up guns, and—*Boom! Boom! Boom!*—the other three tumbled off their pitching horses, screaming.

The man in the black hat got his right boot caught in his stirrup, and his fleeing sorrel dragged him for about thirty yards through the snow, his body bouncing wildly over buried deadfalls, before the horse swerved around a dead birch. The man's boot tore loose of the stirrup and he went skidding wildly off through the snow to slam up against the birch that his horse had avoided, with a resounding *smack!*

He lay flat on his back, arms and legs spread wide, groaning.

The man at Colter's ten o'clock position rose onto his hands and knees. He shook his hatless head as if to clear the cobwebs and glanced over his shoulder. Blood dribbled down from one corner of his mouth, staining his beard.

Colter ejected his last spent shell. It sang into the snow behind him. He levered a fresh one into the chamber but held his Winchester negligently out in front of him.

He shook his head. "It's over."

The man began scrambling forward on his hands and knees, heading for a nearby tree. As he approached the tree, he grabbed the pistol out of the holster on his left hip, and then he gained his feet and ran behind the tree. He kept out of sight behind the tree for an entire minute, and then, when he poked his head out around the side of the tree, Colter painted a red circle in it with a .44 slug, just over his right eye.

The man's head jerked violently back. It straightened, and then he stumbled back away from the tree, lowering the pistol in his right hand. The revolver roared, stabbing flames at the ground, pluming the snow and yellow leaves. The man stood tall for a second and then he fell straight back and hit the ground without trying to break his fall in the least.

Colter watched his pointed-toed boots jerk.

Colter looked around. The man in the black hat lay still now, as well, no longer groaning. The other men lay unmoving where they'd first fallen. One had cracked his head open on a stone previously hidden by the snow but that was now slimy with red slush.

Colter stuffed his right glove into his coat pocket, reached under his coat, and plucked a fresh cartridge from his shell belt. He slowly, calmly reloaded the Winchester, keeping his ears skinned for more riders. Northwest was snorting and stomping around, casting his nervous gaze toward the dead men.

"Easy, boy," Colter said, and ran a soothing hand down the horse's neck.

As he started walking toward the black-hatted man, he wondered vaguely at his own calm. He felt no revulsion for what he'd done. It had been something he'd been forced to do, and he'd done it as purposefully as nailing a new shoe into his horse's hoof.

He had to admit that part of him had almost relished the distraction from his loneliness and anguish over having seen Marianna again, having been reminded of the life he might have had and would forever be denied. He was a killer now, and he seemed to be getting better and better at killing with each man he killed.

It focused his mind, calmed him down. One couldn't accomplish such a task with a busy mind. Killing, he supposed, was a way to clear it.

Only a very small part of his mind was at all uneasy about the person he'd become. The rest of him was practical enough to know that he'd been forced into it, and there was really no other way for him to live now . . . if he wanted to live at all.

The man who'd been wearing the black hat was indeed dead, as were the other three, he learned after a hasty inspection. He paused for a moment on a rock to look around and consider what he should do about the dead he'd left here in these woods and decided the best thing for him would be to leave them here. They did not deserve proper burials. They'd tried to kill him because they thought he was part of some posse. Which meant they were outlaws on the run.

That thought kindled speculation.

Outlaws on the run might have bounties on their heads. And he could use money to tide him through the winter and to help get him down to Mexico in the spring, when some of the fury over Rondo and the dead marshals had died down and bounty hunters wouldn't be scouring the border country for him.

He looked around. Two of the group's horses stood a ways off through the trees, reins hanging. Both were foraging for grass beneath the new-fallen snow. Shouldering his rifle, Colter stepped over the last man he'd killed and walked out toward the horses.

They spooked at the approaching stranger, but one was tame enough that Colter was eventually, after considerable clucking and cooing, able to get close enough to grab its reins. The other near horse blew and stomped, and Colter turned toward the black-hatted man's sorrel that stood bobbing its head nervously.

The sorrel was wearing two sets of saddlebags behind its saddle and bedroll—one atop the other.

Colter studied the creature and then tied the near horse's reins to a branch jutting up from a deadfall log. He walked over to the sorrel, which unexpectedly did not run but watched Colter warily out of the side of its right eye. When Colter approached with his hand out, the horse took a step toward him and sniffed his hand. Colter grabbed the horse's reins, tied them to a pine branch, and then removed the top pair of saddlebags from behind the saddle.

They were heavy. When he dropped to one knee, unbuckled the flap over one of the pouches, he saw why they were heavy. This pouch was filled with greenbacks and two small bags of coins. He found that the second pouch was filled with the same thing—both scrip and specie hastily stuffed into the pouch, as though during a bank robbery and an ensuing getaway.

Now Colter's heart was thudding. He'd never before seen that much money in one place. He ran his hands over the wads of greenbacks secured with heavy paper bands. Their musky smell and the leathery fragrance they'd acquired from the saddlebags were tempered by the tang of ink. He hefted one of the money pouches in his hands.

His ears warmed and his breath grew shallow when without actually counting the bills or the coins he estimated that there must be several thousand dollars here. The bills appeared to be all twenties and one hundreds. Hell, there might be ten, twenty, even thirty thousand dollars here.

Enough money to get a man all the way to the Pacific Ocean without having to work another day for the next ten years!

The horse in front of him lifted its head suddenly and pricked its ears.

Colter dropped the saddlebags and straightened, taking up his rifle. There was a distant, muffled footfall.

And then a man's slightly high-pitched voice called, "Halloo the camp! Drake! Georgie! Sanchez! *Hey, you fellas—it's Billy an' the boys!*"

Chapter 8

Colter heard the riders coming from up the canyon. He could hear a couple of them speaking, but they were too far away for him to hear what they were saying.

He looked at Northwest, who stood where he'd been standing before, in front of and below the cave mouth from which only a little smoke was issuing now. The horse was looking back over his left shoulder, in the direction of the approaching riders.

Judging by the drumming of the hooves, there were at least three, maybe as many as five.

Colter stuck two fingers between his lips and whistled softly. Northwest turned to him with a startled jerk and then came walking toward him, trailing his reins. As the horse approached, Colter watched through the trees until he saw one shadowy figure and then another. There appeared to be two riding ahead of two more.

Quickly, leaving the saddlebags on the ground, he grabbed Northwest's reins and led the horse along the base of the sandstone ridge, glancing back over his shoulder. The ridge bent back upon itself, and Colter followed the bend and then tied Northwest to a piñon sapling angling out of it.

Dropping to a knee, he doffed his hat and looked around the bend toward the approaching gang members, who were now getting within a few yards of where the black-hatted man had fallen. Colter scrubbed a hand across his chin, wondering what to do.

If he tried to flee, he'd likely be heard or spotted. He had no wish to kill more men—just because he'd become skilled at it didn't mean he was about to start inviting trouble—but those saddlebags were tempting. And trying to get away would only make him hunted by more men after these men spotted their fallen comrades, which they were about to do.

The thought had no sooner swept over Colter's brain than the first two riders swung from their main course and rode around the stout birch to stop their horses and stare down at the snowy ground before them. Colter couldn't see what they were looking at, but there was little doubt they'd spied their four dead *compañeros*.

Suddenly, all at the same time, they shucked rifles from saddle scabbards and leaped off their horses, dashing for cover while talking in excited tones and loudly levering rounds into their rifle breeches.

One of the gang members yelled, "I seen a horse moving that way along the ridge!"

One of the newcomers dashed out from behind his covering pine bole and ran toward Colter, dodging and weaving, holding his Winchester straight up in his hands. Colter drew a bead on him and fired, but his bullet merely blew bark from the tree behind which he'd just taken cover.

Colter seated another round but held fire when a man's voice roared in the distance behind the outlaws, "Billy, it's Marshal Dunbar! I come to take you an' your boyos in or kill you right here, you bloody little demons from hell!"

The voice, pitched in what sounded like a thick Scottish or Irish brogue, was loud and clear, though Colter judged the man to be sixty, seventy yards away.

"You boyos throw your guns down and come nice and peacefullike, or so help me, I'll take you back to Justice City belly down across your saddles and that'll be the end of ya but for your poor mother's wailin'!"

"Shit," one of the outlaws exclaimed. "I thought you killed that old bastard!"

"There ain't no killin' me, Billy," said the old bastard. "Me—I've got nine lives, just like a cat. Now, you gonna come peaceful, or do I have to ride in there with my scattergun and put you down like the nasty dogs ye are?"

The man's voice was calm, bemused. He even sounded delighted by his current chore, though he seemed to be alone.

The outlaws must have been thinking it over. Colter could see only the rifle barrel of the one nearest him, poking out slightly from the right side of a tree. The other three outlaws were behind shrubs farther away.

The man nearest Colter, aware of Colter's position, bolted out from behind his tree and ran to Colter's left and slightly away, before hunkering down behind a flame-shaped boulder mantled with fresh snow. There was a tree between him and Colter, but Colter could see an arm and a leg of the outlaw as he raised his rifle and hammered a shot in the direction of the lawman.

Colter snapped his rifle to his shoulder, took a second to aim carefully, and squeezed the trigger. Colter's slug tore into his target's left arm, snapping him around so that his back was against the boulder. He glared at Colter, stretching his lips away from his teeth in an enraged, painful grimace.

Colter ejected his spent cartridge casing. It pinged off the stone wall. He racked a fresh one into his Winchester's breech and yelled, "You boys are surrounded. Follow the man's orders or get it from both sides!"

"Dunbar drummed up a posse?" one of the hidden outlaws shouted. "I don't believe it!"

"Believe it!" Colter said, his voice echoing around the snowy woods. "There's sixteen, seventeen of us out here, an' we got you all in our rifle sights!"

He wanted no part of this, but he'd found himself in a whipsaw, with little alternative but to help the lone lawman. Colter hoped he was worth helping. He glanced at the saddlebags that lay in the snow where'd he'd left them. Part of him wished he'd tossed them over Northwest's back and ridden off, a rich man.

Part of him wondered if that's really what he would have done. He honestly didn't know. He felt a vague relief of having had the decision made for him now.

But what about the lawman?

He likely wouldn't have heard about what had happened in Sapinero, hundreds of miles away, unless he had access to a telegraph, which were relatively scarce in the remote country Colter had been riding through. If Dunbar was federal, that would be another story. Colter would probably have to kill him.

He was already blamed for two dead deputy U.S. marshals. One more wouldn't matter overmuch. They could only hang him once. It was a cold-blooded notion, but being cold-blooded was the only way he'd be able to survive. The guns against him were just too many.

"Do as my friend says, boyos!" Dunbar called. "You hear me now? Or you'll be dancin' with the devil!"

The man nearest Colter was sitting with his back against the rock, breathing hard and glaring at Colter. He'd set his rifle against his extended legs and was clamping his right hand over his upper left arm.

"Throw 'em down, fellas," he shouted in a pain-pinched voice. "They done kilt Georgie an' the others. They got us surrounded! It's a goddamn bushwhack, is what it is!" He looked around as though trying to locate the other posse members. At the same time, he tossed away his rifle.

"All right, Dunbar!" one of the others shouted. "We're throwin' our guns down! We're givin' ourselves up—hear?"

"You're a wise boy, Billy!"

Colter saw the other three outlaws now, rising from behind the deadfall they'd been crouched behind. They tossed their guns away and looked around as the man nearest Colter had done, likely wondering where the others were who'd killed their four partners.

Colter stayed where he was. He had a mind to mount up and light a shuck, but then a horseback rider appeared through the trees, beyond the outlaws. He was a large, stocky man in a bear coat and a high-crowned hat, with a long red scarf wrapped several times around his neck. He was forking a tall cream horse.

He rode crouched slightly forward in his saddle, one hand pressed against his right thigh, and he was holding a rifle across his saddlebow. What appeared to be the barrel of a shotgun jutted up from behind his back where it hung by a leather lanyard.

The lawman lifted his chin, casting his gaze toward Colter. He wore a patch over one eye. Just then, one of the three men in front of him jerked to one side, dropping his arms. He pulled something up from a boot. There was the quiet-shattering crack of a pistol. The man who'd fired the gun took off running toward one of the horses standing a ways off to his right.

The lawman's face turned red as he held the cream's reins taut against his chest. He pinched his eye and bellowed and then lifted his Henry rifle weakly and fired. His bullet blew up snow and leaves well wide of the running man, who snapped off another shot as he approached the horse that had just turned to run.

"Ah, ya bleedin' bastard!" the lawman shouted.

Colter ran out from behind the bend in the ridge, snapped his rifle to his shoulder, planted a bead on the fleeing man's back, and squeezed the Winchester's trigger. His bullet hammered his target between the shoulder blades. The running man screamed and threw his arms up and out as he flew straight forward into the snow, behind the horse he'd been running for but which was now galloping away, trailing its reins.

Colter heard the Henry roar and glanced over to see one of the outlaws facing Dunbar stumble backward triggering a pistol into the ground at his feet. Dunbar bellowed a raucous curse that was drowned by the Henry's next roar, and the outlaw was punched straight back to hit the ground hard.

Meanwhile, the outlaw nearest Colter shoved his hand toward his right boot, eyes bright with cunning. Racking a fresh round in the Winchester's chamber, Colter swung toward him and punched a round through his forehead. He dropped the derringer he'd just pulled from his boot. His head slammed back to smack the boulder behind him before slumping sideways to the ground, arms and legs quivering.

Beneath the Winchester's dwindling echoes, screams rose. Colter looked toward Dunbar, who was aiming his rifle from his shoulder, over his horse's head, toward the last outlaw—a slender lad with long dark brown hair hanging straight down from his leather-billed immigrant cap. He was leaning forward and sort of dancing in place, shielding his head with his arms and screaming.

"Don't kill me, Dunbar! Oh, please don't kill me!"

"You bushwhacked me, boyo!" the man roared from atop the cream that held absolutely still despite the man screaming in front of him, and the man bellowing from his back. "Give me one good reason why I shouldn't carry you back to your bloody pa in pieces!"

"No!" The young man dropped to his knees and flung himself forward, shielding himself with his arms, grinding his head in the snow. "Please, Dunbar! Oh, please don't shoot me!"

Colter looked up from the caterwauling outlaw to the big man called Dunbar. Dunbar returned the look. His thick handlebar mustache with upswept, twisted ends rose taut against his stout nose as he grinned.

Chapter 9

Colter found himself staring in fascination at the young outlaw whimpering like a gut-shot dog on the ground before the grinning marshal. The marshal himself was fascinating. It was hard to tell with him mounted, but he appeared at least six feet tall and built like a bear under his bearskin coat, shoulders broad as a barn door.

His large, round, rough-hewn face was framed by shaggy muttonchop whiskers that were thickest along his jaw. He would have had a definite savage aspect even without the eye patch, though it was tempered slightly by the ostentatious mustache. The fur on his face was strawberry blond liberally threaded with grizzled gray. He didn't appear to have any hair on his head, though of course it was impossible to tell because of the black top hat with a braided leather band.

The lawman's grin faded as he regarded Colter

through the woven tree branches, squinting his lone cobalt blue eye. He turned his head from left to right and back again, taking in the carnage, the snow scuffed around the dead men turned to bloody slush.

"Well, now, who we got here?" His breath puffed around his large, round face. "Who might my *posse* be?"

Colter picked up the saddlebags. He draped them over one shoulder, rested his rifle on the other shoulder, and led Northwest through the snowy brush until he stood near the young man called Billy, who was kneeling on the ground before the lawman's cream gelding. Billy stared fearfully up at the man, his pale, pimply face streaked with tears.

Dunbar continued to scrutinize Colter suspiciously through his one eye, which skidded back and forth between the saddlebags and Colter's own scarred face. The skin around his black leather eye patch was a mass of white knots. One knot dropped straight down beneath the eye to mingle with the bushy muttonchop on that side of his face.

The marshal smiled again as before, narrowing his eye shrewdly. "Aye, a handsome pair we make—eh, squire?"

Colter tossed the saddlebags on the ground near the kneeling, simpering young outlaw. "There's the loot. This kid's gang must have been aimin' to meet up at the cave, not realizin' it was occupied."

Dunbar glanced at the bloody dead men lying around him. "Pity 'em." He looked at the saddlebags and grinned again shrewdly. "Is it all there?"

Colter felt a fleeting wave of guilt wash over him as he remembered how he'd considered stealing it. He shrugged. "Count it."

Dunbar drew a deep breath and swung his broad,

stocky frame down from the saddle. The man's face
had been so fascinating that Colter hadn't fully considered the thick green, bloodstained neckerchief
wrapped around his right thigh. Now he was forced
to consider it as that knee bent, and the big man
stumbled sideways before falling with a bellowed
curse to the ground in front of his horse.

Immediately, the young outlaw tensed optimisti-
cally, his eyes growing cunning, like a wolf pup spy-
ing weakness in an alpha. Colter stepped forward
but stopped when he saw that the firebrand's muscles
were coiled, as though setting himself to spring.

Billy looked up at him with his chocolate brown
eyes that were at once cow-stupid and predatory.

"Give me a hand here, will you, squire?" the lawman asked, lifting an elbow. "Shouldn't have
climbed out of the hurricane deck in the first place,
I reckon. This little bastard—Billy Garrett's his
bleedin' name!—ambushed me while I was collectin' firewood behind the jailhouse, wretched little
lump of Garrett mealworm!" He chuckled as Colter
stepped up beside him and placed a hand on his arm.
"At least they didn't bushwhack me at home and en-
danger me daughter. That's why Billy's still breathin'.
No, he dry-gulched me, all right, but I've been shot
before—many more times than this and far worse."

Colter got the big man to his feet with effort. He
must have weighed over two hundred pounds, though
he wasn't much taller than Colter's five feet nine. His
arms were nearly as thick as his legs, which were as
stout as tree trunks.

Leaning back against his horse, the lawman
glared down at Billy. "If he'd placed a shot anywhere near me home, I'd punch that greasy little head
down betwixt his bleedin' shoulders. After that, I'd

scattergun his knees so he couldn't even dance when I hanged him!"

He turned to Colter. "Help me back to Justice City, will you, squire? There'll be food and a warm place to bed down in it for ya, maybe an ale and a dram of Kentucky bourbon. No Scotch, damn the frontier gods." He cast his lone-eyed gaze at the gray sky. "It'll be snowin' again soon."

Colter looked at the man. Then at Billy, who slid his nervous gaze between Colter and the wounded marshal, who was losing blood quickly from his stout, twill-clad leg and from another wound, Colter saw now, in his right arm. The blood had seeped through the sleeve of his bear coat between his elbow and his shoulder, matting the fur.

"Name's Dunbar," the lawman said with his customary, slightly seedy grin. "Matthew Dunbar, town marshal of Justice City just up the road apiece—oh, six, seven miles. No more than ten."

"You rode six, seven miles with these wounds?"

"Hell, I've walked farther a whole lot worse off'n this, boyo! A spoonful of paregoric, an' I'll be on my feet again in no time!"

Colter gave the man a hand into the saddle, though he wasn't sure how much he helped. Lifting Matthew Dunbar was like trying to move a wheelbarrow loaded with raw ore. As Dunbar settled his considerable weight atop the fine cream gelding, Colter slung the bulky saddlebags over the horse's hindquarters. The man slumped forward, eyelid lightly closed, lips open as he fogged the air around his bullet-shaped, red-faced head beneath the black top hat.

"Give me a minute here, squire," he mumbled, dipping his chin toward his barrellike chest. "Just gonna take . . . take me a little beauty nap. . . ."

"Pssst! Red!"

Colter looked at Billy, who was probably around Colter's own age. The young outlaw's ·eyes were bright with cunning. He said softly but fervently, "There's fifty thousand dollars in them saddlebags. All from my old man's bank. We'll split it!" He grinned as though the money were a trophy and he was cock of the walk for having stolen it. "Twenty-five thousand apiece."

If Colter had been going to run off with the loot, he'd have taken it all himself, not shared it with this young wolf who'd stolen from his own father. He wasn't sure how that mattered—was Colter any better than Billy for having considered running off with it himself?—but it seemed to.

Colter looked around for a horse. He spied movement in the periphery of his vision. He turned to one side as the outlaw bounded toward him. Billy was taller than Colter, but Colter was faster.

Colter stuck his foot out, and the kid dropped in a pile, rolling. Colter strode up to him. As Billy lifted his head, brown eyes flashing angrily, Colter rammed the butt plate of his Winchester against the firebrand's forehead, laying him out cold.

Colter turned to Dunbar, who sat as before, slumped slightly forward, chin dipped toward his chest. "Just a little . . . beauty nap," the lawman muttered. "Then I'll be fine . . . as frog hair. . . ."

Colter gave a caustic chuff and strode off to run down a horse for his prisoner.

He was on the trail half an hour later.

Dunbar rode beside him, half dozing but holding his reins up tight against his chest. He appeared to be in a meditative state. He'd probably lost a lot of blood and was fighting to stay conscious.

Billy rode slumped forward on the zebra dun that Colter was trailing by the horse's bridle reins. Colter had found a pair of handcuffs in Dunbar's saddlebags, and he'd cuffed the kid's hands behind his back. Since Colter had tapped him, he hadn't heard a word out of him.

He rode along the trail, backtracking Dunbar, which wasn't hard in the new-fallen snow. More was coming down now from a low, gauzy sky, slowly filling in the tracks of both Dunbar and one-half of the gang that had apparently split up after robbing the bank, intending to meet at Colter's cave, which they'd done to Colter's regret.

He wanted no part of Billy and Dunbar. He wasn't sure what he would have done with the loot if he hadn't been interrupted back there, and he didn't want to think about it—about the man he might have become. A thief little better than Billy. He just wanted to keep riding and find a good place to hole up for the winter in these remote Utah mountains, for the federal lawmen and bounty hunters would likely be looking for him along the border in Arizona and New Mexico.

In the spring, when their fervor had dwindled, he'd make a beeline for the border and likely stay down there till the end, whenever it came. The way his luck had gone these last three years, that would likely be sooner rather than later.

The trace he followed was probably a wild horse trail, maybe an ancient Indian trail now used by area stockmen, few as they probably were up this high. The path rose and fell through narrow canyons. It climbed saddleback ridges and wound around

fir-stippled mountain shoulders, lifting ever higher
into the Uinta Range. Colter had a hard time imag-
ining a town out this far, especially one with a bona
fide bank.

Dunbar woke up enough to direct Colter into a
side canyon. "Shortcut," the beefy lawmen muttered.
"Steep climb over a rocky pass, but it'll get us to Justice City all the sooner."

Ten minutes later, as they rode along a broad,
climbing riverbed, steep sandstone walls capped
with thick pines rising on both sides, Dunbar roused
again, cleared his throat, blinked snow from the
lashes of his one eye, and said, "Don't believe you
told me your name, Red."

"Red's good enough."

Dunbar chuckled at that. "All right, then. Red it
is." The smile sagged from his face, his eye closed,
and once again his chin dipped toward his chest.

"Red?"

Colter glanced back at Billy riding the zebra dun
behind him. The firebrand had straightened in his
saddle. A blue goose egg had risen on his forehead.
Blood had trickled from the middle of it and crusted
in a short line that ended just above the bridge of his
nose.

"You awake, are ya?" Colter said with a sigh.

"Things ain't gonna go well for you in Justice,
Red." Billy shook his head, sneering, his long
black hair dancing around his pimply, pale cheeks.
"Uh-uh. Not well at all. Gonna go just as bad for
you as it's gonna go for that old barrel of English
ale, Dunbar."

Dunbar's cream stopped suddenly. They were at
the top of a pass looking down into a broad valley.

Colter checked down Northwest and looked at Dunbar as the marshal lifted his chin, rousing from his latest doze. The big man grimaced painfully, casually reached under his coat with his left hand, and hauled out a long-barreled, nickel-plated, horn-gripped Colt Navy revolver. He gave Colter a sardonic look, the man's lone blue eye flashing deviously, and then he twisted around in his saddle and extended the pistol at Billy.

The gun roared.

Billy screamed and clapped a hand to his left ear.

"You *bastard!*" the young outlaw cried as blood oozed through his long hair and between his fingers to dribble across his gloved knuckles. His face creased with torment, he looked at Colter as though for sympathy. "See what he done? You *see* that? You're a witness to this man's depravity!"

Colter had no sympathy for the diabolical kid— likely a rich man's spoiled son who didn't know when he had it good. He'd made the trouble he was in possibly for no better reason than that he was bored with all that high living. No, Colter had no sympathy for one such as that.

To Dunbar, Colter said, "You gonna shoot off the other one, Marshal?"

Dunbar chuckled as he lifted his coat up and shoved the smoking popper down into its holster. "You'll do, Red. You'll do."

He booted his horse on down the slope. Jerking Billy's zebra dun along behind him, Colter followed suit. As they dropped down into the valley, Colter saw a town gradually clarify through the billowing snow veils, rising from the sage, rocks, tussocky sere grass, and widely scattered piñon and ponderosa pines.

It didn't look like much set against the broad valley that seemed to sit up here at the top of the world, rimmed in the far distance by low, dome-shaped hills and limestone outcrops. But as they swung onto a wagon trail and headed directly for the little settlement, it proved to be a healthy scattering of shacks, frame houses, corrals, privies, and stock pens surrounding a business district of clay-chinked log and wooden-frame business buildings, some with garish facades.

Amidst the collection of structures was a white-steepled church and a school with a belfry and a playground complete with a strap swing hanging from a sturdy cottonwood.

There wasn't much snow on the ground up here—judging by the thinness of the air, Colter thought they were probably at around ten thousand feet—but the stuff currently falling was sticking, and the low gray sky threatened more.

They angled into the ragged outskirts of the town from the northeast. The school was sliding up on their right. Its well-trampled grounds were surrounded by a white picket fence, and a smart-looking black leather carriage was just now sitting near the fence gate, where a stone path led down from the school's front steps.

Two people stood between the carriage and the open gate—a well-decked-out man and a tall, young, black-haired woman with an impressively curvy figure swathed in a conservative, lace-edged dark blue frock and purple cape. As Colter, Dunbar, and their prisoner approached, the woman and the man turned toward them.

"Papa!" the young woman cried, hurrying around the end of the buggy, holding her dress above her

finely turned ankles clad in purple canvas, side-buttoned shoes.

"Ah, me dear Victoria," Dunbar said as he reined the cream to a stop.

"Pa, my God—you're *alive*!"

Chapter 10

As the young woman approached Dunbar, Colter felt a half-hitch knot draw tight in his chest. The tips of his ears warmed, though it was probably only about twenty degrees.

The girl was incredibly lovely with her thick, heavy tresses of rich black hair set against the red of her lips and the purple of her dress. She gave a sob, her beautiful face crumpling, and buried her head in her father's injured thigh.

Dunbar winced and groaned.

The young woman, Victoria, lifted her head, and her wide, passionate eyes flashed with fury. "Why, you're nothin' but a bleedin' fool. Goin' out after a whole gang of bank robbers in this weather—with two bullets in your rancid old hide, no less!"

Her brogue wasn't quite as heavy as Dunbar's, but it bespoke the mossy stone castles and rolling green hills clad in British mist that Colter had seen in painted pictures. The young woman looked nothing like her father, who was ugly enough to cause a freight train to take a dirt track, aside from the fact that both her eyes owned the same blue color and sharp glint of unbridled emotion as did Dunbar's sole one.

She turned to Billy sullenly sitting his zebra dun with his hands cuffed behind him. "And you—what a blight on your family. Shame on ya!"

"Yes, shame on you, Billy!" exclaimed the tall, sandy-haired, sandy-mustached young man she'd been conferring with. He walked up to the firebrand's horse. "Haven't you done enough to our family? Now you bushwhack the marshal and steal from our own *business?*"

Billy curled his lip at the young man, with whom he shared a faint familial resemblance, and told him to do something physically impossible to himself.

Dunbar leaned down toward his daughter and grinned, showing his big yellow teeth beneath his upswept mustache. "Girl, do you think ya could fetch the sawbones for your dear old pa? I'd dig this lead here out of me own hide—Lord knows I've done it plenty of times in the past—but since we have a bona fide flesh miner in town, he might as well work instead of loiter about the saloons, pinchin' the percentage girls—don't ya think, now, me daughter?"

The girl gasped, her striking features blanching. "Oh, of course, Pa! I'll get him right away." She glanced at Colter sitting Northwest on the other side of her father. "Can you get him over to the house? Get him inside to bed, while"—she turned to the tall, handsome gent standing behind her—"while I send Morgan for Dr. Crabtree?"

She didn't seem one bit curious about Colter's identity. In fact, she seemed to think, however vaguely, that he was an associate of some kind of her father's. Her keen, lustrous gaze stunned him a little, and, frustratingly shy, he averted his gaze from the gorgeous girl's and muttered, "Reckon."

Dunbar glanced at the redhead and chuckled. And then Dunbar touched heels to his cream and, groaning and cursing against the pain of the holes in his thick body, took off at a trot. Colter glanced back at the girl, flushing a little, and then booted Northwest ahead, jerking Billy's horse along by its reins.

He followed Dunbar around the school and over to a two-story, sandstone, mansard-roofed house sitting on the other side of it, under a sprawling cottonwood. It sat off alone here, a good sixty yards away from the nearest other house or cabin, and it was partly concealed by dead vines and tall yellow brush and grass now dusted with new-fallen snow.

Dunbar stopped his horse in front of the front stoop that needed a fresh coat of paint, and sort of rolled out of his saddle. He'd hit the ground and dropped to one knee with a raucous bellow before Colter could get to him.

"Help me inside, will ya, Red? Feelin' a might peaked, the old marshal is! Need some busthead to soothe me aches an' pains!"

"I don't think you oughta have any busthead, Marshal Dunbar," Colter said as, with the big man's left arm thrown over his neck, he walked him up the three porch steps.

"Hogwash, Red! Nothin' like good Kentucky tangle-leg for cleaning the blood. Oh, but for a bottle of Scotch from my old home country!" Dunbar stopped on the porch and turned to where Billy sat his saddle, glowering. "You stay there, now, Demon Spawn. If you try to run off, I'll hunt you down and *chew* off that other ear."

Through gritted teeth, Billy told Dunbar to perform the act he'd just a few minutes ago told the dandy to do. "Oh, if only I could, boyo," Dunbar said, fumbling with the front door. "If only I could . . . mighta saved me from a few cases of the painful pony drip, don't ya know!"

Colter helped the man inside the roomy, simple but neatly appointed house. Dunbar directed Colter toward a room through a parlor that boasted a small brick fireplace. The room beyond a simple pine door had a bed in it, a bear rug with the head still attached on the floor, and a bobcat hide on the bed. There was one ladder-back chair, a dresser, a marble-topped washstand, several rifles in a gun rack, and the cloying smell of cigar smoke and whiskey. A small charcoal brazier hunched in a corner.

There were several bottles on the dresser. Pearl gray light washed through a single curtained window beside a painting of a beautiful, stygian-haired woman who very much resembled Dunbar's striking daughter, maybe a few years older.

While the marshal leaned against the wall, Colter moved into the room, drew the covers back to expose a pair of worn but clean sheets, and then eased the big man onto the bed. Dunbar pushed the feather-stuffed pillow up against the headboard, and he half sat, half reclined against it. He'd removed his top hat, and a cap of thin, wiry gray-blond hair sat close against his skull, which was shaved up to the tips of his ears.

Colter heard footsteps in the house behind him, growing louder as two or three people approached the marshal's room. The room wasn't very large, and neither was the bed with its halved-log headboard, but both looked all the smaller with the thickset man in them.

Turning to step out of the room, Colter saw the marshal's sublime daughter, Victoria, striding toward him from the parlor, a gray-haired man in a gray suit behind her.

"Red!"

Colter turned back to Dunbar, who hooked a finger.

Colter leaned down. Dunbar grabbed the front of Colter's coat in one fist and held up a town marshal's five-pointed star in his other hand. "You're the marshal now, boyo. Till I'm back on my feet. Might take me a day or two. Ain't as young as I once was."

"Father, the doctor's here," Victoria said, stepping into the room. "We're going to have to get you out of those clothes!"

Ignoring his daughter, Dunbar asked Colter, "Got nothin' pressin', do you, Red?"

Colter didn't know how to answer that. Dunbar winked.

Colter tried to straighten, but Dunbar held fast to his coat and winked. "I know I can trust you, Red. You coulda run off with the loot, but you didn't. Rare to find a man with scruples in this country. And you more than held your own against them tough nuts, and some of 'em were known to be purty handy with their shootin' irons."

"Father, please release your friend so the doctor can have a look at you."

In the periphery of his vision, Colter saw the gray-haired, gray-suited man, Dr. Crabtree, standing behind him, but Dunbar wasn't finished yet. He said through gritted teeth, "Take Billy over to the

jail. Stone buildin' on the main street—wooden second story. Lock him up tight and keep an' eye on
him. Lock the loot up, too. It's evidence. Don't let
nobody see him, and for God's sake, don't let anyone convince you to let Billy go, though they'll try,
sure as the sun'll rise tomorrow!"

Colter shook his head, bewildered by all this.
"Look, I ain't no—"

"Papa!"

Dunbar winked at Colter again. "There'll be a few
coins in it for ya, and a special place in heaven! Go!"

He released Colter's coat. Colter straightened
and stepped back. The young woman stepped up
beside him, glancing over her shoulder at him dis-
approvingly, while the doctor set his black medical
kit on a chair and said, "Well, now, what have you
gone and done to yourself this time, Marshal?"

Colter wanted to protest further, but the doctor
and Dunbar's daughter shielded the thick man from
Colter's view. Slowly, haltingly, Colter backed out of
the room and then turned and ran into the well-
dressed gent whom Victoria had been conferring
with out by the school. The man was about three
inches taller than Colter, but he looked down as
though from an exalted height, his eyes giving Colter
a cold, disapproving scrutiny, from the scar on the
redhead's face to his worn, rusty-spurred boots.

Shaking his head and turning his mouth corners
down, he said, "He's delirious, Red. Best go get
yourself a bottle and a girl over at the Blue Mountain
and then ride on out of Justice City as soon as the
weather clears."

"That outlaw outside—he your brother?" Colter
said tightly, not liking the man's tone or his arrogant
eyes.

"That's right. Black sheep of the family. But he's 'family,' just the same."

"Dunbar says he's gotta be locked up."

Victoria came up behind Colter, said, "Excuse me," in a persnickety tone, and then brushed past Colter and the well-dressed gent, telling the man, "I'm going to heat some water, Morgan. Could you bring some wood in from the shed? And then dismiss the children, will you? Tell them I'm going to be needing a couple of days off but we'll resume classes the first of next week."

She didn't wait for a reply but hurried on through the parlor toward the kitchen.

Morgan had kept his sneering gaze on Colter. "I don't care what Dunbar says. Locking my brother up is pointless. My father will only make sure he's set free first thing in the morning." He grabbed Colter's forearm and squeezed it almost painfully. "I'm warning you, Mr. . . ."

"Call me Red."

"All right, Red—I'm warning you not to get involved in our affairs here in Justice. Like I said, go down to the Blue Mountain, get yourself a meal, a bottle, and . . ." He let his voice trail off as he looked toward the kitchen, apparently making sure Victoria couldn't hear. "And may I recommend the half-breed girl, Delores? The lady will curl your toes." He dug in his pocket and pulled out a Dana Bickford ten-dollar gold piece. "My treat."

Colter stared down at the gold coin in the man's pale, beringed right hand. A diamond cuff link shone on the slick Steve's shirt cuff, an inch beyond the sleeve of his black serge suit coat.

Anger boiled up in Colter, but he kept his voice even as he looked away from the offered coin and said, "Shove it up your ass. Dunbar wants Billy in jail, so that's where he's goin'."

He started to walk through the parlor but stopped when he saw the marshal's beautiful daughter staring at him from the parlor door. She had a towel thrown over her shoulder. She held another one in her hands.

She frowned, looking Colter up and down, pursing her full red lips. "Who are you?"

Colter hated the way young women seemed to tie his tongue in knots. Especially beautiful young women. Especially this one, who was regarding him as if he were no more than horse dung she'd discovered on her parlor floor. "Call me Red, Miss Dunbar. Everyone does."

"I thought my father went after those thieves alone."

"I met your father on the trail."

"And just like that—he trusts you with Billy and the bank money?"

Colter heard the muffling squawk of a floorboard beneath the parlor rug. He glanced behind to see the tall, handsome gent walking toward him, reaching inside his coat. Colter swung around, reaching around his belly for the Remington holstered for the cross draw on his right hip.

"Morgan—my God, *no!*" the girl intoned.

The man shifted his hard brown eyes from Colter to Victoria and back. Colter kept his hand on the walnut grips of his Remington, holding the dandy's hard gaze. "Don't even think about stealing that money, Mr. Red. It belongs to my father's bank . . . and this town."

When Morgan pulled his hand out of his coat, it held only a brown leather wallet. He pulled out a ten-dollar bill and extended it to Colter.

"I'll take the money back to the bank. Here— take this and get yourself a hot meal and . . ." He glanced slightly sheepishly at Victoria. "And a warm bed."

Colter stared past the proffered bill at the dandy's sneering eyes. Anger burned inside him, causing the brand on his cheek to throb. "Next time you reach into a coat around me, expect to die bloody."

He removed his hand from his own gun and brushed past Victoria, pinching his hat brim to her but saying nothing. She did not look at him but kept her cool eyes on the floor, the nubs of her cheeks flushed with chagrin.

Colter walked outside, pulling the front door closed behind him, and stopped on the porch. Billy had dismounted his horse. He was on his knees, head down, mewling. Blood reddened the snow near his left knee. Three men stood around him, quietly conferring. One had the saddlebags containing the loot slung over one shoulder. A black cheroot puffed between his lips.

The three were all dressed in winter trail gear and woolly shotgun chaps, holstered revolvers thonged to their thighs.

"There he is!" Billy raged, glaring at Colter through wings of his long, tussled hair. *"Kill that scar-faced son of a bitch!"*

Chapter 11

Colter hooked his thumbs behind his cartridge belt and stood casually regarding the three men gathered around Billy. Two were younger, mid- to late twenties. The third was older, maybe late thirties, with a hound dog look. He wore a short wolf coat and a black hat.

He said in the throaty, raspy voice of a man who'd smoked and drunk a lot, "We'll be needin' a key for them handcuffs, friend."

Colter said, "Who're you?"

"We work for Billy's pa," said one of the other two—the tallest of the three. He leaned against the hip of Billy's dun, sort of casually shoving back the flap of his rat-hair coat behind the handle of his holstered .44.

"Does Billy's pa know he stole fifty thousand dollars from him?"

"The way Mr. Garrett would see it—if he was

home right now, which he ain't—this is a family matter. He'd want us to bring Billy back to the Garrett Ranch for his pa to deal with the way he sees fit." The older man extended his gloved hand. "Now, kindly hand over them keys, Red . . . and we'll be on our way."

Colter slowly raised his right hand, slid it into his coat pocket, and pulled out the town marshal's badge that Dunbar had given him. He pinned the badge to his coat and said, "Billy's goin' to jail."

"What—you're the marshal now?" The third man—short and thin with a thick cinnamon beard covering half of his pale face—laughed sharply, glancing at the other two. "Has ole Dunbar done kicked off? Don't tell me!"

"No, he's still kickin'. But I'll be town marshal till he gets back on his feet." Colter wasn't sure why, but he liked the way that sounded. What's more, he liked the slight, barely perceptible weight of the badge pinned to his coat. It made him feel like more than what he'd been for the past three years—a scar-faced outlaw kid running with his tail between his legs.

It made him feel like a man with authority as well as a man with a place to call home for a spell, even though from what he'd seen of Justice City so far, it wasn't going to be a place where he'd find much peace and quiet.

The two younger men laughed jeeringly. The taller one pointed at Colter and said, "Why, you ain't nothin' but some raggedy-heeled saddle tramp. How'd you get that ugly scar on your face, Red? Don't you know the brandin' iron s'posed to go on the *calf's ass?*"

Colter ignored the prodding. "Like I said, Billy's going to jail."

"Kid, you don't wanna get mixed up in this," the older of the three said reasonably. "If you do, you're gonna die. You're too young to die." He took several slow steps forward, extending his hand. "Now, just hand over the key to the handcuffs like a good boy, and we'll ride on out of your hair, and you can tell Dunbar we hope he gets well real soon."

He winked.

For some reason, that riled Colter more than the man's words had. He felt his ears heat up.

Colter said, "I'm going to give you to the count of three to mount your horses and ride the hell out of here. If you aren't on those horses by then, some-one's gonna need to call the undertaker."

"Why, you little punk!" yelled the taller of the younger two men, his face flushing with fury. He stepped forward, away from Billy's horse, and dropped his hand to his holster, flicking the keeper thong free of the hammer.

Colter pitched his voice with warning. "I wouldn't do that if I was you."

The tall man stopped, staring at Colter through narrowed eyes. He looked Colter up and down and sideways. A slight grin dimpled his cheeks. He glanced to each of his partners in turn. And then he jerked the .44 out of its holster.

Colter's Remington was in his hand before the tall gent's Schofield had cleared leather. The Remy roared.

"Oh!" said the tall man, dropping the .44 as though it were a hot potato and stumbling back against the dun.

As his knees buckled, the shorter man slapped the pistol thonged low on his right thigh, and had just gotten it raised when Colter's Remy spoke again loudly. The shorter man squealed as the gun flew up out of his hand and over the dun that had fidgeted away from the noise. The short man grabbed his bloody hand, crouching over it, holding it to his belly like an injured little bird he'd found in the grass.

His face was a mask of pain. His hat tumbled forward down his chest to lie in the snow at his feet.

He closed his eyes and sucked a long draught of air through his nose. "Shit, that stings!"

Colter clicked the Remy's hammer back once more, aiming at the older gent's slight paunch pushing out his wolf coat. The older man stood with both hands raised to his shoulders, palms out. He was wagging his head slowly, eyes dark with apprehension as well as awe at the shooting he'd just witnessed.

"Hold up, Red," he said, still shaking his head, dropping his gaze to Colter's smoking revolver. Keeping his hands raised, he stepped to one side and looked at his two companions. The tall man was down on his back, dead, blood oozing from the hole in his chest. The other was down on one knee, squeezing his bloody hand, his bleached-out face turned toward Colter, his eyes bright with agony.

The older gent turned to Colter, his features grim. "All right, Red. All right. Have it your way. Sorry, Billy."

"Get my father," Billy snapped, glaring at Colter from his knees. "Get my father and Burleson pronto, Ray. They'll know what to do." He smiled threateningly at the redhead with the smoking Remington clenched in his fist.

The old gent kept his eyes on Colter as though on a mountain lion he'd stumbled upon in the calving barn. "Get mounted, Demry."

"What about Hagen?"

"Kid killed him. Get mounted."

The older gent lowered his hands as he turned and walked over to the three horses standing out at the edge of the yard, about thirty yards away from where Hagen lay unmoving, the falling snow dusting his filthy chaps from which chunks of wool were missing. He swung into the saddle of a rangy paint, then led a white-socked black toward Demry, who was just now climbing to his feet while holding his bloody hand to his belly.

The blood had oozed onto the front of his coat. His hand shook. He kept his enraged gaze on Colter. "This ain't over by a long shot, Red."

"For now it is."

"Get Pa!" Billy screamed as Demry climbed heavily into his saddle. "Get Burleson. They'll know what to do."

"Shut up, Billy," yelled the older gent. "You wouldn't be in this fix if you hadn't robbed your own father's bank, you cork-headed fool!"

"You'll pay for that, Ray!"

"That's a note you owe me, ya damn peckerwood!"

Ray reined the paint around and galloped off to the west. Demry glanced once more at Colter. His jaw was so hard that Colter thought it would crack. He snapped his head away and put the black into a gallop after Ray, crouching over his wounded hand as he and the older man rode along the rear of several business establishments, weaving around woodpiles and privies, and then disappeared through a break between large frame buildings, heading for the main street and likely the main trail out of town.

Colter tripped the Remington's loading gate, plucked out his spent cartridges, tossing them into the yard, and refilled the empty chambers with fresh shells from his belt. He closed the loading gate, spun the cylinder, and dropped the Remington into its holster.

"You're pretty good with that thing," Billy said. "But you ain't good enough to go up against my pa's men."

"Get on your horse."

"How'm I supposed to get on my horse? My hands are cuffed behind my back!"

"All right." Colter pulled the key out of his coat pocket and removed the handcuffs from Billy's wrists. "You give me any trouble, I'll blow your other ear off."

Grimly, holding one hand to his bloody ear, Billy walked over, grabbed his horse's reins, and swung into the leather. Colter climbed onto Northwest's back and reined the horse away from the hitch rack fronting the Dunbar house. A click sounded. He turned to see the front door slowly open. Dunbar's daughter, Victoria, looked cautiously out. Behind her was Billy's brother, Morgan.

Morgan followed Victoria out onto the porch where the girl stood, clutching her arms against the chill, the falling snow looking pretty in her black hair despite the disgust in her cobalt eyes.

"Good Lord," she said under her breath, shifting her gaze from the man on the ground to Colter, shaking her head slowly and looking as though she'd just swallowed a tablespoon of lemon juice. "Who are you, anyway, young man?"

"Gunman," Morgan said, wrapping an arm around the girl's shoulders and curling his nose at the lanky redhead mounted on the handsome, blaze-faced coyote dun. "Look at that mark of Satan on his face. Your father really knows how to pick 'em."

"Morgan, you send the doc over to the jail so's he can stitch my ear!" Billy shouted from his horse's back, his voice cracking on the high notes.

"You hush, Billy," Morgan ordered softly. "You got yourself into this mess. Now you'll just have to live with a sore ear for a while. Come, Victoria—you'll catch a chill. Let's get you inside, and then I'll fetch the undertaker."

The girl glanced at Colter once more. He watched her and Morgan move back inside the house and close the door. Then he rode over to Billy. "I'm sure you know where the jail's at good as anyone. Show me. Nice an' slow. You try to get away from me, I'll back-shoot you."

Billy scowled at him, pressing one hand to his ear, then reined his horse around and headed south along the two-track street, toward the business district of Justice City. Colter rode behind him, looking around cautiously as their horses clomped through the new-fallen snow. When they arrived at the main drag, Billy turned left, heading east. There were a good twenty businesses in Justice City, Colter estimated. Roughly ten or so false-fronted establishments, including a couple of saloons and two hotels, on each side of the street that was a good fifty yards wide. The bank was on the far eastern side of town, across from what appeared to be a hotel. Both were identified by signs atop poles standing perpendicular to the buildings' facades, extending into the street.

Up and down the trace, smoke issued from brick

chimneys or tin chimney pipes. There was little movement because of the snow—a few dogs, a shaggy cat prowling a trash-strewn gap between a barbershop and a ladies' dress shop.

As Colter followed Billy through the gently falling snow, he glanced behind to see two riders sitting in front of a saloon at the west end of town—a long, low building with a modest facade, the writing on which Colter was too far away to see. The riders he could see well enough. They were Ray and Demry.

Ray was talking to a group of men gathered on the saloon's front porch, and Ray and the standing men were turned toward Colter. Ray was doing the talking, but from this distance of half a block away, Colter could hear only snippets of what Ray was saying.

He heard Billy's name and then, as his prisoner led him to a small, barracklike stone and wooden-frame building on his right, he heard Ray say loudly, "And I'll pay fifty dollars to the man that kills that son of a bitch and turns Billy loose!"

With that, Ray turned forward, touched spurs to his paint, and galloped off down the street and toward the rolling, snowy buttes to the west. Still hunched miserably in his saddle, Demry booted his black in the same direction but at a much slower pace. He hadn't once looked back and he didn't now. That hand no doubt pained him pretty smart.

As Colter stopped Northwest in front of the building whose shingle over the front door read MATTHEW W. DUNBAR, TOWN MARSHAL OF JUSTICE CITY, UTAH TERR., Colter glanced toward the saloon that was half a block away on the opposite side of the street. The six or seven men clumped there were all holding glasses or beer mugs in their hands. Most were smoking. They were staring toward Colter with grim interest. A couple of mouths were working as the men talked amongst themselves, likely opining that fifty dollars was a lot of whiskey and women. Might even get them through the winter without work, if they played their cards right.

Colter removed the saddlebags containing the bank money from over Northwest's back and slung them over his right shoulder. He shucked his rifle from its scabbard, levered a shell with one hand, and stepped down from the saddle.

He kept his eyes on the men on the saloon's front stoop. When Billy had dismounted and dropped his reins, Colter gave him a shove up the jailhouse's porch steps. From the direction of the saloon, a man's laugh rose. On the porch, Colter stopped and turned toward the saloon.

Several of the saloon's customers were chuckling deviously. One stepped forward and, holding a beer schooner in one hand and puffing a quirley clamped in his teeth, held up one hand. He shaped a gun with his thumb and index finger and said loudly, "Bam!"

He and the others laughed.

And then they all turned and strolled leisurely back into the saloon.

Colter turned to Billy, who stood grinning at him in front of the jailhouse's closed door.

"What's so funny?" Colter asked him.

"Nothin'." Billy shrugged, chuckled delightedly. "I just think you're gonna look right smart wearin' a tombstone, that's all, Red."

Chapter 12

Colter shoved Billy through the jailhouse door, followed him inside, and kicked the door closed. He dropped the bulging saddlebags on the floor beside the door.

There were four cells along the rear wall. Stone steps rose along the right wall into the jailhouse's second story. Likely more cells up there, in what was probably an addition. Colter vaguely opined that Dunbar had probably ordered it built to accommodate more prisoners. Dunbar seemed like the type of marshal who would have lots of prisoners, though none currently occupied the four cells along the rear wall. If there were any in the second story, they were mighty quiet.

A rolltop desk was butted up against the front wall, just right of a window between the desk and the door. The desk was neat, a few papers jutting from pigeonholes. The curved butt of what appeared to be an English-made Bisley pistol also protruded from a pigeonhole. A spittoon sat on the floor near the swivel Windsor chair behind the desk. A nail protruded from the chair back, and hanging from the nail was a metal key ring with only one key dangling from it.

The key must fit all the cell doors.

Colter was holding his Winchester on Billy but letting the barrel sag. When he turned to the young outlaw, he jerked back just in time to avoid the kid's right fist, which glanced off Colter's ear. Colter fell back against the wall. He tried to raise the Winchester, but Billy shoved it aside with his right leg, grabbed the front of Colter's coat with both hands, and slammed Colter's head against the wall behind him.

There hadn't been enough room to build up the momentum for a skull-crushing blow, but the rough smack set up a ringing in Colter's ears and made his vision swim and darken momentarily. Billy jerked the Winchester out of Colter's hands just as Colter had tried to tighten his grip on it.

The firebrand gave a victorious yell as he stepped back and started to swing the barrel toward Colter. He froze when he heard the click of the Remington's hammer being cocked, both dark brown eyes riveted on the barrel aimed at his nose.

"I'll take that," Colter said, wincing at the stinging throb in the back of his skull. He'd lost his hat, and his long red hair was sprayed across his face. Breathing hard, he stared at Billy through the strands hanging in his eyes.

He had to make a conscious effort not to tighten his right index finger and detonate the .44 slug seated between the hammer and the firing pin. He felt foolish for having been taken by surprise that way. Would his old friend Lou Prophet have left himself open like that? Would Dunbar? Colter had been on the dodge for a long time. He'd been on the defensive. Being on the offensive was new to him. He'd have to gain his sea legs fast, or die.

"All right!" Billy flipped the rifle over, extending the butt toward Colter while narrowing his eyes at the Remy's maw, a muscle in his cheek twitching.

Colter grabbed the long gun by the neck of its stock, drew it back toward him. He waved the Remington toward the key hanging from the chair.

Keeping his temper in check, he pitched his voice low with menace. "Take the key, open the cell door of your choice, and get your ass in there before I give the undertaker some more business."

Billy glowered at the pistol aimed at him and, stumbling around nervously, did what he was told. When he'd stepped into the second cell from the stairs on the office's right side, he pulled the door closed and smiled through the bars at Colter, eyes taunting.

Colter said, "Latch it."

Billy sighed and pulled the door back until it jerked and the bolt clicked, sounding like a small-caliber pistol in the stone-walled, cavelike room. Keeping his Winchester aimed at Billy through the strap-iron bars, Colter turned the key in the lock, heard the bolt grind through its cylinder and catch. He pulled the key out, retrieved the saddlebags from the floor, and set them on the floor of the cell beside Billy's. When he'd locked the door, he shoved the ring into his coat pocket.

Billy ground his teeth together as he sagged down on the cot, clamping his hand over his ear again. "My ear hurts bad, Red. You best get that worthless sawbones over here and stitch it up for me. Cold in here, too. You're gonna need to build a fire."

Colter glanced at the potbelly stove in the room's front corner, right of the desk, near an empty gun cabinet and a framed map of Utah Territory. Beneath the map stood a washstand, beside an old brocade-upholstered chair so gaudy that it had probably once outfitted a hotel or brothel lobby. The brocade was so worn across the seat cushion that the cotton and horsehair stuffing was poking out through the threads.

There were a few sticks in the large crate beside the stove, and a couple of rolled-up newspapers, but that was all the makings that Colter could see. He was in no hurry to build a fire; he had a more important errand to run first. When he did get around to the fire, he'd have to fetch wood first.

Colter walked over to the desk and began rummaging around in the drawers, all of which he found to be sparsely filled as well as neat and orderly. Dunbar was a large, crude-looking man, but he kept a neat office. Unless Victoria tended it for him.

Victoria. Her image stuck in Colter's brain, just behind his eyes, like a branch suspended by flood-water against a beaver dam. What she thought of him was obvious. He supposed he couldn't blame her. Not only was he ugly, but he'd killed a man in front of her. Besides, she'd apparently set her hat for Billy's dandified brother, Morgan.

"You hear me, Red?" Billy called from the cell. "I'm gonna need that sawbones over here pronto, and I'm gonna need a fire. I've lost a lot of blood here—wearin' it all on my coat—and I've caught a nasty chill."

He shivered loudly as though to support his claim.

Colter ignored him. He plucked a second key ring out of the desk's bottom right drawer and stuck that, too, in his coat pocket. He needed to leave for a while, and he didn't want anyone coming in and finding a spare key with which to free his prisoner.

"You hear me, Red?" Billy said, louder, his irritation growing.

Colter continued to ignore him as he headed for the door, Billy saying, "Red! Cold in here, Red! Don't make me mad, Red, or I'll make sure my pa's men torture you bad before they kill you! Red! *God-damnit, you stop ignorin' me, Red!*"

That last was muffled by the door, which Colter pulled closed as he stepped out onto the porch, holding his rifle in both hands across his chest and looking around carefully. The snow continued to fall in a milky haze. Colter guessed it was midafternoon, but dirty light made it look like a winter dusk.

There was no one on the street, though a couple of horses and a one-horse farm wagon were parked in front of various business establishments. Five horses stood with their heads drooping in front of the hitch rack of the saloon to the west and on the opposite side of the street—the one where Ray had announced the bounty he'd placed on Colter's head. Fifty dollars, eh? Colter gave a dry chuff. Little did Ray or anyone else around here—at least, as far as Colter knew—know about the two-thousand-dollar reward that Bill Rondo was offering.

Had been offering. Who was putting up the bounty money now? Likely, in the wake of the two marshals' deaths, Uncle Sam was.

Would Colter's hell never end?

Why did he feel compelled to stay here in Justice

City? He glanced down at the five-pointed, nickel-washed tin star on his coat. Whatever the reason, he did.

And now he stepped down off the porch, untied the reins of both his and Billy's horses from the hitch rack, and began leading them west along the main street. He'd seen what had looked like a livery barn that way, near the saloon, and he needed to get the horses out of the snow and the cold. No matter what he was going through, sheltering and tending his mount was a man's first job.

He walked along the street's south side, opposite the saloon, leading the horses rather than riding, making himself a lower target, and ready to run and dodge if he needed to. As he came within about forty yards of the saloon, he saw the sign over the porch. FRANK MILLER'S SALOON. Miller's front door opened, and two men stepped out onto the porch.

They were both tall men in shabby hats and wool coats. One of the coats was striped, a torn pocket hanging, and he was smoking a pipe with a white porcelain bowl. Both men stepped out to the edge of the porch, staring at Colter. They were unshaven. The one in the striped coat and smoking the pipe had a full mustache and a long, gloomy face beneath his funnel-brimmed, dirty cream Stetson.

Colter stopped. He had his Winchester in his right hand. He kept the barrel slanted toward the ground, but he placed his thumb on the hammer, ready to rock it back.

"Can I help you fellas?" he asked the two men on the saloon porch.

They stared at him blankly for a time, and then

the one smoking the pipe blew smoke out his nostrils and said, "So, you're the new marshal in town, eh?"

"I'm just fillin' in for Marshal Dunbar's all. He's feelin' poorly."

"We heard about that," said the second man. "You sure are ugly, kid."

"Yeah, well, I've seen dogs' asses better lookin' than you are, mister." Colter held the man's glare while the other man glanced at his companion and laughed jeeringly. The second man—who had a round face and a thick neck, his slouch hat tipped back off his broad forehead—merely scowled at Colter. His eyes were as small as marbles in the doughy folds around his sockets.

The man with the pipe said, "Fifty dollars goes a long ways in these parts. But you know what goes even farther?"

"What's that?"

"Makin' friends with Hawk Garrett."

"That would be Billy's father," Colter said.

"You got it. We're gonna do him a favor. We're gonna drill a bullet through your head so he don't have to look at your ugly face."

The scowling, thick-necked man said, "We figure we'll be doin' the whole world a favor, keepin' it from havin' to look at your ugly face ever again. Ugly enough to curdle milk! I bet that nasty scar makes it pretty damn hard for you to make friends."

"Don't care much for people, anyways," Colter said, his casual tone not betraying the fact that, despite himself, the man's words penetrated like steel pellets what he'd thought was a fairly thick hide. Maybe it never would be thick enough.

"Especially *girl*-friends," said the man with the pipe, grinning. "Bet a girl sees you, she whizzes down her leg, turns tail, and runs home to hide under her bed."

"Well, it's been nice talkin' to you fellas," Colter said. "I reckon we'll be meetin' again soon. When we do, I hope you've made all your final arrangements. If you leave the buryin' up to me, I'm gonna piss on your dead carcasses and toss you in the nearest ravine. Way I see it, mountain lions and wolves need to eat, too. Even if it's just vermin they're chowin' down on. Well, like I said . . ." Colter pinched his hat brim with the hand that held the reins.

He'd just started to turn his head forward when the thick-necked man's hand jerked down to his side. Moving deliberately, without undue haste, Colter turned back toward the saloon and with one hand raised his Winchester and punched a .44-caliber slug through the thick-necked man's belly.

The man grunted loudly. There was a wooden thud as his pistol dropped to the porch floor.

He staggered straight back and sat down against the front of the saloon. His partner had jerked with a start, dropping his pipe, when Colter's rifle had barked, and now he turned to see his friend kicking miserably and groaning, both hands covering the bloody wound in his belly.

"Oh!" the man who'd been smoking the pipe said, staring down at his friend. He turned to Colter but pointed at his dying partner. "Oh boy! Now, kid, you're *really* gonna regret that! Holy shit!" He ran over and crouched down beside his friend, exclaiming, "Ivy, you all right, hoss? Oh, Jesus! Oh, *Jesus*, look what he done to ya! He'll pay for that. I guarantee it, Ivy!"

Chapter 13

When the saloon door opened and several men ran out to investigate the shooting and yelling, Colter lowered his smoking rifle and continued leading the horses up the street.

The livery barn he'd spotted sat on a side-street corner, facing the side street itself. There wasn't much of anything around it except a large side paddock to the left, and several rental wagons and buggies parked against its right side, between the barn and the main street.

It was a simple barn with a hayloft. The loft doors were closed, but the first-floor double doors were open. A half-pint-sized man stood in the open doorway in ragged coveralls and a deerskin cap with dangling earflaps, holding a pitchfork low across his thighs as he stared in the direction of the gunfire.

As Colter approached, he said, "Got two horses here I'd like to stable. The coyote dun is mine. The sorrel is yours, I reckon, since its rider is deceased. I don't have much money, and I was wondering . . ."

"You were wondering what?" the girl asked.

Colter had let his question trail away when he saw that the overall-clad figure in the deerskin hat holding the pitchfork was not a half-pint-sized man, but a girl. One with a ripe, curvy body under all those soiled clothes.

"You were wondering if I'd take that horse in payment for stabling yours. Well, I reckon that depends on if you have a sales receipt or anything that tells me you ain't stolen that critter. Horse thievery is a hangin' offense most anywhere across the frontier, you know, and in Marshal Dunbar's town most of all. But . . ." She let her light brown eyes drop to the nickel-plated star on Colter's coat. "But . . . maybe it's your town, now, eh, Red?"

She looked at him with interest, this raggedly attired girl with a pretty, heart-shaped face and smooth skin colored peach by the sun and wind she'd been exposed to, working outdoors.

"Yeah, that's right," Colter said with vague defiance. He knew what the girl was seeing—a rangy young man in trail-worn duds whose long, straight copper red hair did nothing to hide the grisly scar on his lean, hairless face. "It's my town now. Till Marshal Dunbar heals from a recent bout with lead poisonin', anyway."

The girl didn't seem impressed. In fact, she seemed downright hostile. She leaned her pitchfork against the wall and took Colter's two sets of reins from him. "Well, you're a big man, then. We'll see how big you are when Mr. Garrett comes to town."

Colter scowled at her. Was everyone in this town meaner than a caged mink?

His rifle riding atop his left shoulder, he followed her and the horses into the barn. "If he owns a bank an' all, how come he ain't *in* town?"

"Bank's only open three days a week—Thursday, Friday, and Saturday. And he let's his so-called president, Mr. Beauchamp, run the place, mostly." She stopped the horses in the center alley, stepped up between them, and scratched their ears, cooing to them gently, letting them get to know her. Both mounts sniffed at her, ruffled their lips at her chin, and flicked their ears, responding to her ministrations. "He's got him a big ranch twelve miles out of town. For that, you oughta be right lucky. The twelve miles, I mean."

"How many men does he have ridin' for him?"

"He's probably kept on fifteen or so after the roundup, to see him through the winter. With Hagen dead and Demry out of commission—that was some shootin', I hear—only about twelve, thirteen. The odds are edgin' up in your favor." She gazed at him through the alley between the two horses. Northwest was nosing her left ear under the dangling flap of her cap. Colter found himself envying the horse. The girl was pretty in a rough-hewn sort of way, and her brown eyes seemed to caress him now while still owning a faintly mocking gleam.

"You heard 'em talkin' over at Frank Miller's Saloon."

She nodded and then pulled Northwest's bridle over the horse's ears. "Heard what they said to you, too. Seen what you did to Marlin Ulrich. Can't say as I blame you for that, after what they said, but Ulrich has friends."

"One less to try collectin' that fifty dollars." Colter slipped his saddlebags over his right shoulder and then stood with his rifle on the other shoulder, thumbs hooked behind his cartridge belt, watching the girl slowly, calmly unsaddle the horses.

"Oh, they'll collect it, all right."

"Thanks for the vote of confidence."

The girl gave him a wry look as she tossed a saddle onto a sawhorse.

"What's your name?" Colter asked her, liking the way she moved, wondering how she looked beneath all those bulky clothes. He'd bet she was fine as a young colt, her skin smooth like fresh-whipped cream. It had been a long time since he'd lain with a girl. That had been a percentage girl in Mexico, and then he'd gotten sick from too much tequila and Mexican tobacco and spent most of the evening airing his paunch in an alley.

He'd realized how long ago that had been when he'd met Victoria Dunbar. Even amidst the danger that kept the hair under his collar prickling, his young loins were heavy.

The blonde said, "Sarah Miller's my handle. What's yours?"

Colter started to tell her but stopped himself before he got his first name out and said, "Call me Red."

She gave him another wry look. "All right, Red. Don't suppose you'd tell me how you got that scar, either."

"Nope."

"Well, you and Dunbar have that in common, anyway."

"How'd he get his?"

"Never heard tell." Sarah Miller lifted her chin at him. "It ain't really so bad, not how they were tellin' it."

Colter looked at her curiously.

"That scar, I mean. Any girl worth her salt would see past it. What she saw, then, though, I reckon only you'd know that, eh, Red?"

Colter turned away from her probing gaze. He walked back to the open door and stared toward the saloon on the other side of the main street, off to his left and ahead of him now. Three men were hunkered over the man Colter had shot, speaking loudly, the man who'd been out there with the gut-shot gent now pointing his arm toward the barn and Colter standing in its open doorway. The friend of Marlin Ulrich was talking the loudest.

"Your family run this place?" he asked the girl, vaguely curious but mainly just wanting to make conversation. He felt some comfort in being around her, though he kept his eyes on the saloon, figuring that that's where the next trouble would come from.

"It's just me that runs this place." She was rubbing Northwest down now with a thick piece of burlap, patting the horse as she did. She had a currycomb hanging from a frayed rope around her neck.

Colter glanced at her.

"Pa was a drunk. Had a heart attack fetchin' firewood last winter, froze up solid. He left this place to me. The saloon over yonder, where you gut-shot Ulrich, was his, too. Pete Simon bought it from me but kept the name. I like workin' the barn, won't have nothin' to do with drunkards. It's a livin', anyway."

Colter turned sideways to study Sarah Miller more closely under the light of this new information. Like him, she was alone. "You must be twenty or so. How come you ain't married?"

She kept working, breathing hard with the effort

of running the burlap over Northwest's right wither. "How come you ain't married?"

Properly chagrined, he said, "All right."

"All right what?"

"I see your point."

"It ain't proper askin' a girl why she ain't married."

"I know that."

She paused in her work to smile at him. "There ain't no man I'll take orders from," she said. "That's my problem." She continued working. "Most are lazy and won't work. I won't support one. Just supportin' myself is enough work for me. What's your problem? Since I shared, you can, too. Go ahead." She stretched her pink lips, and her eyes flashed with gentle teasing. "Don't be shy."

The scar in Colter's cheek burned. Embarrassed, customarily tongue-tied, he had to look away from her brash gaze.

"There ain't enough hours left in this day to tell you all my problems, Miss Miller. Well, I got a prisoner to see to. I'd best get back to the jailhouse. Can we settle up later?"

"I reckon I'll know where to find you."

He started walking out away from the barn.

"Red?"

He turned.

Sarah stood in the barn's open doorway, staring out at him, the currycomb in a gloved hand. "Since you're new here an' all, let me give you a piece of advice you might find useful." She shook her head slowly. "Don't get yourself killed for Dunbar. He ain't worth it. In fact, it would have been best for this town if Billy's gang had done the job right and turned him under. The only reason someone hasn't done it before, though a few have tried, is on account of his purty daughter. No man wants to get on the schoolteacher's bad side till she's married up and they figure they no longer have a chance at her."

Colter considered the information as well as the sincere cast to Sarah's gaze.

"All right, then," he said. "Good to know."

He pinched his hat brim and walked back toward the main street and his new place of employment.

Dr. Crabtree opened the door of Dunbar's room and stepped out, looking haggard. One of his white shirtsleeves was rolled down, but the cuff was unbuttoned. He rolled down the other one, his hands still wet from the washing he'd given them after the surgery, and buttoned the cuff.

Victoria Dunbar rose from the piano bench she'd been sitting on, setting her teacup and saucer on the bench beside her, and said, "How is he, Doc?"

Morgan Garrett rose from the overstuffed leather sofa angled in front of the popping hearth, holding his own teacup and saucer in his fine white hands. "Yes, Doctor, how is he?"

"Don't ask me how," Crabtree said, buttoning his other cuff, "after losing all that blood, but I actually think he's going to make it. One of the bullets had gone all the way through without hitting anything vital. The other was lodged against the bone, but the toughest part of digging it out was the fact that it was embedded in so much old scar tissue."

He frowned incredulously at Victoria. "Young lady, how many times has your father been shot, anyway?"

"Too many to count," she said with a sigh. "It's been the bane of my life. I don't know how to thank you, Doctor, but I suppose I could start by paying your fee."

"Don't you worry about that, Victoria." Crabtree pulled his long bearskin coat off the back of the marshal's favorite rocker and shrugged into it. "You just invite me over for pot roast a couple times this winter, and we'll call it even."

Victoria smiled sadly. Crabtree knew that she and her father were always short on money. Dunbar spent it as fast as it came in—on food and what Victoria needed, to be sure. But also on whiskey, women, and gambling. To Matthew Dunbar, money was for spending.

Victoria had been paid only once this year by the school council, and that had gone to lay in a couple of cords of firewood.

"Keep a close eye on him tonight," Crabtree said, donning his beaver hat. He walked back into Dunbar's room and returned a moment later with his medical kit. "He's resting comfortably, but you'll need to keep his temperature down with cold sponge baths. He'll likely wake soon in powerful pain. I'd leave laudanum, but whiskey works the same, and he'd prefer it, anyway."

"Thanks again, Doctor."

Crabtree squeezed her wrist. He hadn't yet looked at Morgan, who stood by the sofa in respectful silence, holding his teacup in one hand, saucer in the other. Now the doctor favored Hawk Garrett's eldest son with a sharp glance, drawing his mouth corners down, dipping his chin cordially, and heading for the door. Crabtree was of that half of the town who did not favor the Garretts, whom many considered to be predatory ranchers at best, rustlers and killers at the worst. Anyone trying to homestead anywhere around Garrett's spread was quick to disappear.

Garrett was evil but he was also shrewd. He'd built the bank here in Justice City to build his power and tighten his stranglehold on the entire county.

"Your brother's just lucky he didn't kill the marshal, young man," the doctor grumbled. "That's a hanging offense even for a Garrett." He glanced at Victoria. "And I doubt his daughter would approve."

"Oh, Dr. Crabtree," Victoria said, placing her hand on Morgan's forearm. "Morgan is every bit as distraught over this as I am."

Crabtree frowned at Morgan. "Whatever could have possessed him to ambush Dunbar and rob his own family's bank?"

"To prove that he could," Morgan said wearily. "And to keep the marshal from running him down— likely the only man around excepting our own father, of course, who could." The tall, well-groomed, well-attired Garrett brother ran his index finger around the rim of the delicate china cup in his hand. "I assure you, Doctor, I do not approve in the least of my brother's behavior. Whatever differences the marshal and I have, they certainly do not extend to law and order here in Justice City. My brother has been allowed to run off his leash for far too long, and this is the capstone to his depravities. I understand that. I know my father does, as well."

"And what do you think he plans to do about it?" Crabtree asked.

Morgan only sighed. A good man with culture albeit a fondness for gambling, he was the black sheep of the Garrett family. He lived out there amongst them, but he was not of them. He didn't even carry a gun most of the time. Usually only a pocket pistol when gambling. He even kept a hotel room in town. Victoria saw the good in Morgan; indeed, she could not have fallen in love with him if he was the man his father and his brother were.

Like Victoria, Morgan enjoyed reading. Victor Hugo was his favorite author, *Les Misérables* his favorite novel.

"I honestly don't know what the punishment will be," Morgan said. "But I guarantee you it will be harsh and swift when he's learned that Billy's been found."

"Will he try to break him out of the lockup?"

Morgan's pale cheeks flushed slightly as he stared down at the cup, troubled. "You know my father. He prefers to handle family matters in his own fashion, and he certainly has locked horns over the years with Marshal Dunbar. I honestly don't know. I'll be conferring with him later this evening, when I ride out to the Eight-Bar-G."

Crabtree scowled distastefully, shaking his head reprovingly at the whole affair. He nodded to Victoria and walked out into the snowy late afternoon.

When he was gone, Morgan turned to Victoria. "You know that's true, don't you?" he asked. "I feel nothing but absolute revulsion for what my brother has done to your father, Victoria."

She placed a gentle hand on his cheek, smiled sympathetically up at him. "I know that, dear Morgan. Please don't fret over this."

"Oh, thank God!" Morgan Garrett wrapped his arms around her shoulders and drew her close against his chest. "I love you more than anything,

Victoria. If this did anything to hamper our getting married in the spring, I think I'd shoot my wretched brother myself!"

"Oh, Morgan—please don't."

Morgan tried to kiss her. She turned her lips aside to peck his cheek, and then with an indulgent smile, she wriggled out of his arms. "Before you go, I'll fetch that book you lent me."

He scowled in frustration as she strode out of the parlor.

Chapter 14

"You're still kickin', eh, Red?" Billy said as Colter walked into the jailhouse, brushing snow off his saddlebags. "Well, not for much damn longer if you don't fetch that sawbones over here *and if you don't build a fire in that consarned stove!*"

The long-haired, dark-eyed, pimply-faced firebrand snarled like a wolf through the bars of the jail cell.

Colter set his saddlebags on the floor near the door, leaned his rifle against the wall, and doffed his hat. He looked at Billy, who was glaring at him through the bars, nostrils wide. Colter wasn't accustomed to taking orders—not since he'd left home, anyway—but he supposed he did have a responsibility to keep his prisoner alive. And the temperature was dropping fast as the afternoon waned.

With a sigh, he walked out the back door at the rear of the stone stairs and found a small lean-to with half a cord of pine logs in it. A splitting maul was embedded in the chopping block near a pile of bark and sawdust.

He used the maul to split enough wood for the next couple of hours, shaving one log into feather sticks for kindling, and carried an armload of the wood back into the jailhouse. As he dropped it into the box beside the stove, Billy watching him from the cot inside his cell, Colter said, "Tell me somethin' while I make you comfortable. I assume you come from a rich family, since your old man owns the bank an' all." He glanced at Billy in the cell behind him. "Why'd you rob the bank?"

Clamping a hand against his torn ear, Billy hiked a shoulder. "What the hell is it to you?"

Colter laid several strips of paper inside the woodstove and began arranging the smallest feather sticks over and around it, building a small tipi. "Your brother's a well-set-up gent. Fine duds an' all. I'm sure he would have lent you a few greenbacks if you'd asked."

The redhead glanced over his shoulder, genuinely curious about Billy's motives. He couldn't imagine stealing when you had no need to steal. Why would a person want to complicate his life like that?

"You don't know nothin' about my brother," Billy said. "Him an' me—we don't get along. He's my pa's favorite, but rest assured he hates the old man same as I do."

"He's a real tough nut, then—your pa."

"Yeah, but I'm tougher. Twice as tough, in fact." Billy grinned. "Especially now that he's gettin' old."

"Your brother don't seem all that tough. He looks like a fancy-Steve to me."

Billy chuckled. "That's a good way to describe

him. No, he ain't tough. Still, Pa favors Morgan over me, though Morgan hardly ever worked a day in his life out on the range. Never really got into the rough work of keepin' a range clear of nesters, neither. Or runnin' down an' hangin' rustlers, which this country's purely damn full of. At least it was before my pa moved in and built up the ranch to supply the little minin' camps around here with beef."

Colter struck a match against the woodstove. It flared to life, reaching high, then shortening and growing dimmer. Colter poked it through the stove's open door, touched the flame to the paper poking out through the leaning feather sticks. "What's he doin' with a bank?"

"Well, the country needs a bank. Pa knew nothin' about bankin', but shit, that didn't stop him from buildin' his own and callin' himself the president." Billy laughed wryly and shook his head. "He advertised in the papers for a chief financial officer—he loved sayin' that and still does—and so here comes Joe Beauchamp and the missus and their two whinin' brats, and Joe pretty much runs things over at the bank. You should see the look on his face when I wagged my pistols in his face, told him I was robbin' him blind."

"I bet he damn near pissed himself."

"Oh, he did piss himself." Billy clapped and tipped his head back, loosing a victorious howl. "I seen piss on his fancy brown shoes. Sure enough, he did. You got that right, Red!"

Billy laughed some more as Colter added a good-sized log to the growing fire inside the stove. "Red, you got a name besides Red?"

On one knee, Colter watched the flames settle around the larger log, wondering if he'd added it too soon. He didn't want to start the whole thing over again. He wanted to get a pot of coffee boiling. "Red's good enough."

"Red, you know, I got a feelin' under different circumstances, you an' me might have been friends."

"You think so?"

"Shit, yeah." Billy paused. Colter could feel the kid's eyes on him, measuring him, probing him through the strap-iron bars. "And it ain't too late."

"Oh, no?" Colter looked over his shoulder at him.

"Hell, no." Billy glanced at the bulging saddle-bags occupying the cell to Colter's left. "There's damn near fifty thousand dollars in them pouches, my friend. The time to rob a bank in ranching country is just after the fall gather and sale."

Colter looked at the fire growing in the stove. Again, the idea of what he could do and how far he could get on that much money poked at him, and then the guilt for his considering it poked him even harder.

"Sorry, amigo." Colter chunked another log onto the fire and closed the door. "You're talking to the wrong—"

The front door opened suddenly. Colter leaped to his feet, and his Remington was instantly in his hand, the hammer clicking back.

"Jesus!" The man who'd just entered widened his eyes at Colter's cocked pistol and fell back against the open door, losing his footing and sliding down the door to the floor. His crisp bowler hat tumbled down his chest.

Another newcomer, dressed as smart as the first, grabbed the falling man's hand and hauled him back to his feet with a grunted, "Christ, Norman!"

Three more men poked their hatted heads in the

door, scowling at Colter, who now lowered the Remington slightly while keeping the hammer cocked just in case. The five men before him didn't look as if they needed fifty dollars, but Colter hadn't remained alive as long as he had by throwing caution to the wind.

Billy chuckled drolly. "He's a fast sumbitch, ain't he?"

The man who'd fallen, Norman, scooped his snow-dusted bowler off the floor, blinking indignantly beneath bushy gray-brown brows at Colter still standing in front of the stove. "You can holster that weapon, young fella. We're not here to collect Ray Beacon's bounty."

The man nearest him, tall and sporting a black handlebar mustache, smiled and said, "And neither are the rest of us."

Colter did not do as he'd been told. "What do you want?"

"We are businessmen here in Justice City," Norman Cantwell said as the four other men continued on into the jailhouse to form a semicircle around him. Cantwell appeared the oldest—somewhere in his late forties, early fifties. The last one in closed the door carefully, as though afraid it might spring open on him, all the while eyeing Colter's well-cared-for Remington.

"That there is the chief financial officer, Mr. Beauchamp his own self," Billy said, mockingly. "How's it hangin', Joe? Well, your money's back!" He added with less vigor, "Wouldn't be if I'd chosen my gang a little better. Damn fools. They let this scar-faced kid who won't even tell nobody his real name take 'em down, just like shootin' ducks on a millpond."

Beauchamp had been the last one in. He was the best dressed—a pale man of average height and build with a trimmed ginger mustache and sideburns. His large brown eyes betrayed little emotion except, when directed at Billy, a tightly bridled loathing.

The businessmen ignored the bank robber, instead keeping their gazes on Colter.

Norman said, "I am Norman Cantwell. I run the hotel—the Summit, down the street to the east. Joe there runs the bank for Billy's father, Hawk Garrett. George Atchison runs the Blue Mountain Saloon, and—"

"Hey, George," Billy said mockingly through the bars, "is Kansas City Jane workin' tonight? Damn, you really found somethin' when you found her. Red, I highly recommend Kansas City Jane. She'll curl your toes!"

Colter ignored Billy, who was getting more and more tedious to be around. The others appeared to have had enough of Billy long ago. No one so much as looked at the pimple-faced firebrand.

"As I was saying," Cantwell continued with a testy sigh, "this is Burt Peebles and the man beside him is Bill Williams. Burt is the land agent, while Williams owns Justice City Mercantile. He is also the postmaster. The reason we are here, Mr. . . . ."

"No mister, just Red."

Norman paused to study Colter dubiously and then continued with "The reason we are here, Red, is that we five compose Justice City's town council. We'd like to know who you are exactly, why you're wearing Marshal Dunbar's badge, why you are occupying this office, and why that stolen bank money has not yet been returned to Mr. Beauchamp, who, as Mr.

Garrett has stated, is the High County Trust's chief financial officer."

Colter holstered his pistol, snapped the keeper thong over the hammer, walked over to a shelf behind the stove, and pulled down a dented tin coffeepot. "I was asked by Marshal Dunbar to fill his position until he feels well enough to fill it again himself."

"How do we know you're qualified?" asked the land agent, Peebles.

Colter had just filled the pot from what he assumed to be drinking water in a wooden bucket hanging from a rusty spike in the wall. He glanced at Billy still standing up against the cell door, watching the proceedings with a speculative delight. He could have been watching girls dance naked.

Colter said, "Well, I got him in there, don't I? And, hell, Dunbar thought I was qualified. I got a feelin' the marshal don't throw his badges around like a percentage girl her charms."

Billy snickered.

"Be that as it may—and I want you to know that I still question your qualifications, young man— why on earth isn't the money that young Garrett stole from the bank not back *inside* the bank but is occupying a cell here in Dunbar's lockup? That money belongs to *all* of us!"

Colter set the coffeepot on top of the stove and shrugged. "That's where Dunbar told me to put it."

Joe Beauchamp spoke up for the first time. "You can turn it over to me, Mr. . . . uh . . . Red." He canted his head at the jail cell. "And while I certainly don't condone young Mr. Garrett's behavior in my bank earlier today, nor his shooting of Dunbar, you'd best let him go. His father knows how to handle Billy."

"You tell him, Joe!" Billy said.

Colter chuckled, not sure he could believe his own ears. "Let him go? Mister, he himself admits to waving pistols in your face as he robbed you and this town and his own father of fifty thousand dollars!"

Beauchamp thrust his arm toward the saddlebags. "We got it back, right? Isn't that it there?"

Colter sat down in the swivel chair behind Dunbar's desk, staring incredulously from man to man. "Are you fellas so afraid of Mr. Garrett that you're willing to forgive armed bank robbery?"

"Mr. Garrett is a very respected citizen of this community," Norman Cantwell said. "Without him—"

"Hold on, now, both of you," interrupted George Atchison, owner of the Blue Mountain Saloon. He was a big, beefy gent whose suit and rings fit him too tightly, and he had sawdust on his knees. "I'm not for turnin' that thief loose at all. We never discussed that, Cantwell. And as for you, Joe—I'm with Red on this one. Keep his ass in jail. The money, now, is a different matter."

The land agent, Peebles, nodded. "No point in turnin' the kid loose. The money, however—that's the town's money as well as Garrett's." He frowned suspiciously at Colter. "Why are you holdin' it, young fella?"

"Dunbar's orders. I'm not releasing the money or Billy there. They'll both be in them cells until I hear from Dunbar."

"What if he dies?" intoned Beauchamp.

"I'll cross that bridge when and if I come to it."

The mercantile owner, Bill Williams, loudly

blew his bulbous red nose with a red handkerchief
and shook his head. "Damn cold weather."

The short, pudgy man with long gray hair stuffed
the handkerchief into his steel-colored suit coat
pocket. "I'm with young Red here on the loot. As far
as Billy goes, I say we turn him out when his father
arrives. If Dunbar was here, I'd say let Dunbar's justice run its course. But with him laid up, possibly on
his deathbed, it's just damn foolish to hold on to him.
Hell, the circuit judge couldn't get way up here for
two weeks. Last I heard he was way down in Provo!"

"Dunbar's justice?" Billy said, hands wrapped
around two steel cell door bands. "You know his justice. The bastard's been waitin' to play cat's cradle
with my head. . . ."

"And you danced right into his trap, you brig-
and!" said Beauchamp, red-faced and wide-eyed
with anger. He shook his head, genuinely baffled. "I
just don't understand you."

"Ah, hell." Billy retreated from the cell door and
sank down on his cot. He leaned back against the
wall, raised a knee, and rested his arm over it. "You
fellas are just piss-burned because Dunbar ain't dead.
Yet." He grinned wickedly, curling his upper lip.

All five of the town council members looked chagrined.

"That true?" Colter asked.

Beauchamp pushed up between Cantwell and
Atchison. "Listen, kid. Turn Billy loose. Keepin'
him in here ain't doin' anyone any good. His father,
Mr. Garrett, will be comin' for him soon. The only
reason he hasn't been here yet is that he had business in a mining camp up north and probably didn't
even hear about this whole affair until just a little
while ago. Hell, maybe he still hasn't heard about it.

But he will when Ray and Demry get back to the ranch."

"And he ain't gonna like it that you got his son locked up," Cantwell added. "Now, he'd expect Dunbar to do that, and them two would lock horns. Terrible horns. Hell, the whole town would likely get shot up before they got through goin' at each other, and the whole damn town would suffer. But Dunbar's laid up with them wounds, so there ain't no good reason in hell for you to hold Billy."

"Go on, turn him loose," Beauchamp urged. "Hell, kid, haven't you heard there's a fifty-dollar bounty on your head? That's a lot of money for some men in this town. Men good with a long gun!"

Atchison rammed his big fist into his open palm. "Goddamnit! Are you tellin' me we just gotta keep on kowtowin' to Garrett no matter what he or his son does? Hell, his men are damn hard on my girls. The only thing been keepin' 'em at all in check is Dunbar. So without the marshal, are you sayin' this town is wide open again, the way it was before Dunbar came to town?"

Cantwell turned his own anger-reddened face to Atchison, who towered over him. "You know as well as I do that it was a mistake hiring that mastodon. He's an ex-bare-knuckle fighter, ex–New York street cop turned vigilante out here in our little mountain town."

"He keeps things civil," said the land agent, Peebles, in a soft, reasonable tone, as though trying to hold the other men's emotions in check. "Without him, we'd go back to the way we were five years ago. All us honest businessmen would be like sheep against the curly wolves that once prowled these mountains . . . and would continue to do so without Dunbar."

"I don't think that's true, Burt," said Cantwell. "That was five years ago. Things have changed. Things have gotten much more civilized. Even up here in Justice City."

There was a high-pitched tinkle followed a wink later by the ferocious crack of a bullet ricocheting off a strap-iron cell bar. A wink after that, the thunder of a rifle rocketed over the town.

Billy screeched and cowered on his cot.

Burt Peebles yowled and grabbed his left shoulder.

"Everyone, down!" Colter shouted, bolting out of his chair and lunging for his rifle.

Chapter 15

The five councilmen dropped to the floor as Colter retrieved his rifle from where it leaned against the wall near the door.

He pumped a round into the chamber. As he did, a bullet slammed into the door to his left, causing the door to lurch in its frame. The slug did not go all the way through, but it almost did. Colter could see the gray slug through a web of bulging splinters.

Another rifle belched, tearing through the window over the desk and *spang*ing off a strap-iron bar of the cell in which Colter had secured the bank loot. Billy screamed again beneath his arms, which he was using to shield his head, "Knock it off, you damn fools!"

Colter opened the door, edged a look around the frame. It was almost dark and the snow was still falling, covering the street. Several shadows milled to each side of the two-story Blue Mountain Saloon on the street's other side.

Something moved behind a stock trough out in front of the place. Colter saw a rifle barrel come up from behind the trough. It flashed and roared, and Colter drew his head back behind the front wall as the slug crashed into the jailhouse's stone wall with a screeching *ping*.

Colter snaked his Winchester around the doorframe and fired four quick rounds, the long gun roaring and lapping frames toward the Blue Mountain Saloon. Three or four man-shaped shadows shouted and yelped and dashed around wildly, heading for cover.

"Hold your fire! Hold your damn fire!" bellowed Norman Cantwell, who sat on the floor with his back to the front wall. He yelled up to the broken window between him and Dunbar's desk, *"You've got five town council members in here, you bloody fools!"*

"Not to mention Billy Garrett!" Billy shouted. "Hold your fire or my pa will have you *gut-shot*!"

Momentary silence. Then one of the men on the other side of the street said, "Shit. Never thought about hittin' Billy."

"Or the five councilmen!" shouted Burt Peebles in his frightened, nasal rasp, crouched by Dunbar's chair and holding his hat to his chest. He held his other hand to the torn shoulder seam of his suit jacket through which blood seeped.

Outside, someone laughed.

"They're drunk," Cantwell said to no one in particular.

Colter aimed the Winchester toward the other

side of the street. He could hear the ambushers conferring. He saw one leaning slightly out from the
saloon's west wall, holding a rifle in his hands. He
was silhouetted against the lilac sky, obscured by
the slanting snow. Their dull tones and intermittent
chuckles told Colter that they were all six sheets to
the wind.

"You hear that, Magoon?" Cantwell shouted, rising to a crouch and jutting his face up near the side
of the window. "Yeah, I know you gotta be one of
the damn fools out there. Call it a night or I'll see
you . . ." He paused, glanced at Colter a little uncertainly, and then finished with ". . . locked up in here
with young Garrett."

"Goddamn idiot!" Billy shouted. "Go on back to
Miller's place. Try again tomorrow when this scar-
faced law dog *is well away from the friggin' jail!*"

Another silence. The councilmen shifted around
on the floor to Colter's right. The snow sifted down
to lie on the jailhouse's front porch and the street.

"Sorry, Billy!" one of the men on the other side
of the street shouted.

The man who'd been standing against the
saloon's west wall took off running in the direction
of Frank Miller's Saloon, to Colter's left. Colter had
an urge to take a shot at him, but then the man's
shadow melded with that of the barbershop beside
the Blue Mountain, and then Colter could only hear
his boots thudding along boardwalks.

Three more men rose from behind the two stock
troughs in front of the Blue Mountain and took off
running, crouching, in the same direction as the
other man. Another had apparently been on the
saloon's porch. Now his shadow leaped over the rail.

He dropped to the ground with a grunt and ran after the others, holding a rifle in one hand.

"Shit!" he hissed, slowing his pace and limping. "Think I twisted my ankle!"

Colter stepped out onto the porch, holding the Winchester across his shoulder, and looked around at the street shrouded in twilight. Shadows jostled in the window of the Blue Mountain Saloon, one man and a girl poking their heads out the saloon/brothel's front door.

"Well, my nerves are shot!" Bill Williams said inside the jailhouse.

Colter heard footsteps and turned to see Atchison step out onto the porch, looking around cautiously. He glanced at Colter. "All clear?"

"For now."

The owner of the Blue Mountain Saloon turned toward Frank Miller's place a couple of blocks west of his own establishment and the jailhouse. He cupped his hands around his mouth. "Drunken fools! Don't none of you ever even *think* about steppin' foot in *my* place again. You hear?"

The big man shook his head and stepped down off the stoop and into the street, staring toward Frank Miller's place as he headed directly across the street to his own saloon and whorehouse, whose chimney was spewing smoke into the lilac sky in which stars were kindling.

A couple of the others shuffled out onto the porch. Cantwell stood behind Colter. He donned his black bowler hat and said softly, "Do yourself a favor and turn him loose, kid." He canted his head to indicate

Colter's prisoner. "Do us *all* a favor. Turn him loose. Tomorrow, those men won't be drunk and I can attest to the fact that they're all good shots."

Cantwell moved on down the steps. Beauchamp glanced at Colter darkly. He had some glass on the brim of his own bowler hat. As he followed Cantwell, Peebles and Bill Williams walked out of the jail-house and hurried after the others, casting dark glances toward Frank Miller's place. Peebles cursed and wheezed as he held his hand over his bullet-burned shoulder.

Colter stood staring toward Frank Miller's saloon, as well. Fury seethed in him. He squeezed his rifle in his hands, heart thudding heavily.

There was nothing lower than a bushwhacker. Maybe it was high time someone taught that lesson to the bushwhackers now settling back down with drinks at the far saloon.

"You all right, Red?"

Colter jerked slightly with a start. He turned to the girl standing just off the west end of the stoop, to his left.

Sarah was bundled up against the cold. Her blond hair spilled down from her round-brimmed felt hat. It was neatly arranged across her shoulders clad in a heavy red wool coat. Recently brushed, her hair shone in the late, feeble light.

"Didn't mean to startle you," she said softly. She had her hands shoved down in her coat pockets. "Heard the shootin'. Figured it might be some boys from Pa's old saloon. The clientele over there has dropped a notch since Pa's passin'."

Colter lowered his rifle, thumbed his hat back off his forehead. "They decided to take some target practice, I reckon. I'll be fine."

Sarah held her eyes on him for a time. Then her mouth corners rose a little and she said, "If you want to get warm later, I got a house behind my barn. If you want to come in out of the cold for a while, I'm sayin'."

Colter stared at her.

She pooched her lips out slightly, shook her head. "That scar don't bite, I reckon." She turned slowly, keeping her eyes on his coquettishly, and then walked back along the south side of the street, disappearing into the shadows of the closed shops.

Colter walked back into Dunbar's office. Billy stood peering through his cell door. He grinned. "That a girl's voice I heard out there? You already sparkin' somebody, Red, when you should be watchin' your prisoner?"

"Shut up, Billy."

Colter leaned his rifle against the wall.

"Maybe your heart ain't really in this thing. Come on, Red. Unlock this door. And then unlock *that* one, and you an' me can ride out of here rich men. I know a place where we can hole up and then light a shuck for Mexico as soon as the snow stops."

Colter ignored him. Water was boiling up out of the coffeepot's spout. Colter used a leather swatch to set the pot on the desk and then grabbed a couple of logs from the wood box.

"Hey, shut the door, Red. You're lettin' all the heat out! You born in a barn?"

"I'm goin' out again."

"Where?"

"Shut up."

Colter chunked a couple of logs in the stove and then closed and latched the door with a shrill metallic squawk. He hauled his saddlebags onto Dunbar's

desk and rummaged around in a pouch before pulling out a second Remington revolver he'd taken off
a man he'd killed a couple of months ago in west
Texas, when he and the notorious bounty hunter,
Lou Prophet, and Lou's beautiful partner, Louisa
Bonaventure, had taken on the gang of an evil dwarf
named Mordecai Moon.

This Remington was a little newer than the one
he always wore, but he preferred the old one because
it had belonged to his foster father, Trace Cassidy.
Over the last few years, the gun had accounted for
the lives of many evil men, and it now felt like a
natural extension of his hand.

"What the hell you up to?" Billy asked, puzzled.

Colter opened the second gun's loading gate,
spun the cylinder. All the cylinders except one
showed brass. He filled the one that had been under
the hammer, closed the loading gate, spun the cylinder, and shoved the pistol down behind the buckle
of his cartridge belt.

Pistols worked best in close quarters. He'd leave
the Winchester here in the jailhouse.

"Okay, Red," Billy said darkly. "What's on your
mind? Come on, tell ole Billy about it. He might just
be able to talk you out of it and save your life."

"Nothin' to worry about." Colter tugged his hat
brim down low on his forehead and started for the
open door. "I'm just gonna buy us a little peace and
quiet tonight."

He went out and closed the door.

Billy's voice was muffled behind him. "Boy, I
sure don't like the sound of that, Red!"

Colter looked around. The street was deserted
except for horses tied here and there out in front of
saloons. In the Blue Mountain Saloon directly

across the street from the jailhouse, someone was playing a jovial fiddle. Colter could see the shadows of men and women dancing in the window right of the closed front winter doors.

He walked along the south side of the street, following Sarah's prints in the freshly fallen snow. Her tracks were already fuzzy with new stuff. It was a pleasant snowfall, and it would have looked pretty on a different, quieter night—when he and Northwest were out alone, say, beyond any town and all the trouble settlements caused. Maybe just sitting around a fire in some abandoned line shack or cave . . .

It was hard being alone. But he was finding it harder being out amongst people.

Maybe it was time to kill a useless few.

He followed Sarah's small prints as far west as her father's old saloon. Then he swung directly toward the saloon, crossing the street, walking between two horses tied at the rack, and mounted the porch steps.

The winter door was closed. Colter turned the knob and stepped quickly inside, drawing the door closed as he stepped to the right, putting his back to the front wall.

Frank Miller's old place was deep and low. There was a woodstove halfway down the long room. The bar was to the right. Four men in fur coats stood at the bar, each separately. Snowbound saddle tramps, most likely.

A dozen or so other men were sitting at several tables—five at one about halfway down the room. Those were the men Colter was looking for. He could tell because one had his boot off and his bare foot propped atop the table. With a cigarette drooping between his lips, he was pinching his trousers up with both hands, showing his friends his swollen ankle and murmuring around the smoldering quirley.

Colter walked forward, stepping around two tables. A short, fat, bald man with a curly yellow beard stood at the bar, holding a towel in one hand against the bar top. In his other fist was a beer schooner. He scowled as Colter continued walking down the room.

"Hey!" the barman called, jutting a fat finger. "No trouble in here, kid!"

The room fell suddenly silent. The five at the table before Colter turned toward him sharply. All ten eyes widened, nearly popped out of their dark-shadowed sockets. There wasn't much light in the place—only a few lamps, a few candles, and the glow of the fire through the stove's open door.

Colter swung to the barman. "You stay out of this, you fat son of a bitch." He'd kept his voice low, but the barman must have heard the menace in it because he merely dropped his head a few inches, like a scolded dog, though he kept watching Colter from beneath his brows.

Colter turned to the five men at the table about ten feet in front of him. "You got somethin' you wanna say to me?"

They all stared at him, jaws hanging, eyes wary as those of a jackrabbit that had wandered inadvertently into a den of hungry brush wolves.

"If you wanna gun me, gun me now, you goddamn cowardly tinhorn sons o' bitches." Colter threw his empty hands out from his sides, exposing his chest and belly. "Here I am. What's the matter? This too close for ya? This too personal? Come on,

I'm only one scar-faced kid against five of you yellow-livered dung beetles."

Very slowly, keeping his eyes on Colter, the bushwhacker with the swollen ankle dragged his foot off the table and lowered it to the floor.

The room was as quiet as a gallows the night before a hanging. The five men before him stared up at him dreadfully. Finally, the man on Colter's far left let a slow smile shape itself on his bearded face, and he said, "Why, Red . . . we was just funnin'. That's all."

"Yeah," said another, clearing a frog from his throat. "We was just tryin' to scare ya."

"All you succeeded in doin' was piss-burnin' me," Colter said. "So you'd best keep tryin'. Now stand up and face me like the men I'm sure your friends here know you to be. Hell, there's five of you. Surely you can take one skinny kid, can't you? I don't have anyone backin' me! I'm all alone here!"

He glanced quickly over his shoulder just to make sure none of the three men behind him was about to back shoot him. He was confident they wouldn't. They all looked as cowed as the five in front of him.

Colter turned his head forward. The five appeared to have turned to stone. They just sat staring up at him, a couple with cunning beginning to drift into their otherwise cow-stupid gazes.

"You got a choice here," Colter said. "You can either slap leather, haul those hog legs up, and try to shoot me from where you can *see* me. Or you can apologize for actin' like back-shootin' cowards out there a few minutes ago." He licked his lips, shaped a slow smile. "What's it gonna be?"

Chapter 16

"You mind if we stand up?" asked one of the five bushwhackers—the biggest of the bunch, who was missing the tip of his nose.

"No, go ahead."

"Shit, I'm barefoot," said the one with the swollen ankle. "I can't get into a pistol fight with a sore ankle. Mind if I sit out this one?"

"Yes."

The man with the swollen ankle—a tall man with sallow cheeks—flushed and glared at Colter from beneath his brows. He grunted, opened his mouth, let his cigarette fall to the floor, where it sparked and rolled.

The others, keeping their drink-rheumy eyes on Colter, slid their chairs back and climbed to their feet, chairs creaking as the weight left them. Colter kept the bartender in the periphery of his vision.

The big man stepped back away from the bar,

looking owly and apprehensive. At the same time, every man in the room behind and beyond Colter scrambled out of his chair and hurried to either side of where the potential lead would fly. One forgot his beer and lurched back to his table to retrieve it, but then he fell over a chair and spilled it, anyway. He cursed and scrambled to his feet and joined the man he'd been drinking with, breathing hard.

One of the five men facing Colter sighed.

The one with the swollen ankle kept glaring at Colter, jaw hard. They'd all swept their coats back away from pistols jutting on their hips or from their thighs. These men were well versed in gunmanship. Their pistols were well cared for. Three of the five carried two. They all wore knives in addition to hog legs.

But they were drunk. And they hadn't counted on a real lead swap this evening. They'd wanted the safe bet tonight. They'd wanted to shoot from a distance and hope they hit their target and collect the fifty dollars so they could keep drinking and whoring for a few more days before they had to look for more legitimate work.

They hadn't expected that there'd be consequences.

But there were. Just as soon as the man missing the end of his nose dropped his hands toward his pistols, they all found that out as both of Colter's pistols filled the room with their roars, flames, and billowing smoke. Only one got a shot off—the man to Colter's far left triggered his own Remington into his own table, shattering a whiskey glass and spraying whiskey in all directions.

Ten seconds after the tooth-gnashing explosions had filled the room, they stopped.

All five men were down.

The man with the bad ankle had sat down on the floor against the bar, blood spewing from the hole in his green-plaid shirt, just left of his heart. Breathing hard, wincing, grinding his teeth, he stared up at Colter.

"D-damn it, you ugly little dog fart." He lifted his chin toward the top of the bar. Tonelessly, he said, "Pete, you make sure they plant me with both boots—you hear?"

The bartender, Pete, had ducked behind the bar. Now he lifted his bald head and looked around with dark eyes, saying, "Yeah, I hear ya, Karl."

Karl's butt slid out from under him and he sagged lower against the bar. He got a glaze-eyed, stupid look on his face as he died.

Colter swung around, both cocked, smoking pistols in his hands, making sure that none of the other customers had gotten the impulsive idea to avenge any of the five dead men. They didn't. In fact, to a man they flinched and pressed their backs tighter against the wall and the bar.

Colter holstered his pistols and, keeping a close eye on the room, went over to the free lunch set up on plates atop the bar's right end, near the door. The barman eyed him pugnaciously. Colter made two ham-and-cheese sandwiches on crusty brown bread, expecting the man to tell him the lunch was only for paying customers.

But Pete didn't say a word. No one did. One of the dead men farted.

Colter shoved both sandwiches into his coat pockets. Out of long habit, he backed toward the front of the saloon, then turned around and walked out onto the porch, hearing a rumble of chatter rise from behind the closed door. He stepped to the top of the porch steps and began removing the spent cartridges in both pistols and replacing them with new from his cartridge belt.

The empty cartridges clinked onto the snowy boards around his boots.

He glanced behind him. The din was rising inside the saloon. One man peeked out, saw Colter, and jerked his head back away from the window. Colter turned his head back forward, shoved his main pistol into the cross-draw holster on his right hip and the other behind his cartridge belt. He lifted his hands in front of him. They were as still as stones. His heart was hardly beating.

He'd killed five men and he didn't feel a thing aside from satisfaction that he'd gotten his revenge.

He chuckled darkly. Jesus Christ, what in hell had he become? Whatever it was, it had become necessary. By God, he wasn't going to take any shit off anyone anymore.

He glanced behind once more. The windows were empty, though he could see jostling shadows behind them and hear boots pounding inside the place, the muffled din of exclamatory voices. He dropped down off the steps and looked toward the jailhouse.

The light of the lamp he'd lit bled through the broken window onto the snowy porch, casting the rest of the place in deep shadow. Dark as it was, he could see that no one was moving around the stone building. No one likely would after the bloodbath in Frank Miller's. Word of such things traveled as fast as bullets even on nights as cold and snowy as this one.

Colter started angling toward the far side of the street, heading east toward the jailhouse. He'd best stoke the woodstove for Billy. With that window having been shot out by his friends, the firebrand was likely getting pretty chilly.

"How many men you gonna kill tonight, Red?" the young outlaw asked as Colter walked back into the jailhouse.

"As many as it takes, I reckon."

"Hey, your name ain't Billy the Kid, is it? I never heard of the Kid sportin' a nasty scar on his face, though, less'n he ran into a brandin' iron of late."

Colter pulled one of the sandwiches out of his coat pocket and thrust it through the bar. Billy looked at it, surprised. "Pete Simon's free lunch, eh?" He chuckled and took the sandwich like a hungry though vaguely suspicious dog. "Thanks, Red. I thought I was gonna have to stomp a rat."

Colter began stoking the woodstove. Sitting back on his cot and devouring the sandwich hungrily, Billy said, "I could hear the pops o' them pistols way over here. You get all of 'em?"

"Yep."

"Christ!" Billy tried to whistle, but he only spat bread and meat. "Who taught you to shoot, anyways, Red?"

"Men like them."

Colter closed the stove door and then took the lamp out back to gather more wood. When he'd stoked the stove to roaring, and made sure the box beside it was piled with split wood dry enough for burning, he shoved the second sandwich through the bars at Billy.

"Here you go. Cold night. Gonna need some tallow."

Billy took the sandwich. "What about you, Red?"

"I'll think of somethin'."

Colter grabbed his rifle and went out.

"What—you think of someone in town you forgot to kill?" Billy shouted through the door.

The girl's tracks were nearly covered by now, but Colter could still see their slight outline in the starlight sparkling off the snow. As he passed Frank Miller's place, he saw men hauling the dead out the front door, down the porch steps, and around the side of the building to the back.

They'd probably store the bodies in a woodshed or stable and have the undertaker tend to them come morning or when the weather cleared.

Colter followed Sarah's tracks around behind the livery barn that was closed up tight for the night, its sloping, shake-shingled roof mantled with snow. There was a cabin behind the barn's rear paddock, sitting all alone in some pines and cottonwoods, flanked by a small stable and a privy.

The girl was outside, sweeping snow off her stoop. At least, Colter assumed it was Sarah. She was a mere shadow against the weathered-gray log cabin, but as he drew closer and continued following the footsteps toward the front door, he saw her blond hair glowing in the light from a window behind her.

Colter paused in the yard before the house. Sarah stopped sweeping, canted her head to one side, gazing into the darkness. "Well, hello."

"Hello."

"You hungry?"

"Oh, I reckon I wouldn't refuse a little bite of somethin'."

"You best come on up to the house, then. I'm not gonna serve it to you out there."

Colter strode to the porch and up the three steps. She stood regarding him wistfully, her broom in her hands. She wore a dress under her coat. Her hair shone in the lamplight. Something told him Sarah didn't wear dresses often but that she'd put this one on for him.

She turned and opened the screen door and then the inside door. Colter grabbed the screen door, hesitating, feeling awkward, bashful. She stomped her feet on the hemp rug in front of the door and then shrugged out of her coat.

"Come on in and stop gawkin' like an idiot," she said as she hung her coat on a peg near the door, smiling at him, her sparkling brown eyes complementing the smooth, healthy tan of her pretty, open face.

Her eyes seemed to be holding a secret that faintly amused her. Colter didn't know if he should be offended by that, but he found himself liking that sparkle in her eyes, and the casual way she swung her hips as she walked around the oilcloth-covered table, brushing the oilcloth with her fingertips, the dress clinging tightly to her narrow waist.

"I've eaten, but I saved you a plate," she said as Colter closed the door and then stomped snow from his boots on the hemp rug before the jamb. "Take your coat off. There's water there behind you. Men must wash before they enter Sarah Miller's shack. Especially men with as much blood on their hands as you have."

"You heard the shootin'?"

"Oh, yes. I knew it was you," she said with a fateful sigh, leaning forward against a chair back. "Your guns have a special ring. Can't quite describe it."

Colter only snorted at that. He felt awkward and bashful, as he always did around pretty girls. The scar on his cheek burned and tingled, making him extra aware of its presence. He hung his hat and coat on a peg next to Sarah's coat and, sweeping his hair back from his face, glanced at Sarah.

She stood behind a chair on the other side of the rectangular table, both hands on the knobs of the chair back, sucking her lower lip as she continued watching with that faint, puzzling amusement. He felt a little annoyed by the patronizing air about her, but he liked the warmth of the kitchen and the smell of the food and he liked how Sarah's hair and eyes shone in the lamplight and how her two front teeth were revealed by her slightly parted lips. A salmon-colored birthmark, like a thumbprint, lay just above the collar of her high-necked dress.

He liked how the dress clung to her breasts that thrust toward him as she rocked back and forth on the heels of her shoes. It was a conservative, gray-and-brown-plaid dress that went well with her blond hair and brown eyes. It was what he would normally consider an old lady's dress, complete with a cameo pin holding the collar closed at her throat.

But on Sarah's firm, curvy, full-busted young body, it grabbed him by the throat and made his tongue feel thick and heavy in his mouth.

She smiled, her cheeks dimpling, and he turned away sharply, realizing he'd been ogling her again. "I'm glad you like the dress," she said. "It was my mother's, and it's the only one I own."

Colter knew he should have something to say in response, but his heart was beating in his ears, and he occupied himself with unbuttoning his shirt cuffs and rolling his sleeves up his arms. He poured water from a pitcher into the porcelain washbasin atop the wooden stand and then splashed water on his face and lathered up with a cake of lye soap and washed his face, neck, and arms thoroughly, taking his time, both wanting to turn around and face Sarah again, whose eyes he could feel burning into his back, and yet not wanting to.

Because he had absolutely no idea what to say to this girl with such frank eyes and such an alluring figure and who seemed to say just whatever came into her head.

He dried with the towel hanging by a nail over the basin—a clean towel, he noticed—and then turned to the table. The water had been warm.

Sarah was setting a plate, topped with another plate to keep the steam in, on Colter's side of the table. She removed the cover, and steam wafted up, rife with the smell of the roasted beef, mashed potatoes and gravy, green beans, and the chunk of buttered bread, heaped before him. It smelled so rich and succulent, the gravy and meat so peppery, that it almost took Colter's breath away.

"Holy moly!" he intoned, the cat suddenly releasing his tongue, gaping down at the plate before him.

"Sit down and dig in. We don't hold with form here in the Miller residence." Sarah reached for a milk bottle that stood with a whiskey bottle, a water glass, and two shot glasses on the end of the table to Colter's right. "Milk?"

"If you can spare it." Milk was often a precious commodity in smaller settlements secluded in the high-and-rocky—especially in the late fall, early winter.

"I got my own cow in the barn out back," she said, removing the cork from the bottle and pouring the rich, buttery substance into the glass. She filled it to the brim.

"You a whiskey-drinkin' man, Red?"

He wasn't, really. As on the road out here, he'd tried to drink like most men he knew drank, but he'd gotten a little too zealous about it several times too many, and the head-splitting, gut-twisting results and decidedly unmanly display it had led to, often in front of pleasure girls, had left a bad taste in his mouth.

"What the hell?" he said, still mesmerized by the food but then catching his manners. "I mean sure. Why not?"

"I'm not forcin' you," she said. "I just like to have a shot or two with a meal. I reckon I take after my pa that way."

He glanced up at her, his mouth already full of the hot, delicious food, and heard the defensiveness in his own voice as he said, "Pour it up."

"All right, then," she said, arching her brows.

She filled two shot glasses and slid one toward him and then sat back in her chair, sipping from her shot glass and watching him eat. He felt a little self-conscious about her just sitting there, staring at him in that amused way of hers, but the food was so good and his belly was so empty that he couldn't have paid much attention to her if she'd been sitting there naked.

When he'd swabbed the last of the potatoes and gravy from his plate with a last chunk of bread and swallowed it, he glanced up to see her smiling at him, her shot glass empty.

"Wow!" she said. "You were hungry."

"I ain't had a meal like that in a month of Sundays."

"I miss watching a hungry man eat."

"Thank you, Miss Sarah." Colter drained his milk glass and wiped his mouth with the napkin she'd provided. "That was dang good!"

"Dessert? I have some cherry pie in the keeper shed."

He shook his head and stifled a belch. "I couldn't eat another bite."

She was leaning forward on the table now, looking almost as hungry as he'd been only a few short minutes ago. His self-consciousness returned. The brand started burning again. Habitually, he turned his head slightly while tilting it forward to let the hair on the left side of his head fall forward to partially hide Bill Rondo's brand.

Keeping his eyes down, he wrapped his hand around the shot of bourbon he hadn't yet touched, and shoved it toward him. At the same time, Sarah rose, walked around the table, and sat in the chair beside him, curling one leg beneath her. She reached up and slid his hair back away from his branded cheek.

Colter flinched and jerked his head back slightly. "What're you doin'?"

"Shhh." Sarah leaned forward, persisting in very gently running the tips of her fingers over the scar. "We all have scars, Colter," she said softly, staring at the brand as though her eyes were caressing his scarred face along with her fingers. "Some folks wear 'em on the inside, others on the outside."

He regarded her curiously. Beneath her touch and scrutiny, he wasn't sure why, but the fire in the scar abated. "I bet you don't have none to speak of," he said. Her skin was flawless. No scars and, except for the birthmark, hardly a blemish.

"Sure I do." Her eyes slid to his. "I had a baby once, two years ago. It's buried out back of the cabin. That there's a scar."

That almost literally threw him back in his chair. Most *married* women didn't even let folks know they were pregnant, let alone those with no men around. None whom Colter had ever known or even heard of, aside from whores, would tell about having lost a child. It just wasn't done.

"I'm sorry to hear that," was all he could say.

She lowered her hand but kept her face very close to his, her eyes flitting around, probing him, the skin above the bridge of her nose slightly wrinkled. "Does that shock you?"

"A little."

"It shocked most folks around here. Shocked my pa prob'ly most of all." She turned away and lifted Colter's shot glass to her lips, took a small sip. "The baby's father was a no-account killed by Dunbar. The marshal caught Donny stealing a horse one night out of Pa's own livery barn, when Pa was still alive. Donny took a shot at Dunbar, and the marshal shot Donny off the horse with that shotgun of his. He's buried now out back, where I buried the baby two months later."

"Oh."

"Donny and me were going to be married, and he was working with Pa an' me in the barn and helping over at the saloon. I guess when the baby started to swell my belly, he got cold feet, decided he'd try his luck elsewhere. The shame of it all's what killed Pa."

Colter looked at her hand resting on her thigh. He placed his hand on it, squeezed it gently. She turned to him, her enticing lips parted slightly. He leaned forward and kissed her, squeezing her hand a little harder. She returned the squeeze as she returned the kiss.

She pulled her head away. "I'd like to know your name, Red. Don't worry—I won't go blabbin' it around."

"It's Colter Farrow." He didn't even pause to wonder if he could trust her—he just did.

She nodded pensively, as though running the name around in her mind for a time. The way her mouth corners quirked and her eyes shone brighter, he could tell she'd found it acceptable.

"And the scar . . .?"

Colter shook his head slightly, picked up the shot glass, and took a small sip, wincing against the burn in his throat. "Not yet, Sarah."

"All right, Colter." Holding his hand, she rose from the table and smiled down at him. "Come on."

He just stared at her, incredulous.

"Yes," she said, smiling brighter, tugging on his arm. "I'm craven and I'm going to burn in hell for liking a man in my bed from time to time. But it's been a long time now since I had one, on account of my reputation, not to mention that I work in a livery barn. But I figure you won't mind. Your reputation around here ain't so good, neither."

She chuckled as she led him around the table, into the darkness of the cabin's living area, through a curtained doorway, and into a small bedroom lit by a single candle.

He watched her undress by the light of that candle, his heart fluttering. Then he, too, undressed, kicking out of his boots first and then shucking so quickly out of the rest of his duds that he tripped and fell.

They both laughed.

"Colter, are you drunk?"

"From one sip? Pshaw! Takes a whole bottle to just get me started!"

They laughed again.

As he approached the bed, they both got quiet. She'd been kneeling on the bed, up near the headboard. Now she clambered forward, her pale breasts jostling, and reached up for him, her eyes grave. He wrapped his arms around her, hugging her closely, feeling her trembling against him.

Together, they sagged slowly into the mattress.

Chapter 17

Colter left Sarah curled in sleep in the warm sheets and quilts of her bed. He dressed quietly, stoked the woodstove in her room, and slipped quietly out of her dark cabin to go kicking through the new-fallen snow, giddy from coupling, toward the jailhouse.

Never mind how many men he'd killed that day. The recent ninety minutes spent in Sarah's clutches had washed his sins away. He wished he could have stayed till morning, but his prisoner might have been frozen up solid as a marble slab by then.

Duty called. He had to stoke the jailhouse's woodstove.

Nothing much had changed on the street since he'd left it a couple of hours ago. Frank Miller's place and the three or four other saloons up and down the broad main street of Justice City were still lit up against the snowy night. The snow had lightened, and now the small flakes danced in the air. It had lightened only recently, however, because the scuffed tracks made by the men hauling the dead bodies out of Frank Miller's had nearly been filled in, as had his own.

Colter walked slowly, his boots thudding and squeaking. He had his coat flaps tucked up behind his pistol butts. He scanned every inky black nook and cranny around and behind him for the sudden movement of a possible shooter.

His ears ached from the cold. He'd need a muffler soon if he was going to spend the winter at these climes. No point in repeating what happened to old Rory Nielsen, a hermetic shotgun rancher in the Lunatics who, too cheap to buy a scarf, had frozen both ears during a brutal winter cold snap many years ago, and spent the rest of his life with twisted white knobs on each side of his head.

Inside the jailhouse, Billy was curled up on his side beneath an army blanket, snoring. It was cold enough that Colter could see his breath, but apparently the firebrand hadn't awakened. The stove was still warm, though cold air was bleeding through the bullet holes in the window. The window would need to be patched.

Glad that he didn't have the full-time responsibility of a job such as this—he'd never figured on all the work it took to keep a single prisoner alive—Colter quietly built up the fire again. He banked it against the winter night, took one last, careful look around outside, and then went back into the jailhouse and curled up in the cell left of the bank loot.

He lay awake for a time wondering about Dunbar. Was the marshal still alive? He'd lost a lot of blood. If Dunbar had given up the ghost, where would that leave Colter? The way the redhead saw it, he was working for the Justice City town marshal. If Dunbar was dead, would Colter then just turn Billy free and be on his own way—head back out on the dodge again, searching for that one perfect place in which to winter before heading for Mexico in the spring?

That would make a lot of people in Justice City happy.

What about Sarah?

From his time in her bed, he knew her to be a free and easy girl. And not one who was ready yet to set her sights on any one man. Not after what she'd been through with Donny. Her and Colter's few hours together had been purely what the doctor had ordered, and he was having a hard time forgetting it and going to sleep—her skin had been soft as honey, her breasts warm and tender—but tumbling together for a few hours meant no more than that.

They'd warmed each other against a cold night. Kept each other company. That's all. It had not meant what his sleeping with Marianna Claymore had meant—that they were in love and intended to marry and spend the rest of their lives together.

Colter's world had grown so much larger and more complicated in the three years he'd been away from home. There were so many different breeds of people in it, all with their own experiences guiding them—their own scars, as Sarah had said, on the inside as well as the outside.

Colter drifted off so gradually that he was surprised to open his eyes and see bright morning light filling the broken window between the door and Dunbar's desk. He frowned. Something besides the light had awakened him.

Outside, a horse blew. He could hear it clearly through the window.

"I say in there—this is Hawk Garrett, and you'd best haul my boy out pronto or suffer the goddamn consequences!"

Colter jerked his head up off the cot with a startled gasp. At the same time, he saw Billy make a similar movement in the cell on the other side of the bank loot.

"Pa?" Billy said, dropping his boots to the floor. *"That you, Pa?"*

Colter rose, blinking sleep from his eyes. He ran his hands through his tangled hair, grabbed his rifle, pumped a cartridge into the chamber, and hurried out of the cell. He pressed a shoulder against the wall between the window and Dunbar's desk and edged a peek out the window.

Seven men straddling horses sat in the middle of the street fronting the jailhouse. They were sitting side by side, about ten feet apart.

The man in the middle of the group was obviously Hawk Garrett—a lion-lean, gray-bearded man with long, curly silver-gray hair hanging to the fur collar of his thigh-length buckskin mackinaw. He wore a sweat-stained cream Stetson with a red scarf over it, knotted beneath his chin. The face beneath the hat was raptorlike, brooding, with shrewd eyes set in deep, bony sockets.

His horse was a tall, white-socked black.

Over his saddlebow, Garrett held a Sharps repeating carbine.

The man's eyes met Colter's through the window. "Come on out here, scar-face!" he shouted. "You tore up one of my men, killed another one. Now you got my boy, worthless as he is, locked up in Dunbar's prison. Get out here. You need killin' and that jailhouse ain't gonna protect you!"

Colter gave a wry snort and donned his hat. He grabbed his spare Remington off the desk, shoved it down behind his cartridge belt, and set his rifle on his shoulder.

Billy stood with his face pressed up against the bars of his cell door. "Be careful, Pa. The kid's hell with a side iron!"

Colter walked over to the door, drew it wide, and stepped out onto the porch, the snow crunching beneath his boots. He looked at the men strung out before him along the street.

The breath frosting around their heads was painted gold by the sun just now splintering above the eastern horizon. Keeping his eyes on Garrett's gang, Colter leaned his rifle against a porch post near the top of the three steps and then walked down the steps and into the street, stopping about five feet in front of the porch.

Hawk Garrett stared at him, narrowing his eyes, canting his head from side to side. He chuckled as he turned to the man sitting to his left and said, "Demry wasn't lyin'. He is ugly enough to make a dog howl." He turned to Colter. "What the hell happened to you, boy?"

"Your wife closed her legs too fast," Colter said without skipping a beat, keeping his face bland. He thought best to communicate the fact that his being young, skinny, and ugly didn't mean he was about to take any shit.

Garrett's face reddened behind the silver-gray beard.

A couple of the men around him chuckled. A

couple more smiled but had sense enough to keep quiet.

Garrett said, "You got a smart mouth on you. A smart mouth to go with that hideous scar. You bring my kid out here and turn him loose, or you're gonna die today."

"Mister, I have a feelin' that if I bring your boy out here and turn him loose, we'll have a hoedown, anyway. What I'm sayin', see, is this: Billy's stayin' where he is, and you can kiss my ass."

Garrett glared at Colter, holding the reins of the black tight in his left fist, his other hand wrapped around the neck of the stout, angry-looking Sharps resting across his saddlebow. "Kid, there ain't no one in this entire county who dares talk to me the way you just did. For good reason. And right here this mornin', I'm gonna show them just how good that reason is."

Above and behind Colter, the porch roof creaked.

A cold breath of warning ensconced the redhead's heart when he saw a shadow move on the sunlit snow to his right—a shadow in the shape of a hatted man holding a rifle.

Across the street, a rifle thundered.

Behind and above Colter, a man grunted sharply. Colter was just then wheeling and pulling both his pistols up when the would-be bushwhacker dropped his rifle and fell forward off the edge of the roof. He turned a complete somersault and then hit the snow to Colter's right with a crunching thud and another grunt.

"Daddy, Daddy, I caught a fish—it's a real big one!" young Victoria cried as she ran along the bank of some creek in northern New Mexico, holding on to her fishing pole for dear life.

Dunbar sat up from where he'd been napping under a pine on his day off from whatever job he'd been working at the time—deputy sheriff or riding shotgun for a stage line, both of which he'd done when he'd taken his wife and daughter West, fleeing the rampant decay and sprawling horror that was New York City in the first few years after the War Between the States.

Dunbar laughed that explosive, resonant laugh of his that sounded like tin wash barrels rolling down a rocky hill. "Bring 'im onshore, girl! Don't let *him* take *you* out to sea!"

"He's too big, Daddy. I can't land him!"

The fish tugging at the end of Victoria's line threatened to rip the cane pole out of the six-year-old's hands. She grunted and groaned and ground her dirty bare heels into the dirt and gravel along the sage-stippled shore. But the fish, heading farther out toward the center of the creek, pulled her forward toward the silver-stitched dark water sliding between low banks.

"Hold on to 'im, little gal!" Dunbar bellowed as he heaved his big, muscular frame to his feet and came running, his heavy tread sounding like thunder behind her.

At the same time, Victoria watched her line twist around the branch of a pine tree that had fallen into the stream. The water-bearded line grew tighter and tighter. Victoria could hear it rasping against the wet branch. The willow pole quivered in her small hands as it slipped through her fingers. She imagined a monster with a hook in its mouth, just beneath the surface.

Victoria screamed. The line snapped and sagged, and she fell straight back on her rump.

"Ah, fudge, Daddy. He's *gone* an' he was the biggest darn fish in the whole *world*!"

"Hold on, me li'l gal!" Dunbar leaped up onto the pine tree that was jutting several yards into the stream, several stubby branches angling off the bole. "He ain't gone too far just yet! You let your old father give 'im a try!"

"Daddy, don't fall!" the girl cried, watching her father walk out along the tree, stepping around the jutting branches. "Let 'im go, Pa. He's just a fish!"

"Just you wait, me li'l gal!" That laugh again as the big man kept walking too quickly for his large size and the too-narrow tree he was tightroping, out toward where the end of the line was wrapped around a branch. The other end was still likely fastened to the monster's mouth, because the line was drawn taut as piano wire where it angled into the sliding, gurgling stream.

"Daddy!" the young girl cried, afraid for her fearless old pa, who, as her dearly departed mother had so often said, threw caution to the wind for the silliest of reasons. "Please let 'im go! He's just a fish!"

Just then Dunbar, who was approaching the branch around which the line was wrapped, pitched steeply sideways. He threw both his thick arms straight up into the air, and his mouth formed a perfect circle as he bellowed loudly and plunged back-first into the stream.

Splash!

"Papa!" Victoria climbed to her feet and ran along the shore, sobbing and screaming, *"Papa! Papa! Oh, Papa!"*

She leaped over the tree and stared into the water

where her father had disappeared. Drowned, for sure!

The water slid on by.

Dunbar's big head came grinning up out of it, eyes and mouth wide, yelling at the top of his lungs as he held the huge trout high in the air above his head, "Got 'im, me gal—and he'll fill a roasting pot, that one!"

In the dream, Victoria screamed at the size of the fish. Sitting in the rocking chair in the house she shared with her father in Justice City, twenty-three-year-old Victoria Dunbar gasped and lurched forward. The blanket she'd wrapped herself in, fully dressed, fell down to her waist.

The chair runners creaked. A whistling sounded. Or had been sounding . . .

That would be the teapot she'd set to boil after waking earlier to check on her father and to stoke the range. Wondering how long she'd been asleep—the water had likely taken a good half an hour to boil while the stove heated up—she glanced out the parlor window. Full light now, with golden sunlight washing through the snow-limned branches, making all the nearly leafless trees appear clad in sequin-studded wool.

It was still relatively dark in the house.

Victoria went into the kitchen, lifted the pot from the range, and filled a small china teapot that had belonged to her mother. She dumped in a small handful of English tea and then, yawning, sat down at the linen-covered, halved-log table to get awake and to wait for the tea to seep. Her father had never taken to coffee. Irish or English tea for him, often with a jigger of Kentucky bourbon but only because way out here he couldn't get the authentic Scottish whiskey he loved so much. To him, Southern bourbon was the only American spirit that even remotely resembled the nectar of the Scottish gods.

As Victoria sat alone in the quiet kitchen, the fish swam up out of the dreamworld once more. She saw her father's laughing eyes, the water streaming down his face as he stood in the waist-deep water, showing her the fish "she'd caught," and she laughed out loud, remembering that day so long ago.

Her mother had died only the year before when a stray bullet fired by a drunken miner had torn through the wall of the tent shack they'd been living in at the time, in Nevada City, Nevada, where Dunbar had been working as a deputy town marshal and a bartender. They'd been alone then, when she'd caught the fish—just Victoria and her larger-than-life father.

Her father whose eye had been carved out of his head with his own badge at the hands of a gang that had corralled him in a New York City alley.

Her father who had hunted down and killed each member of the gang in turn and then, knowing he'd compromised the safety of his family, turned in his resignation and headed west.

And he and Victoria had been alone ever since that stray bullet had killed her mother.

Except now Victoria had promised her hand to the son of her father's fiercest enemy.

Chin resting in her hand, the black-haired, blue-eyed Scottish beauty frowned down at the table, a dark mood winging over her. That's how she showed her gratitude to the man who'd raised her in surprising comfort for one of his own crude, violent, and impoverished origins. He'd grown up in Old Nichol, the most notoriously savage of the London slums.

He continued to live a hard, uncompromising life because it was the only life he knew, violence being the only way he knew how to survive.

In the distance, a rifle cracked, and Victoria jerked with a start. The report echoed flatly, eerily in the quiet morning. Every shot she'd ever heard and continued to hear she unconsciously assumed was meant for her father.

Not that one, however. It couldn't have been, because Dunbar was . . .

She turned her head slowly, dreadfully toward the front door. Her father's big bear coat was not hanging from the hook she'd hung it on when she and Dr. Crabtree had taken it off him yesterday. His nearly knee-high fur boots were gone, as well.

Victoria bounded up from her chair, strode quickly through the parlor, and opened the door to her father's room.

The bed was empty, the covers thrown back.

Dunbar was gone.

Chapter 18

The would-be bushwhacker, lying spread-eagle in the snow four feet to Colter's left, gave one last hic-cupping death grunt, his coat turning red over his chest, as the rifle spoke again.

Pa-chewww!

Hawk Garrett's hat flew off his head to lie in the snow near the dead man.

Three seconds hadn't passed since the first shot had thrown the would-be bushwhacker off the porch roof behind Colter, and all of Garrett's men were sitting their horses, stunned. But now, as the echo of the second shot bounced off the false-fronted, snow-mantled buildings lining the main street, they all whipped their heads around toward the far side of the street, Garrett exclaiming, "Goddamnit! Who in the hell . . . ?"

He let his voice trail off. He was likely seeing who Colter was seeing—the broad-shouldered gent with the thick walrus mustache, muttonchops, black top hat, and thigh-length bearskin coat sidled up against the wall of the Blue Mountain Saloon, aiming a Winchester from his shoulder.

"Dunbar!"

The Scotsman loosed a wild guffaw. "Come for the oozin's of your evil ole loins, eh, Garrett? You keep on like this and I'll be handin' him over to you, all right. I'll be handin' him over to you in itty-bitty little pieces you can carry home in a pickle jar! No need for dressin' him out—just pour him right into the grave!"

Dunbar laughed again, keeping his cheek pressed tight against the walnut stock of his Henry rifle, squinting down the barrel at Garrett.

"I thought he shot you, you old bastard!"

"Shootin's one thing, boyo. Killin's another."

Billy's voice sounded hollow from inside the jailhouse. "Pa, what's goin' on out there? Is that Dunbar?"

"Shut up, Billy!" both Garrett and Dunbar shouted at the same time.

Garrett said, "Turn him loose, Marshal. You know I'm the last person on this mountain you want to rile!"

"That boy robbed your bank, Garrett."

"That's right—my bank!"

"It ain't just your bank. You got the town's money in there. Besides, the law's been broke. You can press charges if you want to, but it don't matter one damn bit. The law's the law, and when the law's been broke, I step in and fix it. That's what the town council hired me to do five years ago, and that's what I do. You know it and I know it and the whole damn town knows it. And that's why Justice City's been livin' up to its name!"

"Marshal Dunbar!" someone called from up the street on Colter's right.

It was Norman Cantwell. He was walking toward the jailhouse from the direction of the Summit Hotel on the east end of town and on the same side of the street as the jailhouse. Joe Beauchamp was walking with him, and they were just now passing in front of the bank on the opposite side of the street from the hotel, where they must have been having breakfast together when they'd heard the shooting.

The men were walking quickly, kicking up the fresh snow around their knees clad in fine black broadcloth. They both wore fur coats and bowler hats. Cantwell had a thick scarf wrapped around his head so that Colter could only see his face from his red nose up.

"Please!" Cantwell pleaded. "Stop this right now! I am so tired of hearing gunfire in our fair town, I could hang myself!"

Colter could hear Dunbar say something beneath his breath on the far side of the street.

Loudly, the marshal said, "Stay where you are—both you and Beauchamp! This ain't no Sunday picnic down by the friggin' river! I'm out here doin' my job." He grinned at Colter. "Me an' the squire."

Colter spied movement in a second-story window of the Blue Mountain Saloon. A face peered out. It was hard to tell from this distance, but Colter thought it looked an awful lot like the handsome face of Morgan Garrett, Hawk's dandified son and Victoria's chosen.

Another face appeared beside young Garrett's. This was a girl with her hair pinned up. Her bare shoulders told Colter she wasn't wearing much, if anything. Morgan shoved the girl away from the window and then he, too, backed away while staring furtively down into the street.

Colter gave a silent snort. He'd instinctively disliked Morgan Garrett the instant he'd laid eyes on him. Now he knew why. He was taking tumbles behind his girl's back. Vaguely, Colter wondered what else he was doing.

As Cantwell and Beauchamp stopped in their tracks, scowling toward Dunbar, the marshal kept his attention on the seven horseback riders, most of whom had turned their horses around to face him.

"I got my sights laid plumb square on your black heart, Garrett. If you don't want my finger squeezin' this trigger, like it's itchin' to do, you throw down every last gun you're carryin'. Have your men do likewise. Every last one. If any of you buckos got a derringer keepin' his balls warm, you toss that out, too. Come on, now. Don't be shy!"

Garrett's head was turned toward Dunbar. His longish pewter hair blew in the slight breeze that lifted the bright snow like dust around the horses' legs. Apparently seeing the threat in his adversary's eyes, Garrett whipped his head toward the men around him. "Do as he says!"

He tossed his rifle over his horse's head. The Sharps dropped into the street and out of sight, painting a thin gray line in the snow. The others did likewise, and then they began unbuckling their cartridge belts and tossing them down along with guns they hauled up out of their boots.

When all seven of the Garrett riders sat slouched and scowling like scolded schoolboys, Dunbar grinned at Garrett. "Just makes you wish that worthless pup of yours would have done it right—don't it, Hawk?"

"Sure as hell does," Colter heard Hawk growl.

Dunbar turned his blue-eyed gaze on Colter. "Fetch our prisoner, will ya, squire? Time to get his trial out of the way. Oh, and bring the money he stole, too. As soon as it's booked into evidence, we can return it to Mr. Beauchamp over yonder. He'll be glad to have it back."

Colter stared at the big man, incredulous. Trial?

"Forget it, Dunbar!" Garrett shouted, leaning forward in his saddle and pounding his thigh with his gloved fist. "You ain't no judge and jury. The boy is mine, and I say how he's punished!"

Dunbar kept his mischievous gaze on Colter. "Squire, fetch the prisoner, if ya will."

Garrett whipped his head toward Colter, face crimson, jaw set hard with fury. "Don't do it, scar-face!"

Colter had been hesitating. Now he turned and walked back inside the jailhouse.

Billy stood in the middle of the cell, arms crossed on his chest. "Nope! I ain't goin' out there, Red! I go out there, that bastard's gonna play cat's cradle with my head!"

Colter dug the key out of his pocket and retrieved the loot-filled saddlebags. Then he opened the door to Billy's cell and stepped aside. He unholstered his pistol, clicked the hammer back.

"Out. Or I'll shoot you in here, Billy." He wasn't sure what he was doing, or why he was doing it. All he knew was that for some crazy reason he'd found himself admiring Dunbar enough to side with him—one man against the world, not unlike himself—and hating Hawk Garrett, though in many ways he and Dunbar probably weren't all that different.

"You know I can do it, Billy," Colter said, when the pimple-faced kid just stared at him, lips stubbornly pursed. "To me it don't mean a damn thing. And you know that, too." At the moment, it really didn't. Maybe it never would again.

Billy stared at him, blinked. The kid's chest rising and falling sharply, he shrugged into his coat and donned his leather-billed immigrant cap. He moved out of the cell slowly, like a condemned man walking to the gallows, which might very well be what he was doing. Colter didn't know what Dunbar had up his devilish sleeve.

"There you are, boyo!" Dunbar said, lowering his Henry, pressing the stock against his hip as he walked out from the side of the Blue Mountain Saloon. He was dragging his right leg. Colter saw a white bandage peeking through the round hole in the dark brown, bloodstained twill of the man's pant leg.

Dunbar waved the rifle. "Back! Back up. Give me some room, and crawl down off those horses or I'll shoot you out of your saddles!"

Garrett stared at the pugnacious lawman for a full five seconds, the rancher/bank owner's long, thick gray hair continuing to blow in the breeze. He did not look at his men but reined his horse out of Dunbar's path, swung his right leg over the black's hindquarters, and dropped to the ground.

His men did likewise, the horses' hooves crunching snow.

Moodily, Garrett's men dismounted and held their horses' reins. Garrett walked forward, scooped his hat out of the snow, brushed it off, batted it against his thigh, and set it on his head. Then he

walked back and stood by his horse, grave eyes on
Dunbar.

The marshal limped forward.

He stopped when sounds rose behind him, and
he turned toward where Garrett's older son, Morgan, was just now walking down the boardwalk
from the east. Colter curled his lip at the dandy's
subterfuge. He must have left the Blue Mountain
Saloon by a rear door and circled around so that he
now appeared to be walking from the direction of
the Summit Hotel.

He wore a long wool coat with a cinnamon bearskin collar and a black planter's hat with a brown
silk band. A thick black muffler was wrapped
around his neck, and he had his hands stuffed down
in his coat pockets.

In the window from which Colter had spied the
dandy looking out a few minutes ago was the pale
face of the girl Morgan had left. Her hair was down,
and she was brushing it while gazing into the street
with what appeared to be a bored air.

Dunbar yelled toward the fancy Dan, "Get a
good night's sleep, Morgan?"

Morgan stopped and canted his head to one side.

"Come on over." Dunbar beckoned. "You're just
in time for the trial."

Morgan stood staring at Dunbar from in front of
a millinery shop sharing space with an assayer's
office half a block away.

"You can't have a trial out here, you old coot!"
This from Morgan's father, Hawk Garrett.

"You watch me, bucko."

Dunbar continued forward, keeping his brightly
belligerent gaze on Garrett's men. He stopped

twenty feet from the jailhouse and jerked his chin back, beckoning.

Colter shoved Billy forward with his rifle barrel. Billy started forward, dropped slowly down the steps. "You can't have no trial, if that's what you're fixin' to do, old man. You got no judge and no jury."

"You know I don't need none o' that fluff." Dunbar looked at Colter. "Them the saddlebags you found on the gang that young Billy here was ridin' with, Red?"

Colter couldn't help enjoying himself. He couldn't help enjoying all of this—Dunbar cowing maybe seven of the most ruthless bastards in the entire county and going up against two prominent members of the city council. With two good-sized holes in his old body.

What balls!

"Yes, sir, they are."

Dunbar turned toward where Cantwell and Beauchamp stood still as statues. "Mr. Beauchamp, kindly get your ass over here, sir!"

Beauchamp glanced at Cantwell as though for help. Cantwell didn't look at him. Beauchamp came forward reluctantly. As he approached Dunbar, the marshal said, "Take a look in them saddlebags, Mr. Banker, sir."

Beauchamp turned his mouth corners down and then walked over to Colter, who handed him the saddlebags. Beauchamp set the bags on the ground and, looking around at Garrett and his men and then at Dunbar, unstrapped the flap over one of the pouches. He peeked inside.

"Yes, okay."

"That appear to be the money stolen from your bank yesterday morning?"

Beauchamp gave a peevish look to Billy. "It does."

"Is that there the lad who led up the gang who stole it?"

"He is," Beauchamp sighed, casting a wary look at Hawk Garrett.

Dunbar said, "I myself will testify that that there is the younker who shot me out back of the jailhouse when I was collectin' wood for me fire, yesterday mornin' . . . just before he and his gang went over and held up the bank. Fired three rounds. Two struck home—more or less, though I'm certain sure he'd have aimed better if he hadn't been whizzin' down his leg while he was shootin'. Then he run off like a headless chicken."

Dunbar ground his jaw at Billy, who averted his gaze, looking as though he'd sucked a lemon.

"Well, I reckon that pretty much seals it." Dunbar looked around. "Anyone here have any doubt that young Billy Garrett here done robbed his father's and Mr. Beauchamp's bank?"

"All, right, Dunbar," Beauchamp said, casting another wary glance at Hawk Garrett. "You've proven your point. Billy robbed the bank. But I for one do not intend to press charges. I'm sure his father will punish Billy in his own fashion and likely rehabilitate the boy, as well. I've no doubt he's just going through a phase, as so many his age do."

Dunbar looked at Colter. "You ever rob a bank, squire?"

"No, sir," Colter said, standing at the top of the porch steps, aiming his Winchester negligently out from his left hip. "Never have." *But you considered heading to Mexico with money that someone else had stolen,* a voice whispered in his ear.

"There you have it."

Garrett said quietly, "Dunbar, you're crossing a line here."

"Shit, I've never been on the other side of that line," Dunbar said, chuckling. "Not one goddamn day of my life." To Billy, he said, "Boy, as the chief law officer here in Justice City who five years ago was granted certain . . . uh . . . what one might say extraordinary privileges by the town council who wanted to bring law and order to their fine village at any cost, I hereby sentence you to death."

Billy blinked and dropped his lower jaw nearly to his chest. A murmur rose from Garrett's men while the rancher himself looked stony.

"Marshal Dunbar!" Cantwell intoned, striding forward. "As the chief sitting member of the Justice City town council, I hereby revoke any and all such privileges!"

Dunbar shook his head. "No point in waitin' on the judge. He won't show up till spring, if he shows up at all. I heard he's been sufferin' from a particularly painful bout of syphilis. Even if he did show up, he'd likely be three sheets to the wind an' swillin' that tarantula juice he favors.

"No, no. I've considered the evidence. My sentence will stand. Billy, I'm too shot up to do this good and proper. Besides, the hangin' tree was struck by lightnin' last fall. Split in half. I'm gonna give you two options. You can take it from either the front or the back. Which will it be?"

Dunbar pulled out a bone-gripped, silver-chased Smith & Wesson revolver from his coat pocket and clicked the hammer back.

Billy stumbled backward. "Pa, you can't let him do this!"

Garrett lurched forward. Dunbar swung the pistol on him. Garrett stopped.

"Wouldn't wanna make your Nancy boy Morgan over there an orphan, now, would you, Hawk?" Dunbar gave him a wolfish wink. "Or maybe his stepma would step in and raise him up proper."

"You an' me been at war since about two months after you got here, Dunbar. Cleanin' up a town is one thing. This . . ." Garrett glanced at his son, whose pimpled face was as white as the new-fallen snow, his eyes about to pop out of their sockets. "This here's cold-blooded murder. And you'll pay for it. You'll die bellowin' like a poleaxed bull, Dunbar!"

Dunbar grinned and turned to Billy. "Either turn around, boyo, or take it from the front."

Billy screeched and dropped to his knees. He threw himself forward and buried his head in the snow beneath his arms. "Pa, don't let him do it. Oh, please don't let him do it! I don't *wanna* die, Pa!"

Dunbar limped up to the kid, planted his boots about six inches away from the kid's head and tangled black hair. He glanced once more at Garrett, who narrowed his eyes at him, flaring his nostrils. His gaze promised all-out war if Dunbar followed through with the execution.

Colter could tell that Dunbar didn't care a bit. In fact, Garrett's presence at his own son's execution made it all the merrier for the big marshal. Colter watched the proceedings without judgment. It wasn't his town. He was just passing through. Apparently, the town had hired Dunbar to do this sort of thing. And he was doing it.

How big of a loss would Billy Garrett be to the town—to the world—anyway?

Still, Colter's heart raced. His hands tingled inside his gloves. If and when Dunbar squeezed the trigger of his silver-chased Smith & Wesson, a powder keg would be ignited. And he, Colter, would be right in the thick of it.

Chapter 19

"Please, don't kill me!" Billy screamed, grinding his forehead into the snow, against the leather bill of his cap.

"Sorry, boy," Dunbar said, aiming the Smith & Wesson at the back of the kid's head. "But this is what you bought and paid for—dry-gulchin' me and robbin' your daddy's bank."

"Dunbar!" Hawk Garrett shouted but holding his ground, knowing he'd get a bullet in his belly if he tried to intervene.

Dunbar was about to squeeze the pistol's trigger. Colter could see it in his eyes, and the redhead steeled himself for the shot. He could even see the man's finger start to squeeze the trigger—the marshal had cut the tip of the right index finger out of his glove, as did most men who wielded pistols in cold weather.

But then he removed his finger from the trigger

guard altogether when a young woman's voice rose from the far side of the street. "Dad, don't!"

Colter stretched his gaze across the morning-bright street to see Victoria Dunbar, clad in a long marten coat, standing near where her father had been standing only a few minutes ago. She had her hands stuffed into a rabbit fur hand warmer, which hung from her neck by a lanyard. Now she removed her bare hands from the warmer and came running through the snow in her high-topped black boots. She was not wearing a hat, and her thick black hair was alluringly messy as it bounced across her shoulders.

"Dad, don't," she said beseechingly as she approached, slowing to a walk when she was halfway across the street. She shook her head, scowling, shuttling her gaze from Garrett's men to the dead man in the snow near the porch, and then Billy and his father. "Don't do this."

Dunbar swallowed. He'd turned away from Colter, but the redhead could have sworn the old lawman had a sheepish look. "Victoria," he said with uncustomary softness, "this is no place for you. Go on back home."

"Please, Pa—look. You're bleeding." Victoria had glanced down at the man's thigh. The bandage peeking through the hole in his trousers had turned red. "Besides, you don't want to do this. Shoot this boy in the street in front of his own father."

"And brother," Colter couldn't help interjecting, though he wished he'd just stayed out of it. Whom the girl had given her hand to was no business of his.

Victoria looked at Colter with those eyes that seemed to see right through him, as though he were no more than a shadow. And then she looked around until her gaze held on Morgan Garrett, who now left the boardwalk and began walking toward her, taking long, hurried strides as though he'd been heading this way all along.

"Yes," Victoria said to her father, stepping up close to him. "In front of his brother—the man I've chosen to marry." She put a little steel in her voice now, and for the first time Colter could see that she'd gotten at least a little of her father's rugged toughness. At least enough to stand up to him when she deemed it necessary.

Dunbar depressed the pistol's hammer and lowered the weapon to his side. "Ah, hell."

Colter couldn't quite believe what he was seeing. Matthew Dunbar cowed by a woman! If the marshal were a dog, he'd be giving her his belly!

Despite his shock—and yes, his disappointment—at seeing Dunbar cowed, Colter was relieved that the burly marshal had heeded his daughter's entreaty. Nothing good would come of his killing Billy. The town—hell, probably the entire county!—would explode.

"Come on, Pa," Victoria said, wrapping an arm around her father's waist. "Let's get you back to bed."

Garrett said, "He free to go?"

Limping back in the direction from which he'd come, Dunbar merely threw up his arm. He continued dragging his right leg as he allowed his daughter, who looked like a fawn beside his bullish frame, to lead him in the direction of home. Morgan Garrett had stopped a ways away, uncertainly glancing at his brother and father, but then hurried after his girl and Dunbar.

Garrett gave a wry snort as he watched Morgan

go. Then he walked over to where he and his men had dropped their guns in the snow, and began kicking around for his shell belt and rifle, cursing under his breath. Meanwhile, Billy rose from the snow and dusted off his trousers. He stood straight and threw his long black hair back.

"Whew!" he said. "That was close." He grinned over his shoulder at Colter, dark eyes flashing. "You heard him, Red. I'm free to go. Reckon I'll just walk back inside and collect my gear."

Colter stepped aside. Billy brushed past him with that irritating grin on his pale, thin-lipped mouth though his eyelids were red from bawling. Colter was still standing in the same spot when Billy came back out strapping his shell belt and two holstered pistols around his waist, beneath his coat. He had his Winchester carbine clamped under his right arm.

"Well, it's been fun, Red." Billy turned to Colter and adjusted his hat, his eyes jeering and haughty. "Just so's you know, I don't harbor no ill feelin's over this. You was just doin' what you saw as your job." He winked. "Next time I see you, though, I'm gonna kill ya."

Colter held the firebrand's cold stare. "You try that."

"Billy, get your ass out here!" This from Hawk Garrett, who'd collected his weapons and was walking toward where his and his men's horses stood ground-tied up the street to the west. "You can ride Fletcher's horse. We'll collect yours later."

"Yes, sir, Pa!" Again, Billy gave Colter that mocking smile, and then he dropped happily down off the porch and into the street, tramping over the patch of yellow snow he'd left straight out from the porch steps.

* * *

Billy stepped over Larry Fletcher's dead body lying belly up in the snow, and ran down Fletcher's horse.

Fletcher's gelding didn't like anyone riding it except Fletcher, so it took Billy an embarrassing two or three minutes to get the horse settled down so he could toe a stirrup without risking being dragged halfway across town and making a spectacle of himself. More than he already had done in front of the jailhouse, that is.

Billy looked around self-consciously, glad that the only one out in the street now was the lanky redhead watching from the jailhouse porch. Shame from his earlier display still burned his ears and the back of his neck and set up a high-pitched screaming in his ears. It would take him a while to live that down, but he would. Oh, he would.

To hell with that jailer kid, anyway. Billy would teach him soon enough. Show him who was faster with a shooting iron.

As he settled himself on Fletcher's gelding's back, Billy cast a glance over his shoulder toward the jailhouse. The redhead pinched his hat brim to him. Billy pinched his own brim back. He touched spurs to the gelding's flanks and rode off after his father and his father's men, who were on the outskirts of town and heading off toward the west and the Garrett Eight-Bar-G spread out on Cottonwood Creek.

Beneath Billy's natural braggadocio, however, he wondered if he was good enough to take down Dunbar's deputy. Young as he was—even younger than Billy—Red had steely eyes and a cool, confident way of carrying himself. He was obviously also fast with a shooting iron. Faster than anyone Billy had ever seen. And he wasn't one damn bit afraid of anyone. Maybe of any*thing*.

Vaguely, aware of the cold, wet chill in the crotch of his long-handles, Billy wondered what that would be like. To live without fear. Not having to kowtow to any man, including his father.

Billy's jaw tightened as he brooded. Then his thoughts returned to his jailer.

No, Red was fast. Billy might have to dry-gulch the kid, the same way he'd dry-gulched Dunbar. Billy had his pride but not so much that he was going to let it get him killed.

Thinking of getting himself killed, he turned his gaze to his father. Hawk Garrett rode straight-backed in his saddle about a hundred yards ahead of Billy. His men rode around him. None of them was saying anything. None looked back toward Billy. They all rode with a grim air, breath frosting around their heads in the bright morning sunshine, fresh snow spraying up around their horses' knees.

Billy felt a stone drop in his chest. He didn't like it when his pa wasn't speaking. That usually meant something bad. He was sure his father would forgive him for robbing the bank, though. Hell, Billy had figured the old man might even approve of what he'd done. Or if not admire, at least *respect* him for it.

Wasn't bank robbing what the old man himself had done when he was Billy's age?

Hadn't Billy overheard Hawk Garrett mentioning to his foreman recently that robbing a bank or two was how a kid cut his teeth and put some iron in his balls? Sure, Hawk and his foreman, Hal Burleson, might have been drinking, but hell . . .

Billy started to wish he'd ridden the other direction

out of Justice City when he caught up to the group as they stopped to rest their horses in a grove of pines along Juniper Creek. As they loosened their saddle cinches, slipped the bits from their horses' mouths, and strapped feed sacks over their ears, no one so much as looked at Billy riding in on Fletcher's owly chestnut.

His father drifted off with Burleson, both men conferring in low tones. Billy tried to joke around with a few of the men standing around their horses, hauling out their makings sacks or pipes, but he might have been a pinecone for all the attention they paid him. No one would lend him any tobacco and papers, either, including one man he'd counted as a close friend, Rick Church. Church only shook his head and gave Billy his back.

"Hey, come on, Rick!" Billy tried to pull Rick back toward him, but his friend jerked his arm from Billy's grip. "What the hell you fellas so sore about?"

No one said anything.

They continued to say nothing after Hawk Garrett and Hal Burleson had returned to the group and they all mounted up, headed back out to the main trail, and continued on toward the Eight-Bar-G. Billy struggled with his mount again. He whipped the ornery beast with his reins ends, cursing. When he'd finally forked leather, he continued riding drag, a sullenness as well as deep apprehension shrouding him, like a cold, wet blanket.

Christ, they were all taking this pretty serious!

Would Pa or the other men ever speak to him again?

He was wishing more and more that he'd headed east from town instead of west. But he didn't have a dime to his name. Besides, he was hungry, and since

Red and old Dunbar had wiped out his gang, he was alone, too. The only place he had to go was the Eight-Bar-G.

Well, he'd pay his dues. He'd likely be due a whipping. And then he'd probably be cutting and hauling firewood all winter as well as driving the supply wagon to and from town—likely all by himself!—when the trail was passable.

He'd probably also be sleeping out in the bunkhouse with the hired men instead of in his room in the main lodge with Pa, Pa's wife, Angelina, Morgan—when Morgan wasn't staying over in Justice City to gamble and spark Dunbar's precious daughter—and Billy's two half sisters. Morgan had Pa believing that he was reading for the law with a local attorney, Owen Crebbs, but Billy knew that if Morgan was doing any reading it was only the local paper in the morning over coffee and brandy after gambling and whoring the previous night away.

Morgan had pulled the wool over Pa's eyes. Over Victoria Dunbar's eyes, too, for that matter. But most likely not over the eyes of old Dunbar himself. No, the marshal knew what Morgan was up to. Morgan and Victoria might think they were going to be hitched as soon as the first crocuses lifted their purple heads above the melting April snows, but Billy was damn confident they had another think coming.

The young firebrand grinned at that. The thought of Morgan's ruse being foiled by Dunbar warmed him and distracted him however briefly from the punishment he was due for robbing his father's bank.

Big mistake, that. The truth was, he'd wanted to pull that job for a long time. He figured he'd had his chance when Morgan mentioned in passing one night in the Blue Mountain that the safe was fairly bleeding scrip and specie after the fall roundups and sales. Billy had wanted to take that money and head to Mexico and spend the rest of his life grinning over how he'd beaten the old man. He'd never intended to see Hawk Garrett again.

Nor his brother.

Nor Justice City.

Only, that damn redheaded pistoleer had thrown a wrench into his wheel spokes.

And the kid would pay for that one, by God. For every whipping the old man gave Billy, Billy would strap the redhead double!

Before shooting him.

Chapter 20

It was midafternoon when Billy reached the ranch headquarters behind his father and the six hired hands.

He'd ridden slowly, in no hurry to get home to the whipping in front of his half sisters that he likely had coming. By the time he reached the ranch yard nestled between two stony mountain walls, the other riders had finished tending theirs and Hawk Garrett's horses, and were just now leaving the barn, heading for the long, shake-shingled log bunkhouse just beyond it.

They were all just as quiet as they'd been before. One—Roland Trilby—cast Billy a dark glance over his shoulder as he walked with the others through the snow over to the bunkhouse.

The sun was now hidden behind high, steel clouds, lowering a deep, early-winter gloom over the ranch yard and the two-story lodge house on the opposite side of the yard from the bunkhouse, barn, and corrals. Gray smoke unfurled from the lodge's large stone hearth, scenting the air with the smell of pine.

Billy dismounted in front of the main barn and then led the chestnut inside, where he tended the beast thoroughly, as was the tradition at the Eight-Bar-G. Billy had known many a man who'd endured his father's iron-fisted, whip-happy wrath when he'd neglected his horse. Billy had endured that whip once himself, when he was only eleven years old, but that was a punishment a fellow took heed to never endure twice.

The punishment he was due now would probably be as bad as that. Oh, well. He'd live. In the spring he'd steal one of his old man's horses and fog it the hell out of these god-forsaken mountains. With a fistful of greenbacks he'd swipe from the old man's office safe. . . .

Finished tending the horse and turning it out into the main paddock with the others, Billy walked over to the ranch house. The hair along the back of his neck pricked in anticipation of the punishment he had coming, but the smoke wheeling from the chimney beckoned with its promise of warmth. And food. Whatever Pa had in store for Billy, he wouldn't withhold food. Hawk Garrett knew he couldn't get as much work out of a hungry man as he could one with his belly sufficiently padded.

As he walked up the low front porch set on stone pilings, and which had been swept clear of snow likely by Hawk Garrett's Indian cook and housekeeper, Henry Three Wolves, Billy heard a horse approaching. He turned to see his brother Morgan coming along the trail from town, astride the handsome ovaro pinto he claimed to have won in a poker game from some horse rancher from the southern mountains.

Morgan turned his head toward Billy and then turned away, heading for the barn with that bland, snooty look all the rest of the men had been giving the firebrand. Billy curled his lip, crossed the porch, and threw the stout oak door open. He was starting to get his neck up. He could feel the anger burn down deep in his loins.

All right, he'd robbed the bank. He'd had some fun. If he was going to be punished, then the old man best make it quick, but he'd better not expect Billy Garrett to put up with no whipping or anything of that nature. He might have been resigned to it a few minutes ago, but on deeper consideration, he wasn't now, by God. He was a man, and he wouldn't be whipped by no one. Not even his father.

Shit, if the old man tried taking a whip to him, he might just find himself with a .44-caliber slug nestling between his eyes.

"Billy?"

Henry Three Wolves, the stooped old Ute who'd been working in the main house for years, had appeared in the kitchen doorway. Beyond him, Billy could see his stepmother and two half sisters milling about in the kitchen's deep shadows, helping Henry prepare supper. An ominous silence issued from the kitchen behind Henry. None of the women turned toward Billy, though they'd probably heard him come in. There were only the sounds of the women moving about and setting bowls down on the table or prying up stove lids.

"Yay-up," Billy said with a casualness not altogether feigned.

"Your pa wants to see you in his study, Billy."

"Thanks, Henry." Billy grinned. "Figured he would. I'd like a word with him my own self. Think I'll just freshen up a bit first."

"I'd just go on in there, if I was you, Billy," Henry said in his low monotone, a thick wing of salt-and-pepper hair hanging down over one eye. Henry had skin the red of a scorched brick, but he dressed like a white man.

"And I do appreciate your sage advice, Henry. I really do. Just the same, I believe I'm gonna freshen up a bit before I go in and powwow with Pa. Splash some water on my face and whatnot."

Henry just gave him a dark look, turned, and shuffled back into the kitchen, heading for the range with its smoking kettles and gurgling coffeepot.

Billy went into the mudroom adjacent to the front entrance and took his time washing, scrubbing his face, neck, and arms, and drying with the clean towel that Henry kept hanging from a nail over the basin. When he was through washing, he ran his damp fingers through his long dark brown hair—the brown of Pa's first wife, who some said was part Indian, though Billy didn't know for sure. Pa never talked about Billy and Morgan's mother. Garrett's second and current wife was Mexican, so it was likely the old man had married up with a savage the first time around, too.

Savage. Right fitting. Billy was starting to feel some of that savage come out in him, the way he was suddenly being treated around here. Yeah, he was starting to feel a hump in his back.

He threw his hair behind his shoulders, hitched his two pistols and cartridge belt a little higher on his narrow hips, and headed off down the main hall. He approached his father's study humming "Abilene

Saturday Night" just under his breath, walking with a swagger, swinging the guns jutting from his hips.

His father's study door was partway open. Billy knocked on it loudly and poked his head in. "Howdy, Pa. Henry said you wanted a word?"

When Morgan Garrett had finished rubbing down the Appaloosa, he turned the horse out into the main paddock and headed for the house.

He felt a pricking under the fur collar of his coat, and a fluttering in his chest.

What would his father's reaction be to Billy's having robbed the bank? So far, nothing that had happened in the past twenty-four hours had gone as he'd hoped it would. Oh, he'd known of Billy's plans to rob the bank, all right. He'd gotten word of those plans from one of Billy's drunken cronies, whom Morgan had paid to keep him informed of his impetuous kid brother's doings.

In fact, the bank robbery had been Morgan's idea, one that he'd voiced in passing to Billy one night in the Blue Mountain Saloon. He'd also suggested that if Billy had anything "ill-advised" in mind, he'd best figure on doing something first about the town's crazy Marshal Dunbar, who saw himself not only as judge, jury, and executioner in their fair town, but as God himself.

All of Morgan's own plans over the past seven months had been centered on Billy, which was anxiety-provoking. If Billy was one thing, he was undependable and unpredictable. Crazy, violent, headstrong, and with as much control as a runaway train. That was Billy. Still, Morgan's younger brother was the motor at the center of the locomotive Morgan had begun trying to set into motion ever since he'd decided that Victoria Dunbar would one day be his.

Not so much because he loved her, but because she was the most beautiful woman around—the most beautiful woman he'd ever known and would likely ever know. And he had enough of his own father in him to want to possess the very best that he could find. He also had enough of his own father in him to want to go against the wishes of his father and those of Victoria's own father, who'd long ago forbade Morgan to see her, let alone marry her.

Morgan was determined not only that he would marry Victoria Dunbar in the spring, but that he and she would live very comfortably out here on the ranch forever after. With Billy out of the way, his father's fortune, including the ranch, would be his. His father would soon be out of the way, as well. Morgan had found a letter written to Hawk Garrett by a doctor in Salt Lake City, where Garrett had gone to be examined last fall. The cancer the doctor had found was inoperable, and he'd given Garrett only two years to live.

Billy, however, was the variable Morgan couldn't depend on. Imagine the kid not only botching the robbery but leaving Dunbar alive!

Now, with all those thoughts swirling around in his semiconsciousness, making his shirt collar feel extra-tight behind his black cravat, Morgan climbed the lodge's porch steps and pushed through the heavy-timbered door to find Henry Three Wolves standing in the broad entrance hall, near the kitchen doorway, wiping his big hands on his flour-speckled apron.

"Morgan, your father wants a word with you in

his study. Billy's already in there. Said he wants you there, too."

"Good Lord," Morgan said under his breath, unwrapping his thick scarf from around his neck while shaking his head with phony graveness. "What now?"

Henry shuffled back into the kitchen as Morgan hung up his coat, scarf, and hat. He glanced into the kitchen. His stepmother, Angelina—a tall Mexican beauty even now, pushing forty—was rolling out piecrust dough on the table while his two plump, round-faced, dark-haired half sisters, Calico and Esmeralda, fifteen and thirteen, respectively, chopped apples for the filling. The girls looked up from beneath their brows as they worked.

All three wore dark, worried looks. Morgan's father was often like a wounded bear glooming around this bear den of his, keeping everyone in it thoroughly cowed. His having recently taken ill with severe stomach cramps hadn't helped Garrett's demeanor.

That's why Morgan had gotten away—at least, partly away. His father allowed him to stay in town while still collecting a monthly allowance, because Hawk Garrett believed Morgan to be reading for the law, though Morgan only paid his so-called instructor to lie and report that he was reading and having the law explained to him whenever Garrett inquired.

It wasn't hard for Morgan to deceive the old man. Morgan was Garrett's firstborn and therefore his favorite. Morgan had not been very good at working the range—or at work of any kind, for that matter—but he was intelligent and he was good at cards and women, and for some reason his father respected that. Maybe he was reliving his own youth through

Morgan, who, as he walked through the big house now, which was turning dark with the early mountain evening, felt as though he were on the cusp of war.

He felt a thrilling anxiety tapping at his heart.

He had no idea what was about to happen in this game he'd been wanting to see played out, leaving him a rich man and married to Dunbar's beautiful daughter, but he felt it would be big. And he had a feeling it would be in his favor.

He walked to the end of the hall and paused at the half-open door of his father's office. He could smell cigar smoke from inside, but he heard no voices.

He tapped on the door very lightly and was met with his father's booming voice. "Morgan, get in here!"

Morgan pushed the door open, stepped into the spartanly furnished office, and nodded at Hawk Garrett, who'd been standing at the window behind his desk to Morgan's right. Garrett wore a sheepskin vest, his twill trousers secured with a thick black belt and a large gold belt buckle. He held a long stogie negligently in his beringed right hand.

"Come on in and have a seat beside your brother there."

Billy sat in one of the leather armchairs angled in front of Garrett's large though plain pine desk appointed with only a reading lamp, an ink bottle and pen, a small leather-bound brand book, and a cloth-bound ledger book. There were no bookshelves, which was fine because there were no books to put on them. Hawk Garrett was not an educated man. Billy had never seen the man read a newspaper.

The only ornament in the room, which was not very large, was a painting of a beautiful red-haired, cream-skinned woman riding a white horse without a saddle through a green pasture surrounded by green trees and flowers of every color. The woman's nakedness was painstakingly, erotically charged, and it had been a source of endless fascination to both Morgan and Billy when they were younger.

It could still give a tug to Morgan's groin when he gave it more than a passing glance, which he did not do now, but stepped up to the empty chair to the left of Billy, who sat back in his own chair looking like a man awaiting a haircut on a slow Saturday afternoon in Justice City.

Billy's legs were extended before him, spurred boots crossed at the ankles. The kid had his hands entwined behind his head, and he was staring past his and Morgan's father and out the window, moving his lips in a fidgety, bored sort of way, as though it were summer and he were waiting to head to town for a night of whoring.

"Glad you're here, Morgan," Hawk said in his low, rumbling voice, blowing smoke at the window. "I wanted you to be here for this."

"Uh . . . for what, Pa?" Morgan asked, tension causing his voice to quake.

Chapter 21

As he eased into his chair, Morgan inwardly smiled at the thought of his smug younger brother getting the bullwhip—ten, twenty lashes to his bare back.

Hawk Garrett continued to stare out the window for a time as though purposely holding his sons in suspense, though it appeared that only Morgan felt any tension. Billy continued to lounge back in his chair as though his mind were miles away. Totally unconcerned.

Garrett took another puff off the stogie and then, blowing the smoke out of his mouth as well as his nostrils, swung around and sagged with a sigh into his leather swivel chair. He stared hard at Billy for a full minute. Maybe it was longer than a minute. Morgan's heart was beginning to beat in earnest with anticipation while Billy just sat staring over

his father's head and out the window behind the
old man.

However, Morgan noticed that a single sweat
bead was rolling slowly down from the end of his
brother's left eyebrow.

Morgan himself was ready to leap up and throw
himself out the window before Garrett finally said
one word, which flew like a hatchet through the
pregnant silence: "Why?"

Billy sat as before. Then, dully, he said, "Why
what?"

"Why'd you rob me, boy?"

Another sweat bead rolled down the side of Billy's cheek. He sat up straighter in his chair. "Ah,
shit, Pa . . ."

"You was tryin' to ruin me. That it?"

Billy raised his hands chest high, palms out.
"No." He shook his head. "No, no . . ."

"I tried to raise you right." Garrett slid his gaze
briefly to Morgan, who sat in his own chair tensely,
his heart throbbing in his ears. "Tried to raise both
you boys right. Tried to whip some sense into you,
every chance I got. Whenever you stepped out of
line, you got that strap. Ain't that right?"

Billy's throat worked as he swallowed. "Sure, Pa,
but . . ."

Garrett slid his gaze again to his older son. "Ain't
that right, Morgan?"

"You did as well as you could, Pa. As well as any
man could." Morgan canted his head toward Billy,
said gravely, "This is not your fault."

Garrett's eyes were on his younger son again.
"Didn't do no good, did it? Much as I tried to bring
you to heel, you just wouldn't heel."

Garrett stopped. Hands laced across his belly,

over the sheepskin vest and the blue plaid shirt beneath it, he rolled his brown eyes back and forth between the two young men before him. His face was long and craggy, etched with fine lines.

His nose was straight and long and with a bulging red tip. There was a scar on the left side of the tip from where the doc had cut a growth off it several years ago. That scar turned a darker red than the rest of his nose when he was angry.

"Pa," Billy said, his voice growing high and whiney, "I was just funnin', mostly. I didn't mean nothin' by robbin' the bank. I was just—"

"Gonna head on out of the country with that money. My money."

Billy shook his head adamantly. "No."

"What, then?"

Billy's lips moved, but no words came out of his mouth. He sat up straight in his chair now, boots tucked beneath him, staring across the desk at his father. His eyes were wide, dark with stupidity, liquid with mute pleading.

"Ruin me—that was your intention," Hawk Garrett said. "Somehow, you found out that Melvin Stuart's Fence Post payroll was in there—the money he intended to pay off his fall roundup hands. You knew, must have known, that if you stole Stuart's money, you were as good as ruinin' me, since he's the second biggest investor in that bank after myself."

Billy's lower jaw dropped and he drew a shallow breath. "No, Pa." He shook his head adamantly. "I had no idea that was his money in there. I just knew . . ." He glanced fleetingly as Morgan, whose gut drew taut.

"Ruin me. That's what you tried to do."

"No. No."

"You're a bad dog, Billy. And you know what happens to my dogs that don't heel."

"Oh, Pa," Billy said, sobbing. "Please don't see it that way. Please let me make this up to you."

"You want to make it up to me."

"I sure do."

Hawk glanced at Morgan. "How can your brother make this up to me, Morgan?"

Morgan's mind raced as he stared across the desk at his father. The bloodred scar on the side of the man's nose fairly pulsated. Haltingly, Morgan said, "Well . . . I reckon you could have him cut firewood for the rest of the winter. Keep him from going to town for a couple months." He almost laughed at that himself.

Morgan flinched under his father's dark, brooding gaze. "Is that what you would do to a son that tried to ruin you, Morgan? Would you keep him about the place?" Now his voice rose gradually with increasing menace. "So that you could look at his ugly face all the goddamn winter—because he robbed your bank and tried to run you into the ground after all you done for him?"

Morgan didn't say anything, because Garrett wasn't really expecting an answer. Garrett already had the answer. And whatever it was, there would be no changing his mind or tempering his anger in the least. Morgan's heart beat faster, faster . . .

The way he saw it, the more Billy alienated himself from his father, the closer Morgan and his father grew together. It had always been that way, though Billy had mostly been too stupid to see the subtle ways that Morgan had always played them against each other.

And now it was growing more and more clear that Morgan had succeeded at last. He'd won the game. Hawk was going to write Billy out of his will and send him packing.

Without a dime. . . .

The old man's gaze had returned to Billy, and now he said, "You know, I could actually tolerate a son stealin' from me, showin' he had some pluck in him, after all. But then him gettin' caught only a few miles out of town. . . . And you're havin' the chance of killin' Matt Dunbar and not takin' full advantage, and then pissin' on yourself in front of half the town when Dunbar threw down on you . . ."

Hawk shook his head darkly. "That pill's just a little too bitter, boy."

Billy was speechless.

Morgan stared across the desk at his father. It was hard for him to maintain a concerned expression when he wanted to laugh out loud.

Garrett pulled a Starr .44 revolver out of a desk drawer. He hefted the gun in his hand and considered it with an almost wistful expression before clicking the hammer back. He gave a fateful sigh as he extended the pistol straight across the desk and blew a neat, round hole through the bridge of Billy's nose, between the kid's wide, staring eyes that blinked as the slug punched his head back with such force that Morgan heard his brother's neck crack.

Billy and his chair flew back to strike the floor with a thundering boom.

Morgan stared as though in a dream, the shot echoing in his head, down at his brother quivering on the floor, still seated in his chair, spurs ringing as they banged against the chair legs. Billy's eyes had rolled up into his head. As he continued to quiver violently, as though he'd been struck by lightning, Morgan could see only the eggshell whites of his brother's eyes.

Screams sounded in another part of the house. A dish shattered. Several people were running toward Garrett's office. Morgan just stared down at his dying—no, *dead*—brother, unable to wrap his mind around what had just happened. When the realization began to trickle in, Morgan covered his mouth, feigning shock, though he was really quelling the impulse to laugh hysterically at his unexpected good fortune.

Hawk had sent Billy packing, all right!

This was far, far more than he'd ever even hoped for.

Morgan looked at his father, who was still holding the pistol straight out across his desk, lips pursed disdainfully inside his shaggy gray mustache. Smoke curled from the barrel. As the muffled thunder of running feet approached the office, Garrett turned to the office's open door and gave a sour expression.

"Ah, shit."

Garrett's wife, Angelina, screamed as she bounded into the office and dropped to her knees beside Billy. Morgan's two half sisters ran in behind her, screaming and sobbing as they, too, dropped to their knees around the young man whose blood was gushing out of the hole in the bridge of his nose.

"Hawk, what have you done?" Garrett's Mexican wife screamed, glaring up at him, tears streaming down her face while Morgan's half sister, Calico, cradled Billy's bloody head against her thigh.

Morgan kept his hand across his mouth, shuttling

his gaze quickly from his father to the women to Billy and then back to Garrett as the old man dropped the pistol back in its drawer, slammed the drawer closed, and rose from his chair. He turned to Henry Three Wolves standing in the open doorway. Even the Indian's normally opaque, dark brown eyes were bright with shock.

"Henry, take care of that." Garrett turned to Morgan, who was still sitting in his chair as though glued to it. "Morgan, let's take a walk."

When Morgan finally managed to rise to his feet that felt like wet sponges, he walked around the bawling women hunkered over dead Billy, and followed his father out of the office and down the dim hall. Hawk's tall, broad-shouldered figure long-strode into the parlor adorned with mounted trophies of nearly every four-legged beast native to the Uinta Range, including two silver-tipped grizzlies and a massive cutthroat trout mounted over the popping hearth.

Morgan was tongue-tied, his mind and heart still racing.

He was a wealthy man. Not only that, but he would soon marry beautiful Victoria Dunbar. At least, he would after Hawk Garrett killed Dunbar, which was bound to happen now, sooner or later. . . .

He really had to work hard to keep himself from coming unglued and leaping around the room like a wild mustang.

When his father turned to him, caution entered the mix of emotions washing through him, tempering his delirium. Garrett smiled, but only with his mouth beneath his scraggly mustache. The scar on the side of his nose continued to throb.

Morgan thought, *Uh-oh*.

"You were the only one outside of Beauchamp who knew about that extra money we had in the vault," he told his older son, wicked lights flashing in his eyes. "And you told Billy. That's why he robbed the bank."

A scream that had nothing to do with the women now sounded inside Morgan's head. That knot in his tongue was drawn tighter. "Oh, Pa . . . ," he finally managed, though he wasn't quite certain he'd made it audible.

Garrett said, "And I know that you and Owen Crebbs ain't been gettin' together for nothin' but maybe red dog or five-card stud over at the Blue Mountain Saloon. I bet you ain't cracked one law book."

"Pa, that's just not true!"

"And as for your dalliance with Dunbar's purty daughter—let's see how far that goes when she learns you been wrote out of my will."

Morgan's feet once again felt like sponges. His knees did, too. He could only stare at his father and feel the blood run out of his face as his father placed a firm hand on his shoulder, winked, and said, "Get the hell off my land. Do it fast before I give you what your brother got. And don't you ever come back—you hear me, boy?"

Hawk squeezed his older son's shoulder until Morgan nearly winced. It was a threatening parting squeeze. And then Hawk Garrett walked over to a liquor cabinet against the far wall, under one of the silvertip grizzlies he'd shot several years ago with Henry—neither of his "Nancy boy" sons had been invited along—and started building himself a tall drink.

Morgan stole numbly out of the room and out of the house, hearing the women's muffled bawling and bellowing behind him, though he couldn't distinguish it from the screaming inside his own head.

Chapter 22

Sitting forward in Marshal Dunbar's chair behind the marshal's desk, Colter painstakingly dribbled chopped tobacco onto the two cigarette papers he carefully troughed between the first two fingers of his left hand. He sprinkled a line of tobacco along the crease between his fingers, stopping to jostle the bag a little, mixing the tobacco, working purposefully, taking his time.

When an overlarge piece of the Duke's Mixture got hung up at the edge of the bag, he jostled the small elk-skin pouch again and then continued working, pressing his tongue against his lower lip as he concentrated, wanting desperately to perfect the art of quirley building. It seemed that every man over the age of twenty worth his salt knew how to build a cigarette.

What's more, they knew how to smoke one without coughing up half their lungs, as Colter nearly always did. Add the tobacco to too much tangle-leg, and he had a recipe for disaster—*embarrassing* disaster when there were others, especially ladies, present. More than once a kind doxy had held his head while he'd aired his paunch after mixing the drink with too much tobacco and prolonged mattress dancing, which was another art he was still working to perfect. (He was hoping to get a little more practice with Sarah Miller in the not too distant future.)

When he had the right amount of tobacco lined out on the paper, Colter set the bag on the desk and began the complicated procedure of rolling the two papers closed while keeping the tobacco inside the cylinder. He was grinning in satisfaction as he finished closing the tube, rolling both thumbs in unison against his index fingers.

But he almost ripped the near-perfect cylinder in half when someone hammered the door so loudly that it sounded like the blast of a .45.

Dropping the quirley, he grunted with a start and swept his Remington off the desk, extending it out in front of him while cocking the piece, aiming at the door. He waited for another knock. It didn't come.

"Who's there?" he said, keeping the pistol aimed at the door, his heart quickening its pace.

Since Billy Garrett had headed off with his father, the town had been relatively quiet in the wake of the snow. But there'd been tension in the air, like a held breath, and when Colter had drifted outside the jailhouse to take a tramp around the town, he felt eyes boring holes through him.

Beyond the boards he'd nailed over the broken window just left of Dunbar's desk, he could hear someone walking through the snow—quick, furtive steps. They dwindled quickly to silence.

Colter rose from the chair and, keeping the cocked pistol aimed half out in front of his belly, grabbed the doorknob. He jerked the door open quickly and then, suspicious of a trick, stepped back behind the wall. As the door squawked open on its rusty hinges, a paper fluttered from a nail that had been driven into the front of it.

It appeared to be a wanted circular.

Colter edged a look around the doorframe. When he saw nothing suspicious in the street that was turning dark now at the end of the day, he ripped the circular down from the door. Stepping back away from the opening in case someone was arranging rifle sights on him from cover, he stared down at the paper in his hands.

He frowned, his insides writhing anxiously.

Beneath WANTED in large blocky letters across the top of the coffee-stained, age-yellowed leaf was his own sketched likeness complete with his hat and the grisly S on his left cheek, though the illustrators always made the scar much larger and more pronounced than it actually was. They also made his eyes smaller, and they set them too close together, casting them with a wolfish cunning that, after obsessively appraising them in looking glasses, he didn't believe was really there except maybe when he was facing men wanting to give him a bad case of lead poisoning.

His name, COLTER FARROW, had been printed just below the sketch in letters only slightly larger than those at the top of the page.

As he read the words below the sketch and his own name, ". . . for the crippling of Sheriff Bill Rondo, the cowardly murder of Deputy Chico Bannon, and for sundry other depravities, a $2,000 reward has been offered for this gun-savvy, cold-blooded firebrand—ALIVE!"

Those last two words adorned the bottom of the page in the same-sized script as WANTED across the top. Below them, in much smaller print, had been added "$1,000 for DEAD."

Colter lowered the crumpled sheet to his side and looked around outside again. A horseback rider bundled in a knee-length red blanket coat was passing the jailhouse, crouching forward to light a quirley. As the rider rode off to the east, Colter looked down to see fresh tracks, dark with gathering night shadows, angling off to the right of the porch. He dropped down the steps he'd shoveled earlier, and followed the tracks—a man's boot tracks—around the far corner of the jailhouse and into the gap between the jail and a boarded-up shop beyond it.

Colter quickened his pace, but by the time he reached the rear of the jailhouse, the man was gone. His tracks angled off through the brush and around what appeared to be an abandoned original settler's shack toward pines lining the town's southern perimeter. Colter considered following the tracks.

But what would he do once he'd run the man down? The man hadn't taken a shot at him, only told him that someone in Justice City knew who Colter was and that he had a price on his head, albeit an old price. By now the bounty for killing Rondo and the marshals had likely grown much higher and it was probably as high for "dead" as "alive."

Would someone come collecting? If so, he was a fool to have tipped his hand this way.

Puzzled by the man's intentions, bothered that someone knew who he was and that others likely would, as well, Colter headed back toward the front of the jailhouse. As he approached the corner, retracing his and the mysterious caller's own tracks, he heard the tread of someone atop the porch. Automatically, actions honed from three years of running and killing, Colter brought up the Remington and cocked it as he aimed over the porch rail toward the front door.

The girl who'd raised a hand to knock on the half-open door turned her head toward Colter. She gasped when she saw the pistol aimed at her head, and lurched back, slapping her hand to her chest. "Good Lord!"

Colter depressed the Remy's hammer as he lowered the weapon. "Sorry." Still wary, he looked around. He doubted that the marshal's daughter could be the bait of a deadly trap someone was setting for him, but, while life hadn't turned out the way he'd want it to, he wasn't yet ready to throw in his cards.

Still a little rattled by the wanted dodger, he said, "You'd best not skulk around the porch like that, Miss Dunbar."

"I was not *skulking* around the porch, Mr. . . . Mr. . . . uh . . . Red. I was sent by my father to invite you to supper at our house this evening."

Colter walked around the front of the porch, gazing at her. She was even prettier today than yesterday. It had something to do with the old blanket coat she was wearing over a plain housedress, with worn rabbit fur boots on her feet and a shabby red scarf wrapped over her head to protect her ears from the cold. Her hair was windblown. It hung in her eyes, which were flashing angrily above the ruddy flush in her cheeks.

Her less-kept, more natural appearance with those

blue eyes of her fathers and the thick tresses of coal black hair ensconcing her face were savage, hammering blows to Colter's heart, and her disdainful gaze instantly cowed him.

"Sorry about that," Colter said, staring up at her from the bottom of the steps. "And I wouldn't want to put you out, intrudin' on you and the marshal, an' all." He wondered if Sarah was expecting him for supper again this evening.

It was almost as though Victoria were reading his mind. "Do you have other plans?"

Did she know about Sarah? But then he saw by her look that she assumed that he would have no plans. Not a scar-faced young killer her father had inexplicably invited in from the cold to help him keep law and order in his town.

"No, ma'am."

She frowned at the paper he held low against his right leg and that fluttered in the chill breeze that rose now just after sunset. "What's that?"

Colter looked down at the leaf, thought quickly. "This here? Oh, just a piece of scrap paper I found in the alley yonder. Thought I'd use it for kindling."

"Kindling, huh?" Again, there was the skepticism and casual disdain in her voice.

"Yes, ma'am."

"Please don't call me ma'am. You make me feel old. Would you like to walk over to the house with me now or is there something you need to do first?"

Colter shrugged. "I won't keep your supper waiting, ma'am . . . I mean, Miss Dunbar. I'll just shut the damper on the stove and be right along."

Colter was nervous. He was also a little peeved because this girl disapproved of him for little better reason than that he was ugly and he'd killed several men in her town—men who were trying to kill not only him but her father, as well.

It wasn't fair. But then, beautiful young women often weren't fair, he thought as he closed the damper on the stove, turned down the wick of the rusty lamp on Dunbar's desk, and then walked out onto the porch, pulling the door closed behind him. She waited at the bottom of the steps, arms crossed on her chest.

Colter had hoped that she'd go on ahead. He wasn't sure what they'd talk about if they walked together to her and Dunbar's little house. He didn't particularly like getting the cold shoulder even from a girl as pretty as she. And he didn't like this compulsion he felt to truckle before her like a dog wanting only to stop being kicked.

Obviously, Dunbar had sent her to fetch him. She had no desire to endure the young stranger's company in her neat little house at her neat little supper table.

As Colter walked down the porch steps, she gave him a chill glance, threw her hand out as if to indicate the way, and then began walking at a western slant across the street. When they were halfway across, walking side by side in awkward silence, Victoria slowed her pace.

Colter saw that she was looking west toward where a man was riding a steeldust horse toward her and Colter. The man, positioned against the florid western horizon, was a shadow atop the horse, but as Victoria stopped walking altogether, Colter also stopped and scrutinized the oncoming man until he recognized the rider's fine bear coat as well as the crisp felt slouch hat and the heavy scarf wrapped around his mouth and nose. The man rode stiffly in the saddle, staring straight ahead.

As he came to within twenty yards of Colter and the girl, Victoria stepped toward him, saying, "*Morgan?*"

Only now did Morgan Garrett pull back on the slow-moving steeldust's reins and turn his stony gaze to her. He slid his gaze to Colter and then looked at Victoria again, who said, "Morgan, is something wrong? I thought you'd gone back to the . . . ranch. . . ."

Morgan Garrett stared down at her blankly, his face pale against his dark brown, immaculately trimmed beard. At first, Colter thought he was asleep with his eyes open, but then the man said in a dull monotone, "It's finished, Victoria. Done. *Fini*, as they say in Spanish. My father was holding that ace I'd been looking for. The old bastard. Imagine that. Why, he's damn near as smart as I am . . . or thought I was."

"Morgan, what are you . . . ?" Victoria let her voice trail off when Morgan reached into his coat pocket and pulled out a small, flat brown bottle. He popped the cork on the bottle, tipped it back, his throat rising and falling several times as he drank and then lowered it. He smiled, smacked his lips, his glazed eyes on his bride-to-be, and then replaced the cork in the bottle's mouth and returned the bottle to his coat pocket.

"Morgan, what ace are you talking about?" Victoria said, staring up at him in shock.

Chapter 23

Morgan did not answer Victoria's question. He was looking at the Blue Mountain Saloon to Colter's right, on the north side of the street. "If you'll excuse me," he said. "But I really need some proper consoling, which, I'm sorry to say, is just not in your dear but chaste heart, my dear Victoria. Prim and proper schoolteacher lady."

Colter glanced at the Blue Mountain, turned toward Morgan, and then turned back to the saloon and whorehouse, shuttling his gaze to the second story. A girl stood in an upstairs window looking out. The same girl Colter had seen Morgan with earlier that morning, when Hawk Garrett had come to pull Billy out of jail.

Following Morgan's gaze, Victoria slid her own glance to the saloon, as well. Colter could see by the way she frowned that she saw the girl looking into the street.

Again, Morgan said, "Well, then, as I was saying
. . . I need a proper tumble," and booted his horse
over to the hitch rack fronting the Blue Mountain.

Victoria stood staring with her mouth open as the
well-dressed young Garrett threw his shoulders
back, as though steeling himself for a grand maneu-
ver, and then swung his right boot over the steeldust's hindquarters. As he lowered that boot to the
ground, he got the other one hung up in the stirrup
and fell.

His head and shoulders struck the ground on the
left side of his horse, which sidestepped nervously,
nickering.

"Morgan!" Victoria exclaimed.

She and Colter hurried toward him. Morgan
cursed as he rolled from side to side, his face red
and swollen. But before Victoria and Colter reached
him, he'd worked his boot free of the stirrup, and he
held up a hand to waylay them. They both stopped.
Morgan picked up his hat, placed it on his head. He
climbed to his knees and then pushed himself to his
feet, holding one open palm out toward Colter and
Victoria, though not looking in their direction.

He brushed snow off his pants and his coat and
then turned, wobbly on his feet, and stumbled up
the steps of the gallery fronting the saloon. As he
reached the top gallery step, the front door opened
and a girl in a black and red corset and bustier and
with long fishnet stockings and garters on her long
legs stood in the doorway. She wore pink feathers in
her hair. Colter could tell by the shape of her rather
plain-featured face that she was the one he'd seen in
the second-story window.

As Morgan walked toward her, the girl stepped
back, drawing the door wide. Morgan walked

through it. The girl glanced at Victoria, her eyes vaguely sneering, then drew the door closed. Colter stood, shocked, embarrassed for Victoria. Stiffly, he turned to her, but before he could say anything, she'd swung around and begun walking up the street in the direction they'd been heading when they'd spied Morgan.

Colter stayed where he was. The girl would likely want to be alone now, after such a defeat. But then she said without turning around, "This way, Mr. Red. My father is waiting."

Colter glanced back at the Blue Mountain Saloon and then followed Victoria through a gap between two buildings and around a privy, a woodshed, and a buckboard wagon. She was about thirty yards ahead of him, and he did nothing to close the gap between them. He didn't know what to say to her. He had no idea what he'd say to her through supper, for that matter, but he followed her dumbly, anyway, not knowing how to get out of the awkward evening he was facing.

Vaguely, inasmuch as how it might affect him, he wondered what Morgan Garrett had run into back at his father's ranch.

In the meantime, Victoria long-strode ahead of him angrily, black hair bouncing on her shoulders. The girl had pluck—Colter would give her that. He couldn't tell if she was crying, but if she was, she was crying silently. Mostly, judging by her speed and the set of her shoulders, she was angry.

He discovered at whom she was angry only minutes later, when he followed her up onto the porch and then through the front door of the house she shared with her father. He followed her footsteps into the kitchen off to the left of the entryway. Dunbar sat in a rocking chair near the black range on which several pots bubbled, his wounded leg propped on a footstool. Also on the range was a smoking iron skillet. On a counter between a dry sink and the range sat a plate loaded down with three large, raw steaks smothered in onions ready to be cooked.

Dunbar wore a ratty plaid robe, red balbriggans, and heavy knit socks. He was leaning back in his chair, one arm in a sling, a drink and a whiskey bottle on a small table to his right.

He had a stogie in his right hand. A rifle leaned against the wall near his drink, within easy reach.

Dunbar frowned as his daughter walked straight past him, on the far side of the linen-draped table from her father, and stopped suddenly, facing the far wall. Colter stopped in the kitchen door, feeling out of place and uncomfortable and not wanting to be here but not knowing how to discreetly take his leave. Certainly, the evening's stakes had changed since Victoria had fetched him from the jailhouse.

Dunbar slid his befuddled scowl from Victoria to Colter and then back to his daughter. "What the hell happened?"

She wheeled on him suddenly, hair flying, her cheeks flushed with rage. "Why didn't you tell me? You had to know. You know everything about this town. You know everyone in it. You know everyone's secrets."

Dunbar just stared up at her through his lone blue eye, his gray brows pinched. The scar around his eye patch drew deeper into his cheek and forehead. The long groove running from beneath the patch and down his cheek and into his whiskers was pale as paraffin against his ruddy face.

He opened and closed his mouth like a fish, as though trying to find his voice.

"Morgan!" Victoria said. "Why didn't you tell me? Certainly no one else was going to tell the schoolteacher that her beau was a lecher. A whore-monger. That wouldn't have been in good taste. But you'd think that the girl's father would inform her of this nasty little secret. Especially when said father didn't want her marrying the whoremongering son of a bitch in the first place!"

She waited. Her face was nearly hidden now by her badly mussed hair, though Colter glimpsed the rose of her cheeks through the messy black curtain. She threw her arms out as though in beseeching but said nothing more as she waited for her father's response.

"Ah, shit." Dunbar glanced out the curtained window on the far side of the table, and raked a thumb and index finger through his muttonchops. "How . . . how in the hell did you find out, me dear one?" His voice was thin and weak, despondent.

"I just got lucky, I guess. I was fetching this young killer for you, like you asked, and we were walking past the Blue Mountain Saloon when . . ." Her eyes filled with tears. She sniffed, raked a sleeve across her nose, and shook her hair back from her face. ". . . when I saw him. He was drunk and he was returning from his ranch and muttering something about his father holding the ace. And then he fell off his horse and stumbled on into that . . . that place . . . and into the arms of a *young lady* who I got the distinct impression was no *stranger.*"

"Ah, hell. Ah, shit on me and all the poor, wretched fools."

"Yes, shit on you, Papa!" she raged, snarling like a lioness and then wheeling and striding back past the table. Colter stepped aside as she brushed past him through the doorway and into the hall.

He could hear her footsteps and feel their reverberations through the floorboards as she stomped up a stairs to the second story, where they continued for several more seconds before a door slammed.

"Yes, shit on me, then," Dunbar said, sagging back in his rocker, his stogie smoldering in his right hand.

Colter stood against the wall beside the kitchen door, holding his hat in his hands, pinching the brim as though working dough around the lip of a pie plate. He stared at the floor until he heard Dunbar chuckling very softly. Colter looked up. Sure enough, the man was laughing, narrowing his lone eye as he lifted the stogie to his mouth and took a puff.

"You know, I believe that was the first time I've ever heard me sweet little gal cuss. She was always the proper lady, don't ya know? Tryin' so hard to set an example for me all these years, takin' over for her dearly departed ma."

Colter knew it wasn't any of his business, but his curiosity was too great to hold the question inside. "Why didn't you tell her?"

"Didn't want to hurt her feelin's. They are such tender feelin's, though she often don't let on. A stoic one, me sweet li'l gal. But her heart is large and tender. Just like her old man's. Oh, yes, it's true, for all my blow an' bluster."

"She would have found out eventually."

"I thought she'd see through him to the rotten-
ness at his core and I wouldn't have to be the one to
break her heart. Or that Morgan himself would have
broken it off. I knew what a randy one he was, his
practically livin' over at the Blue Mountain, but I
knew my good gal would share none of her sweet
desserts till she was proper married. Her ma made
her promise, and when Victoria promises—well, a
locomotive at full steam couldn't blast through the
girl's resolve."

"You think she'll be all right?"

"Oh, she'll be fine. Just needs a good cry. She'll
be down in the mornin' and headin' off to the school
to raise the flag and get her stove a-roarin' for the
children." Dunbar looked at his cigar. "I think we
only need to cook the steaks, squire. The rest—the
beans and potatoes—is done. If you still have an
appetite after all that."

"I think I should go, Marshal."

"Nonsense. We got somethin' to talk about. Why
don't you set those steaks on the range, add some
butter, and get 'em fryin'? I like mine bloody. How
do you like yours, squire?"

Colter wasn't sure why he did what he did next.
As though of its own accord, his left hand reached
into his coat pocket. It came out with the balled-up
wanted dodger bearing his own likeness and dropped
it on the table in front of Dunbar.

"What's this?" the marshal asked as Colter used
a fork to transfer two of the onion-covered steaks to
the smoking skillet. Each chunk of meat crackled
loudly when it hit the hot iron. Colter used a wooden
spoon to add a plop of butter to each from a small
stone jar, and the butter melted almost instantly,

bathing the beef and the onions and sending the intoxicating aroma of the butter and the beef and onions into the smoky air over the range.

Colter forked the meat and the onions around in the pan, keeping his back to Dunbar. The old marshal was silent as he perused the wanted circular. Colter kept expecting to feel a gun barrel rammed into his back, but it didn't come.

When he finally turned around, Dunbar was sitting back in his rocker, the dodger lying faceup on the table. Dunbar was taking a sip from his drink. He set the glass back down on the small table, flicked ashes into an ashtray, and poked the stogie back into his mouth.

"Had a feelin'," the marshal said finally. "That S brand has turned up from time to time in the past. How is ole Rondo, anyway?"

"Dead."

Dunbar nodded thoughtfully, staring through a front, pink-curtained window on his left. "Then I reckon that reward has grown, hasn't it?"

"Most likely. Especially since I've been blamed for two dead U.S. marshals now, too."

Dunbar looked at him sharply. Then he glanced at the smoking steaks and said, "Don't burn that beef, now, Master Farrow!"

Colter flipped the steaks, let them cook another minute, and then forked them onto plates. He added pinto beans and potatoes to the plates and set each plate on the table. A percolator was chugging on the range, and from it he poured piping black coffee into two stone mugs and set those on the table, as well.

He and Dunbar were well into their meal, each man leaning hungrily over his plate, forking food into his mouth, before Dunbar said, "You kill them lawmen, Colter?"

Cutting his steak with fork and knife, Colter shook his head. "Rondo killed 'em because he knew I'd get blamed for it. I don't blame you if you don't believe me. I'll be ridin' on."

"I believe you, squire," Dunbar said, forking a large chunk of meat into his mouth and chewing, showing his large, square teeth beneath the big walrus mustache. "But you'd best pull your picket pin from here, anyways. Ride on. That's what I was meanin' to talk to you about. After what we put him through here today, Hawk Garrett will kill you or have you killed for sidin' me. He knows men good with their shootin' irons. After hearing about how Morgan rode back into town—hell must've popped out to the Eight-Bar-G—Garrett won't rest till we're both strung up by our little toes over pots of hot tar."

Colter looked up from his plate at Dunbar, who was busy chewing and rolling a forkful of meat and onions around in his buttered potatoes. "What about you?" Colter said. "You gonna run?"

"Hell, where would I run? I got Victoria."

"Then I'll be sidin' you, Marshal."

Dunbar looked at him, scowling, narrowing his lone eye incredulously. "Why? You don't owe me nothin', Colter. You're lucky I haven't gotten you killed yet."

Colter thought it over. Yes, why? Simply because he admired the blustery old mossyhorn—one man against the world. And because Colter had nowhere else to go and nothing better to do than to continue siding Matthew Dunbar, one of the few who'd called him friend over the past three long, lonely years.

That town he'd been looking for in which to hole up for the winter?

He'd found it.

But all he said as he hiked a shoulder and stared down at his plate was "I reckon 'cause we're both ugly as sin."

Dunbar slammed his fist on the table and roared.

Chapter 24

Morgan Garrett flicked his thumb across Jane Delancy's left nipple and sang, "My life is over. All hopes for fortune gone. What is there to do now, dear Jane, but sing silly old songs?"

Jane looked down at him from where she lay back against the headboard of her bed in the second story of the Blue Mountain Saloon. Her bedcovers were pulled down beneath her exposed breasts and Morgan's head, which lay between the firm, pale orbs.

"Is that a real song, Morgan, or you just makin' it up?" The whore slurred her words. They'd both shared a bottle of George Atchison's best brandy, which wasn't all that good but as good as one could get this far from Salt Lake City.

Morgan chuckled as he lifted his water glass, which was a third full of the brandy, and poured half a shot over the girl's pebbled nipple, and licked it off. "Was rather good, wasn't it?"

"Not bad at all, hon."

Jane ran her hands through Morgan's thick hair, rolling his head from side to side against her breasts. "But don't you think you're bein' a little overly dramatic about all this?"

Morgan lapped up a drop of the liquor that had rolled down over the bottom of the girl's breast, and lifted his head, arching one dark brown brow at her. She was nineteen and rather plain faced but well endowed and missing only one tooth.

"Dear Jane, you think that watching my own brother gunned down before my very own eyes and then being run off the family ranch on a greased rail, or what amounted to a greased rail—after all, I had to saddle one of the lesser horses in my father's remuda, because my precious ovaro was blown out from the previous ride!—is being 'overly dramatic'?"

Jane sandwiched his face in her hands. "Oh, Morgan, Billy was bound to take a bullet sooner rather than later. Yes, it's too bad your father did it, but someone was going to, and you might as well keep it in the family, right? Wouldn't it really be worse if a stranger did it? I had this old dog once, and when he—"

Morgan jerked back in shock and said thickly, squinting to keep the girl's plain face from doubling up on him. "Dear Jane, you're not equating my brother with a . . . with a *dog*, are you?"

She stared down at him, thin lips stretched amusedly. He stared back at her with much the same expression. They laughed at the same time, devilishly, and she sat back against the headboard once more. "To tell you the truth, Morgan—and don't take this wrong, I know he's passed an' all—I've known some dogs I'd much prefer to take into my home than your brother. When he came to bleed his oysters here in the Blue Mountain, we girls were downright afraid for our lives. Especially when he'd been drinkin'."

Morgan rolled onto his back and stared at the ceiling that candlelight shunted shadows across, and said, "Indeed, I only jest, dear Jane. How right you are. Billy truly was a dog that needed to be put down. Too much of my father in him, you see, whereas I take after my much more couth mother. Only now I feel like such a fool. Such a damn fool."

Morgan rolled over, dropping his bare feet to the floor, and leaned forward, resting his elbows on his knees. "I was playing both ends against the middle, only to get crushed for my efforts. And now I no longer even have a brother to hate. Soon, I will no longer have a father to hate. Where will that leave me? What games will be left for me to play?"

"Not sure I understand you, honey," Jane said, running a soothing hand down his bare back.

"You see, Jane, I'd hoped Billy would kill Dunbar and abscond with enough money to hurt my father very badly. Not badly enough to ruin him, of course, but badly enough for him to write Billy out of his will. Then, when he died . . ." He groaned, lowered his head, and scrubbed both hands across his scalp.

"Well, hell," Jane giggled as she plucked a cigarette from an ashtray on the bedside table, "that was a helluva plan, hon! What went *wrong?* You saw what happened out on the street today as good as I did, or better!"

"Yes." Morgan felt a single sob bubble up from deep in his chest. "And I have lost the love of my life, dear Jane."

When Jane said nothing, Morgan glanced over

his shoulder at her. She was frowning at him, pooching her thin lips out in a pout. "You really love that teacher, Morgan? I thought you was just lettin' on 'cause she's so purty. You said yourself you been sparkin' her for over a year and have gotten only a couple of quick pecks out of her." She smiled deviously. "And none where it really counts."

"Did I say 'love of my life'?" Morgan flipped the covers up from the edge of the bed, dragged Jane's bare foot toward him, and kissed it. "Shame on me. So right you are, Jane. The girl was about as warm as a stone buried under six feet of snow atop Blue Mountain in January."

He rose from the bed, nearly lost his balance, caught himself, and walked over to the room's single dresser. "My father has filled our parlor out at the ranch with the heads of many beasts." Morgan picked up his hat and set it on his head, though he was wearing nothing else. A gun had been lying under the hat. He scooped it up and hefted the pearl-gripped Bisley—more gambling booty that he'd won off a drunken Irish stock detective—in his hand. "They're not really decorations. No, they're trophies. The old man placed them there to show all and sundry who visited the ranch what a crack shot he was with a rifle. What a great hunter he was. What a stalker!"

"So you don't really love Miss Dunbar, Morgan? Purty as she is?"

Morgan stared down at the gun in his unsteady hand. "No, I don't love her. I merely wanted to bring her back to the ranch and show her off to the guests. After my father and her father were six feet under, you understand. And I was running things—both the ranch and the bank whose reputation I would rebuild with my business savvy."

He chucked ironically at his own folly.

"Now what?"

"Now?" Morgan flicked the Bisley's loading gate open. "Now I'm going to squeeze whatever satisfaction I can from the situation. First, I'm going to kill both those warrior sons o' bitches—my father and Dunbar—and save the other the trouble. Show my pa he made a big mistake when he didn't kill *both* his sons. And then I'm going to kill that scar-faced young deputy of Dunbar's." He drew a deep breath, tipping his head back and blinking at the ceiling. "And then I'll ride back to the ranch, pick up my prized ovaro, and ride far, far away from here."

Jane sat up straight in the bed, widening her eyes desperately. "Take me with you? Oh, won't you, please, Morgan!"

Hefting the loaded Bisley in his hand, he walked back over and sat on the edge of the bed. He lifted his glass, took a sip, and swallowed, staring into the deep amber liquid. "Sure. Why the hell not? We'll head for California and live like English royalty."

He gave a droll chuckle.

He felt the bed wobble, and glanced behind him. Jane had risen onto her knees, raising her pillow above her head.

"*Liar!*" she screeched, smashing the pillow down over his head and knocking the drink from his hands. "You would if I was as pretty as that cold-hearted Victoria Dunbar. But I make *love* to you, you son of a bitch!"

His mussed hair hanging in his eyes, Morgan stared at his glass rolling across the thick Oriental rug onto which the last of his brandy had spilled.

Rage like boiling acid welled up within him. It made his ears and his eyeballs burn. He swung around quickly, flinging his right hand back behind him and smashing the butt of the Bisley against Jane's left cheek.

The whore screamed and flew off the far side of the bed. She struck the floor with a loud thump. From his vantage, he could only see her shoulder and part of an arm as well as her tangled hair. She didn't seem to be moving.

"Jane?" Morgan said thickly, his heart thudding.

He waited, staring dumbly at the floor on the far side of the bed. The girl didn't move.

"Jane?" he said again, wheeling when the possibility that he could have killed her made its way through his alcohol-fogged brain. He ran around the bed and stopped.

Jane lifted her head and sat up, one leg curled beneath her. Her light brown hair was like a thin curtain over her face. She held a hand to her cheek that was turning bright red while the skin around her eye was darkening.

Eyes shocked and hurt, she stared at Morgan through the curtain of her messy hair as she slowly gained her feet, her chafed breasts jostling.

"Jane," Morgan said, standing naked before her, slowly shaking his head. He couldn't believe what he'd done. He hadn't known he'd had that kind of violence inside him. "I . . . I don't know. . . ."

The whore backed away from him, keeping her hand pressed to her cheek, her wary eyes on him. And then she grabbed a black-and-red silk wrap off a chair back, wrapped it around herself, and hurried out the room's only door. In the hall she glanced back at him, her eyes incriminating, and then slammed the door before he could hear her bare feet running off down the hall.

Her muffled sobs seeped through the door for a few seconds before fading.

Slowly, Morgan lifted the gun in his hand. Staring down at it, he arched a wistful brow. "Well, I'll be damned."

Since he'd committed himself to working for Dunbar for as long as the marshal needed him or until they were both planted in the Justice City boneyard, Colter followed up his supper at the marshal's house with a professional tramp around the town. All was quiet in Justice City this clear, cold evening in the wake of the storm. Every saloon he walked into got especially quiet, and he was given twice-overs and cold stares.

That was all right. He was used to them.

When he'd walked through Frank Miller's old place that boasted fresh red stains on the floor in front of the bar, he went back out into the cold and rattled his spurs in the direction of Frank Miller's pretty blond daughter. He had nowhere else to go this evening except the stone jailhouse, but those cold stones seemed especially unwelcoming in contrast to the night he'd spent with Sarah the night before.

He hadn't been formally invited, and she might even be entertaining another caller. But his young man's warm juices, not to mention the loneliness of the chill, starry night in this little town high in the Utah mountains, compelled him to find out.

"Well, well, well," she said when she drew her cabin door open a few minutes later. "Look what the cat dragged in." She leaned against the door, and it was hard to read the expression on her face. Did she have another caller?

"Don't mean to intrude," he said, fidgeting as he always fidgeted around pretty young women. He opened and closed his hand around the neck of his Winchester's stock, the barrel of the long gun resting across his left shoulder.

"Well, you *are* intruding. You didn't tell me you were coming, so how was I supposed to know?" Sarah's voice was cold, her eyes narrowed.

Colter looked past her, but only her tiny kitchen was lit. The living area was cloaked in shadow. If someone was sitting in there, Colter couldn't see him.

"In that case, I won't hold you."

Colter pinched his hat brim to her and started turning away.

"You think so, do you?" Sarah grabbed his arm, pulled him into the cabin, closed the door, and stepped into him, wrapping her arms around his neck and mashing her mouth almost painfully against his.

Chapter 25

Colter and Sarah kissed for a long time in front of the closed door.

When she pulled away, she licked her upper lip, flicked her finger against his hat brim, and wriggled out of his enfolding arm. "You must be starving, Colter. I bet you haven't eaten all day. Let me take your hat. You get out of that coat and sit down at the table. I've been keeping a plate warm for you."

Colter saw the plate with an iron lid over it atop the oven's warming rack. He'd had plenty to eat over at Dunbar's place only an hour ago—a thick steak, pinto beans, and potatoes—and he wasn't one bit hungry. But he wasn't going to tell Sarah that. She'd fixed him supper, and he wasn't going to tell her he'd eaten over at the Dunbar's. Sarah might get the wrong idea, think that Colter had something going with Victoria.

That was about as likely as a snowball making it

through a Texas summer, but women saw the world differently. Colter's sap was rising—he loved how her lips felt against his and how supple her fragile body felt in his arms—but he'd have to pack down another meal before he was getting any farther than her kitchen.

She swiped his hat off his head with a chuckle, pegged it, and then, wiping her hands on the apron she wore over a simple gray-and-brown-plaid housedress with several of the top buttons undone, she walked around the table to the stove. He watched the sway of her rump behind the clinging dress, and then pried his eyes off the girl, who wore her blond hair in a loose coronet atop her head, long enough to wash at the basin, noting that the pitcher was filled with warm water and that the soap cake beside the basin had been scrubbed clean.

Inwardly, Colter smiled at that. He washed thoroughly. When he'd dried himself, he turned to find her sitting across the table from where she'd set his smoking plate, leaning forward, watching him, smiling, obviously enjoying having a young man in the house, enjoying having cooked a meal for him.

"Hot dang, that looks good!" Colter said, though his insides recoiled a little when he stared down at the large, thick steak on the uneven, fat-marbled surface of which grease and melted butter had puddled. Beside the steak was a good-sized pile of corn and an even better-sized plop of mashed potatoes and rich brown gravy. Beside the plate sat a smaller plate with two steaming hot cross buns.

"I made a little extra tonight. I know how hungry men can get at the end of a hard day." She hiked a shoulder as she leaned forward on her folded arms, pushing her breasts up enticingly.

"I sure *am* hungry!" Colter's jaw ached with the effort of grinning as he tightened the rolls of his shirtsleeves above his arms and picked up his knife and fork.

Sarah gasped and leaped to her feet. "I forgot the milk!"

"Oh, that's all—"

"Just never you mind, mister. A man's meal is not complete without milk. How 'bout some coffee, or do you want to wait for dessert?"

Inwardly, Colter groaned, but he smiled up at her as with heavy hands he cut into the steak that was larger than one of his own size-ten feet. "Yeah, I think I'll just wait . . . for dessert. You really shouldn't have, Sarah. Really . . . shouldn't have . . ."

With that he began eating with feigned hunger, and by the time he was only half-finished he was afraid he'd explode right here in front of her like an overloaded tick. His moaning and groaning by the end of the meal was for real, though the smile was faked. By the time he'd finished up the peach pie smothered in whipped cream washed down with a cup of hot black coffee, he didn't think he'd be able to climb out of his chair.

Sarah got his sap running again, however, when she walked over, sat on his lap, nibbled at his lips for a time, then at his ears, and nuzzled his neck before sticking her tongue between his lips. She kissed him with a moaning, groaning passion he'd rarely experienced in a girl before. Shortly, she climbed off him, hooked her finger at him, and he found out just how limber he still was even with all that grub pressing at the buckle of his cartridge belt.

He followed her into her small bedroom, lit with

three candles, at the back of the house. She stood by her bed, undressing, the candlelight sparkling in her eyes. Colter hoped his belly wasn't too noticeably distended as he walked to her after having shucked down to his birthday suit. Naked, she was still letting her hair down as he touched his lips to hers, knelt down before her, and poked his tongue into her belly button.

"Oh!" she cried, stepping back with a shuddering jerk, giggling and then pressing his face to her belly again. "Oh, God. That feels . . . *so* . . . *good!*"

He remembered that Marianna Claymore had enjoyed having her belly nuzzled. Maybe all girls did. He wouldn't know. But it worked Sarah into a near frenzy, and they spent the next forty-five minutes toiling together in her bed, under the sheets and quilts.

Colter did not think about Marianna anymore after that one time—except to notice the absence of her memory—so intoxicated was he by this warm, passionate girl who moved to his own rhythms beneath him. Together they made the bed's leather springs creak slowly, almost melodiously, both of them grunting and groaning and sighing softly. Sarah stared up at him smokily, half smiling, wincing, squeezing her eyes shut, sometimes biting her knuckles and turning her head to one side as he worked between her spread knees.

Later, straddling him, she stared down at him between the wings of her blond hair, the ends of which slid back and forth across his chest as they moved together.

Colter's chest fairly exploded with his passion for Sarah. Aside from his brief time long ago with

Marianna, he'd never realized that making love could be this consuming and pleasurable. In the past, he'd mostly only slept with percentage girls, and that had only been for the release as well as the short-lived company after weeks alone on the desperado trail, trying to outdistance the bounty hunters here in his own country and for long stretches in Mexico.

Nothing had tied him to the whores he'd lain with. They'd seemed as eager to get away from him as he'd been to get away from them, after the transaction had been completed, the one or two or, rarely, three dollars having changed hands. But he had no wish to leave this room after he and Sarah had had their pleasure. Instead, he lay back against her pillow, stretching luxuriously, feeling the rich languidness of fulfilled desire spilling over him, pressing him deeper into the mattress, toward a long winter night's slumber.

"How long you gonna stay here, Colter?" she asked him after they'd lain entangled together, dozing, for at least twenty minutes, the charcoal stove ticking in a near corner.

He pressed his lips to her forehead as she rested her chin on his own shoulder and caressed his chest with her fingertips.

"Hard to say," he said. "I told Dunbar I'd stay as long as he needs me." He turned his head toward her, though he could only see her forehead from this angle. "Why?"

"I like you."

"I like you, too, Sarah."

"It would be nice if you could stay for a while." She looked up at him and smiled. "I reckon I'm going to have to know who you are eventually, though. I mean, where you come from, what brought you here."

"I'll tell you." Colter gave her a warm look. "Eventually."

She lowered her head to his chest again and was silent for a time before she said, "You should look for someone else to work for, maybe."

He kissed the top of her head. "I know you don't understand, but I like workin' for Dunbar."

She seemed to think about that for a while, and then she got up and walked naked to the small stove in the corner. He looked at her slender back flaring to her pale, round hips. Her heart-shaped rump was the color of a nearly ripe peach. He could stand looking at Sarah for a long time, he thought, feeling the urge to settle down.

She glanced back at him as she stooped to open the stove door, and her eyes were suddenly grave. "He's not the man you think he is, Colter."

"We already talked about that. I can understand how you feel, but he's had to be strong to stand against men like Hawk Garrett."

Sarah threw a shovelful of coal into the stove, closed the door, and walked back to the bed. Her breasts jostled as she crawled back under the covers and turned to him and ran a hand through his long red hair.

She slid her face down close to his. "I see what you see when you look at him. A big, impressive hombre. A man as good with words as he is with his guns and his fists. Yes, he *is* impressive. He's larger than life. But he's a *raw* man. A *crude* man. A man who thinks the law needs to be hammered into Justice City."

"Well, from what I heard—"

"Yes, at one time outlaws had a strong hold on the town. It took a man like Dunbar to pry it loose. And believe me, Dunbar stretched some hemp under that old cottonwood he loved so much. He spent some lead and used up some brass, as my old man used to say. He damn near filled up the grave-yard. But those times are over. And Dunbar knows they're over. But he loves the power those times gave him, and he can't let it go."

Colter studied her. "You really got your blood up over him, don't you? Is it because of Donny?"

"No, you idiot!" Sarah leaned farther forward, smoothed Colter's hair back, and pressed her lips to his forehead. "It's because of you, Colter Farrow, whoever-in-hell-you-are." Her nose was nearly touching his as she stared into his eyes. "I'm afraid he's going to get you killed. And I really, really don't want that to happen, Colt—"

There was a sudden screech of breaking glass.

Sarah screamed and buried her head in Colter's neck as something arced over the bed several inches above her bowed back and slammed against the wall. Colter rolled over Sarah and, grabbing both her arms, rolled once more, rolling her with him as he dropped off the edge of the bed. He struck the floor that was covered by a bearskin rug, and she fell on top of him with a grunt.

He rolled over her, caught a glimpse of a fist-sized stone on the floor nearby, and reached up to slide his Remington from the holster he'd hung from a chair back.

"Are you all right, Sarah?"

"What *was* that?" she said, hunkered over her knees and casting a frightened glance at him.

"Not sure!" He only meant he wasn't sure why someone had thrown a rock into her room, and that he wasn't sure that something else wouldn't be behind it. A bullet, say. "Stay down while I check it out!"

He ran at a crouch around the bed and blew out the candles on the dresser. Cocking the Remington, he slid the curtain away from the window with the back of his hand and stared out into the night above the ragged hole in the pane. It was too dark for him to see anything but the pearl snow and the stars. Behind the house were only brush and pines and a few sorry-looking outbuildings—all liquid dark against the velvet sky.

Whoever had hurled the rock could be anywhere, cloaked by the shadows.

But he would have left tracks in the snow.

Fury throbbed in Colter's temples as he tossed the pistol onto the bed and quickly started dressing, breathing hard.

"You aren't going out there?" Sarah said.

"Sure as hell I am."

She knelt on the floor by the bed, her eyes flashing fearfully in the ambient light from the window. "He might have a gun!"

"That's all right. I got one, too."

Colter stomped into his boots and dropped the Remington into the holster on his hip. He shoved his second gun behind his cartridge belt and headed for the curtained doorway. "Stay in here and keep your head down."

"Colter!" she rasped behind him as he stumbled through the dark house to the front.

He pulled on his coat and hat and stole silently outside. He crouched behind a bush ahead and right of the door, and looked around, holding his pistol low so that starlight wouldn't flash off the steel. Nothing moved. There was no sound, not even a dog barking in the distance. As far as Colter could tell, there were no tracks on this side of the shack.

Moving quickly and staying close to the weathered cabin, hoping it would absorb his own shadow, he walked around to the west side. He took his time looking around from this vantage, and then he walked to the rear where Sarah's bedroom faced north. Straight out from the broken window were tracks. They angled up to within twenty feet of the window from the east and then trailed away in the same direction.

Striding quickly, Colter followed them east as far as the main street, where they disappeared in the maze of tracks left by the previous day's horse, foot, and wagon traffic. Beyond lay the town that was quiet now at midnight. Lights glowed on the snowy street fronting Frank Miller's Saloon and the Blue Mountain, but the rest of the buildings were dark.

Whoever had thrown the stone was most likely long gone.

Now a coyote howled, a plaintive wail from far away.

It howled again as Colter started back toward the cabin, grinding his molars, vexed by Sarah's broken window. Who would throw a stone instead of lead? Someone who hadn't wanted to kill him but only frighten him, he supposed.

Still, it didn't make sense. Why try to frighten him when killing was so much more efficient? Besides, hadn't he made it obvious he didn't frighten easily?

He went back inside and stopped in front of the door.

Two lamps had been lit. Sarah sat at the table dressed in a powder blue robe. She'd built up the fire in the range, and the coffeepot sighed as the water warmed. The stone was on the table before her. Beside the stone was a leaf of paper. The paper was a wanted circular.

Colter's gut clenched.

Staring up from the circular was his own scarred, menacing face.

Sarah looked up from the paper, her expression somber. "This was lying beside the rock. Apparently, it came wrapped around it."

Colter didn't know what to say. He sighed.

"That's a lot of money on your head."

Her tone caused his guts to draw tighter. And then he realized with the sudden force of an avalanche sweeping over him and carrying him down a steep hill that he'd been a fool to think anything could come of him and Sarah. He was on the run, for Christ's sake. He'd always be on the run.

She looked down at the circular again, the coffeepot hissing quietly behind her. She studied the paper for a long time. She raised her eyes to him, frowning as though seeing him for the first time. She wasn't seeing *him*, however. She was seeing the face on the wanted dodger. The face of a killer with a stiff bounty on his head.

Her eyes filling with tears, she shook her head. "I knew this. I didn't want to know it. But I knew you were something like this."

Colter stood staring at her, a knife through his heart.

"Not again," she rasped. "I can't . . . I won't do that again."

"I know," he said, feeling a sharp knife twisting

in his guts. "It's all right, Sarah. I'm sorry. I never meant to hurt you. I shouldn't have . . ."

He shook his head, not having the words to express what was on his mind. He should not have come here. He should not have started anything with Sarah. He'd come with too much on his shoulders. She'd been through that with one man whom Dunbar had had to put down like a rabid dog. She couldn't do it again.

Colter turned around, fumbled the door open, and left.

Tonight, a heavy depression dogged him. It was a stout black dog with soft yellow eyes following from only a couple of feet behind. He could hear the critter panting back there, its breaths rasping in and out of its tired, old lungs. Its breath smelled like a pent-up attic littered with mouse droppings. The smell got into him, made his shoulders ache as though he were carrying a heavy load.

Colter tramped along the south side of the street, kicking at snow clods, heading east past Frank Miller's Saloon and three other false-fronted buildings to the north. There were four on the right, all dark. Ahead, across from the Blue Mountain Saloon, sat Dunbar's stone jailhouse with the wooden second story. The stout black hovel looked about as welcoming as a cave. It would be dark and cold inside.

That was all right.

Colter went inside and lit a lamp and worked out his frustration fetching wood from the woodshed, first splitting enough to get him through the night. Then he built a fire. He put a pot of coffee on to boil and rolled a sloppy cigarette and then he drank a hot cup of tar black coffee and smoked the quirley.

He had good reason to feel sorry for himself. But he'd be damned if he would. At least he had a place out of the cold for now, and he had a job to do. He'd met Matthew Dunbar, and he didn't care what Sarah had said about the old marshal. Colter liked him. There were lots of bad lawmen out there. Bill Rondo had been one. Some of the good ones straddled the line of the law, but in some places it was the only way you could keep a town out of the hands of the savages.

Rondo had been one of the savages who'd taken over his town. The fact that he'd donned a badge hadn't made him any less a savage. Dunbar was fighting against the possibility of that happening here in Justice City. Sometimes it took killing to get the job done. But no man whom Colter had seen Dunbar kill—and no man Colter himself had ever killed—had ever *not* needed killing.

The frontier was a tough place. Colter knew that from personal experience. Men lived and died by the gun. You had to be a tough man to survive in it.

Colter had a friend here in Justice City. And he had a job to do. And, by God, he'd side Matt Dunbar for as long as the one-eyed old hammerhead wanted him to.

By the time he'd finished his coffee and cigarette, he felt as if he'd swallowed a horse apple and inhaled coal smoke by sucking a chimney pipe. He banked the fire, kicked out of his boots, went into one of the cells, and rolled up in the blankets he'd laid out on the cot. He forced his mind away from Sarah and Marianna Claymore and his foster mother, Ruth, and everyone else from his past. He gave no thought to his future.

He let the warm darkness seep into his every pore, fill him up, and pull him down deep into the soothing ocean of sleep. He woke up to a quiet morning in a quiet town, and the next several days were much the same. Marshal Dunbar's wounds were healing well enough for him to get back to work.

He didn't speak of it, but he tired easily, so Colter worked half of the daylight hours and took several tramps around town during the night. Dunbar might have a tight hold on "his" town, but Colter had learned that outlaws passing through the mountains had been known to slip into Justice City under cover of darkness and rob the shops and steal whiskey out of the saloons.

Colter ran into no such trouble, however.

Indeed, the next few days after Sarah had discovered his true identity were quiet around Justice City. A couple of the afternoons warmed up to melt the snow, though the nights froze the street puddles. During the day, the streets were mud, and shop owners had stretched boards across them to accommodate foot traffic at several strategic places.

Wood smoke lingered in the air over Justice City. So did a strange pall, as if the entire town were collectively holding its breath. Maybe it was just Colter's imagination, but he sensed that everyone was waiting for the powder keg of violence between Dunbar and Hawk Garrett, whose fuse had been lit the day Billy had returned home only to be killed by his own father.

Word of that had spread fast. Everyone—at least those few who would talk to Colter, as everyone sort of saw him as a young Dunbar (especially after word about his identity also spread)—seemed to think it was just the beginning of more, bloodier violence to come in Justice City. So did Dunbar, who spent the bulk of his days on the jailhouse's front porch, obsessively cleaning his pistols and rifles and sharpening his two bone-handled bowie knives, which he wore in sheaths strapped to his shell belt.

He kept his lone, shrewd blue eye skinned to the trail spilling down out of the pine-carpeted mountains to the west. Few men entered town from that direction, none of them Eight-Bar-G riders. Colter had been told that Hawk Garrett kept a dozen or so men on his roll through the winter—mostly men good with guns, as nesters and rustlers were always a problem even in the winter out that way—and that most of them rode to town every couple of nights, either to Frank Miller's old place or the Blue Mountain Saloon or one of the two or three lesser saloons. None did now, and the saloon owners not only lamented the lack of business but dreaded what it meant.

Hawk Garrett seemed to be keeping his men at the ranch, biding his time, waiting to make a move on Dunbar and his young deputy, Colter Farrow. There was no way in hell that the indignity that Garrett had suffered the day he'd come to town for his son would go unavenged.

"Why do you think he killed Billy?" Colter asked Dunbar one day. "On account of the bank robbery?" He was standing in the jailhouse's open front door, smoking a quirley, while Dunbar sat on the porch, his wounded leg propped up on the porch rail. He held a rifle across his thick thighs, and he had twelve .44 cartridges lined up on the rail before him.

"Nah, not the robbery, squire," Dunbar said, glancing back at Colter, squinting his eye with cunning. "Shamed him . . . gettin' shamed by me. Yellowin' the snow an' such."

"Shame?"

"Worst thing in the world you can do to a man like Hawk Garrett."

"Then, why'd you do it?"

"'Cause I knew once I did it, I'd have to kill him."

Colter studied the man who sat staring westward along the muddy main street along which horseback riders rode and several farm wagons bounced and rattled, splashing mud. Several shopkeepers were clumped out in front of the Blue Mountain Saloon, glancing gravely toward Dunbar, who ignored them.

"You expected this?" Colter said at last, coughing a little on the peppery smoke in his lungs.

"You can bet the royal whiskey on that, squire. Time we got this thing between us settled. Been needin' settlin' for years now. Him killin' Billy and kickin' Morgan off the ranch . . ."

Dunbar let his voice trail off as he waved to Morgan staring down at him from the whore's window in the second story of the Blue Mountain Saloon. Morgan did not return the gesture but only lifted a cigar to his lips. "Him killin' Billy was as much a message to me as a punishment for Billy. Hell's gonna pop. Gonna pop soon, squire. Be on your toes . . ."

The marshal let his voice trail off again as several of the men who'd gathered on the front gallery of the Blue Mountain Saloon started walking down the steps. Norman Cantwell, owner of the Summit Hotel, was in the lead. The four others were all town councilmen, as well—Burt Peebles, Bill Williams, Joe Beauchamp, and George Atchison.

They made their way over to where a boardwalk crossed the street, the boards so narrow that most of the finely dressed men held their arms out for balance. Cantwell stepped off the boards and plunged his right foot in the mud up to his ankle. He cursed, was helped back onto the boards by Peebles, and they all continued until all five of the councilmen stood at the bottom of the jailhouse steps.

"Fine afternoon to ye, gentlemen," Dunbar said in his deep, resonant voice that was always pitched with strained tolerance when he addressed the businessmen. This was the second time this week that they'd all visited the jailhouse as a group. The first time, they'd beseeched Dunbar to do what he could to defuse the battle brewing between him and Garrett.

Colter had a feeling they were here again about the same thing, and he was partly right.

Cantwell usually spoke for the group, and he did so again today: "Marshal, the town council has met again to discuss this situation."

Dunbar sighed and loudly racked a round into the breech of his Winchester, which he continued to hold across his thighs, the barrel aimed toward the west. To a man, the councilmen jerked with a start, scowling fearfully at the rifle in the big man's hands.

"I'm all ears, boyo," Dunbar said, though his tone belied his words. He depressed the Winchester's hammer but clicked it softly, with subtle menacing, against the firing pin.

Chapter 27

Cantwell gave Dunbar's twitching thumb a sour look and said, "As you know, Marshal, business is down in Justice City. All the saloons and my hotel and even the mercantile are hurting. Not only do we not have the Eight-Bar-G's business, but other farmers, ranchers, and miners in the area have heard about the trouble brewing and are simply not coming to town."

Bill Williams said, "Why, my mercantile's business has plummeted. Many of the folks in town won't even come to the main business district out of fear of getting pinked by a stray bullet!"

Atchison said with a reluctant air, shrugging his heavy shoulders as he stood behind the others, "My business is down, too, Marshal. I've been on your side through this whole thing with Garrett. I appreciate what you've done for this town, giving folks confidence to open businesses here and, what's more, to patronize those businesses without fear of getting shot by owl-hoots." He shook his head in frustration. "But now . . . with this feud you and Garrett have goin' . . . folks are afraid of you two."

Beauchamp stepped forward and, red-faced, piped up with "And if you kill Garrett as you seem so bound and determined to do, what will become of the *bank?*"

"Worried about your asses, eh? Every last one of you." Dunbar shook his head in reproof. "Never seen the like. You'd as soon that outlaw did whatever he damn well pleases. And he would, too, if it weren't for me."

Beauchamp rose on the toes of his muddy brown shoes. "Everything would be fine and peaceful if it were not for you, Dunbar! Don't you see that?"

Dunbar rose awkwardly from his chair, wrapping one ham-sized hand over the top of the porch and leaning forward, his face swollen and red. "Now, that ain't true an' you *know* it! It was me that wrestled this town away from no-accounts like Hawk Garrett. If it wasn't for me you'd all still be pissin' down your legs every night an' every mornin'! If I had jurisdiction over the whole damn county and didn't have to leave that up to that prissy Sheriff Moynihan in the county seat, I'd run Garrett out of the county, too! He's a land-grabber, a common stock thief, and a killer! You know that as well as I do. Leastways, you *used* to know it . . . before Garrett used his stolen money to build the bank. Buyin' himself respectability in his old age was all he done. Only it's a lie. I'm smart enough to see through it. You men should be, as well."

The five councilmen stared up at Dunbar in dire frustration. Dunbar sagged back down in his chair, picked up a bottle from the porch floor beside his chair, and took a liberal swallow. Colter heard the air bubbles chug.

The marshal lowered the bottle, sighed, raked a hand across his mouth and bushy side whiskers. He set the bottle back down on the floor. Cantwell glanced around at the others as though for backing.

The hotelier cleared his throat and said with a sheepish air, "We have a proposal for you, Marshal Dunbar."

"Can't wait to hear that!"

"We'd like to make you an offer. An offer to buy your house from you and your daughter, and to pay you an entire year's salary—one thousand dollars—to turn in your badge."

"The offer for the house is right smart, too, Dunbar," said Burt Peebles, the land agent, who'd just bit the twist off the end of a fat stogie. "Two thousand dollars. We would also pay out the full sum of your daughter's teaching contract. That would be close to another five hundred dollars."

Bill Williams said, "You two could move anywhere and live very comfortably on that kind of money, Marshal."

Atchison said, "All you have to do for it is turn in your badge right here and now."

Beauchamp reached into a pocket of his brown camel hair coat and pulled out a lumpy brown envelope. He held it out, the sunlight glinting off his round spectacles. "It's all right here. Money for your and your daughter's contracts and money for your house. The sums you were just quoted."

Sitting straight backed in his chair, Dunbar studied the men. His back was to Colter, so the redhead couldn't see his expression. Dunbar reached up and very deliberately lifted his top hat from his head and inspected the high crown, flicking crusted mud from the smoke-stained felt just above the braided leather band.

"Mighty tempting offer, buckos. Mighty temptin'." Dunbar raked a thick fingernail across the mud stain.

The five councilmen looked as hopeful as yearling calves around feeding time. Their faces dropped in unison as Dunbar added, "And I'm sorry I'm going to have to turn it down. 'Cause that's a coward's offer. Matthew Dunbar has never been an' never shall be a man to shirk his duties, even when such fine, upstandin' citizens as yourselves try to buy him off."

"Oh, come on, Marshal!" Cantwell was incensed. He doffed his own bowler hat and held it down by his side, the bald top of his head glowing golden in the west-angling sun. "This is an extremely attractive offer. We're not firing you, you understand. We are paying you to leave Justice City so that the town can once again know peace!"

"The peace you admittedly did bring to it!" Atchison said, holding his hands up, palms out, in supplication.

"This feud between you and Garrett has just gone too far!" added Williams. "Now you're endangering all our livelihoods."

Dunbar carefully set the top hat back down on his head. "You men are the ones endangerin' your livelihoods. By kowtowin' to men like Hawk Garrett. You don't understand men like ole Hawk. I do. If I leave, him and his men will have the run of this town, and so will every outlaw in Utah and western Wyoming. I don't aim to see all my hard work come to nothin'. No, sir. Not fer all the tea in China. I do apologize, gentlemen, but I'm going to have to refuse your offer . . . attractive as it is. But, since we're on the subject of money, I do have a request."

"What's that?" asked Cantwell, who looked as though he was about to break down, sobbing. The others looked the same.

"My deputy here. Mr. Colter Farrow. He ain't been paid an' he's been on the job nigh on two weeks now."

Cantwell and the others looked incensed. Cantwell said, "We are not going to—!"

"Indeed you are going to pay the squire."

"We did not hire this man," Joe Beauchamp said. "You did! You pay him!"

"He's done this town a great service, and I want him paid right now." Dunbar went back to flicking the hammer of his Winchester against the firing pin. It made a very low pinging sound.

Colter wasn't sure what to say, so he kept his mouth shut. It was true that only Dunbar had hired him, not the town council. But he was doing a job for the town, and he did need money to survive on, like everyone else. As it was, he was eating mostly Dunbar's food and sleeping in the jailhouse.

Cantwell said quietly, pointing at Colter still standing in the open doorway flanking the marshal. "This is a wanted man. Everyone in town knows it. Why, you yourself should have arrested him by now, Dunbar!"

"The only thing Master Farrow is guilty of is avenging his own pa's murder. Woulda done the same myself." Dunbar pitched his voice with menace. "Now pay him ten dollars—a dollar a day, just like me. Do it now, out of Beauchamp's little package there, before you piss-burn me more than I already am, and I drill every one of you cheap bastards where you stand in the muddy street. Leave you there for the hungry curs!"

The town councilmen looked around at each other. Then the four turned to Beauchamp. Cantwell tossed his head at Colter.

"I will *not!*" the banker said, exasperated.

They only stared at him, as did Dunbar and Colter himself.

Beauchamp looked as if he were about to puff up and explode. But then he relented, reached into his coat pocket again, and pulled out the brown envelope. As he did, another paper fell out of the same pocket. It fluttered in the air before dropping into the mud as the banker stepped forward, holding two greenbacks in his soft white hand.

Colter moved to the top of the porch steps. He looked at the paper that had fallen out of Beauchamp's pocket. It was folded and crumpled, but enough of it showed for Colter to see his own likeness on the face of it, staring up from the mud on the street near the banker's muddy shoes.

Colter accepted the greenbacks as he stared down at the wanted circular.

"Well, I'll be," Dunbar said. "Lookee there, squire."

Beauchamp stared sheepishly down at the circular. He gave a nervous smile, hemmed and hawed, and then stepped abruptly back as Colter descended the porch steps. Colter looked at the banker skeptically and then reached down to pick up the paper. He brushed mud off his own likeness and then extended it to Beauchamp.

"Dropped somethin'."

"I, uh . . ." Beauchamp cleared his throat and glanced at the other councilmen, who studied him curiously. "I, uh, found this in the bank . . . where the Wells Fargo men occasionally post dodgers. It was behind some others. I remembered it . . . and . . ."

"Thought it would be a good way to run my deputy out of town, eh?" Dunbar said. "Only, the squire don't run so easy."

Colter stared at Beauchamp, whose spectacles glinted, obscuring his dung-colored eyes. "You don't have nothin' better to do than run around at night, throwin' rocks in girls' windows?"

Dunbar chuckled. "Oh, he probably didn't do it himself, Red. Probably hired some younker to do it for him—bein' the upstanding citizen that he is, don't ya know?"

Cantwell gave a disgusted chuff and turned away. "Come on, Joe. Our business here is finished."

The town councilmen headed back across the street, Beauchamp following the others with a hangdog air.

Dunbar chuckled as he watched them. Colter stuffed the greenbacks in his pocket, grateful to Dunbar to have gotten paid but not sure he liked how it was handled. He had the uneasy feeling he'd come by the money dishonestly, despite the work he'd been doing.

Colter said, "That's a lot of money they offered."

Dunbar had just taken another pull from his bottle, and grinned with half of his mouth. "Think I should take it, squire?"

Colter shrugged. "I don't know. I reckon I'd take some time to think it over."

"We Dunbars are Scots, squire. And no Dunbar ever run from a battle—not before or after we run the English out of our fair land." Rising from his chair, cradling his bottle with his wounded arm, picking up his rifle with the other hand, Dunbar added, "Don't reckon this Dunbar's gonna start now. Tellin' it to you straight, boyo. . . ."

The old marshal glanced at Colter, a devilish light in his lone eye. "I aim to grow old and die here in this town o' mine. And mine it is, too. I fought for it, won it back from the wolves. And when I kill ole Hawk Garrett, the last big wolf in the woods, I aim to drag his carcass through these very streets and leave it on the steps of his own bank. And then I'm gonna piss on him and enjoy watchin' Beauchamp piss down his own leg while I do it, too."

He extended his good hand to Colter. "Honored to have you aboard, squire. Nice meetin' another one like me, a man who'll give no quarter." He smiled, showing his teeth. "Must have some Scot in ya!"

He laughed as Colter shook his hand, regarding the man a little uncertainly before watching the stout Scot walk tenderly down the steps and into the street, not bothering with the boards. "I'll be retirin' for the evenin', squire," he called behind him. "If you see any trouble, remember to fire two quick shots in the air, and I'll be there quick as the duke's hounds on a red fox in county Fife!"

Colter watched Dunbar walk away, limping on his bad leg. The redhead felt soft fingers of uneasiness brush the back of his neck. He was so lost in thought that he didn't hear the approach of footsteps until a girl's voice said, "A right impressive man, isn't he?"

He whipped his head to the left with a start. Sarah Miller stood in the street, about twenty feet west of the jailhouse, on a plank bridge across the mud. She had her hair up, and she wore a blanket coat over a plain brown dress and the heavy brown boots she wore in her livery barn. The handle of a wicker basket covered with oilcloth was looped over her right arm. She lifted that arm, indicating the basket.

"Brought you a sandwich," she said.

"You didn't have to do that."

"I know that. I had meat left over from last night, and extra bread, and I figured with no one to cook for you, you were wasting away to nothin' but bone and sinew."

"You don't have to do me no favors, Sarah."

"Oh, God, I hope Dunbar's pride isn't rubbing off on you now, too!" She mounted the steps and thrust the basket at him. Her eyes were pleading as she said softly, "Please don't let him get you killed, Colter."

Colter took the basket. "Why would you care, anyway?" He couldn't help that his feelings were hurt by the girl's rejection. He liked to think he was strong and independent, but he'd thought about Sarah many times over the past few days. Those thoughts were like the edge of a dull knife probing his belly.

"I care," she said. "That's the trouble with me. I'm always caring about the wrong kind of man."

That riled the redhead. "You don't know anything about me!"

She gave a somber nod, wisps of golden hair blowing about her smooth cheeks. "I know enough. Take your sandwich inside and eat it with a cup of coffee, and don't get your neck up about a girl tellin' you what to do."

She turned and started walking back the way she'd come, her head down, pinching her skirt above her ankles so it wouldn't drag in the mud.

She stopped suddenly and turned toward him

again. "Hell's coming, Colter. Everyone in town knows it." She dipped her chin solemnly. "And you know it, too. I just hope none of the wrong people get killed."

Colter threw up his hands in frustration. "What can I do about it?"

"Ride out of here tonight." She swung around and continued walking west.

Colter watched her go. And then, holding the basket, he turned to where he'd watched Dunbar disappear. His gaze was cast with a growing doubt. A doubt that his stubborn pride, not all that different from Dunbar's own, wouldn't let him admit to.

He cursed under his breath, hauled the basket inside the jailhouse, and slammed the door.

Chapter 28

Colter enjoyed Sarah's roast beef sandwich so much that the next morning he found himself hungry for more good food.

Mainly, he'd been eating jerky, bread, cheese, and beans from the mercantile, and washing the store-bought food down with Arbuckles' coffee. That was getting old, but in light of how she felt about him, he couldn't very well walk over to Sarah's and ask for another round. He'd heard the grub was good over at Cantwell's Summit Hotel, which had a dining room. Since he had a few extra dollars in his pocket, he decided to splurge on a big breakfast.

After he'd hauled in a load of firewood and built a fire in the stove, he made his morning rounds about the town, ending up on the west end of Justice City. The hotel was on that end of town—a two-story white-frame building directly across from Hawk Garrett's Summit County Bank & Trust. Colter angled toward the hotel from the bank, whose door he'd just made sure was locked, the windows unbroken. He didn't much care for Garrett's holdings, but the bank was part of his rounds.

As he crossed the street that was a maze of iron-like ridges of mud frozen in the shapes of wheel furrows and horse prints dusted with soot from chimney smoke, he slowed his pace to inspect the six horses that stood tied to one of the two hitch racks fronting the hotel. As he continued walking toward the veranda, he paused to give the horses—sleek-looking mounts that were blowing as though they'd been ridden into town just that morning—a closer scrutiny.

He ran his hand along the left wither of an apple-wood bay into which an 8 over a bar G had been burned. Colter's heart increased its pace. He ducked under the bay's reins and quickly looked at the withers of the other five horses. Only the bay was wearing the Eight-Bar-G brand.

Only one mount from Hawk Garrett's spread, but it was in the same group as the other five. All six had rifle scabbards strapped to their saddles. All of the scabbards were empty. Colter brushed his hand across the butt of his second Remington that he'd wedged behind the buckle of his cartridge belt, and was glad he'd remembered to arm himself double. He'd left his Winchester in the jailhouse, and he wished he had the long gun now, as well. He'd gotten careless during the time he'd been waiting for Garrett to make his move, and here the rancher had made it—ridden into town with five other men before Colter was awake—and the redhead wasn't as thoroughly armed as he wanted to be.

He wasn't as hungry as he'd been a minute ago,

but he headed on up the steps of the hotel's white-painted front porch, anyway. The only way to meet trouble, he'd learned over the past several years, was head-on.

He went on inside to find a central hall that led past a carpeted lobby with a long oak desk flanked by pigeonholes, to a stairway with deep purple carpet. On the right, under a large elk head, was an open doorway through which Colter could hear the typically quiet hum of morning conversation and smell fried eggs and bacon and boiling coffee.

He ground the mud from his boots on the hemp rug fronting the door and walked into the dining room, pausing just inside the door, where the smell of the food hung as heavy as a blanket.

It was a large room floored with halved logs. There was no carpeting, but the dozen or so square tables were covered in white linen. A cuckoo clock ticked loudly near the door. Colter was surprised to see Morgan Garrett sitting alone at a small table to Colter's left, just now looking up at Colter over his stone coffee mug, a strained look on his pasty, sallow face.

He had a newspaper half-open on the table before him, though the man's haunted eyes told Colter he hadn't been reading it. The older and sole-surviving son of Hawk Garrett was too distracted by the six men gathered on the other side of the room from him. All six, including Garrett himself, sat at two linen-draped tables that had been shoved together to make one long one.

Hawk Garrett sat at the far end, facing Colter. Two of the six men sat with their backs to Colter, facing the west wall. Three sat facing Colter, with their backs to that same wall.

They'd been the only ones in the room talking

above the sound of pots and pans clattering unseen in the kitchen beyond. Garrett had just taken a drink of his coffee, and now he set his cup down on the table with a flourish, looking at Colter, his thick, wavy gray hair swept straight back off his broad, freckled forehead.

The others at his table turned toward Colter. They were a seedy-looking bunch, rifles leaning against the wall or against chairs, within easy reach. They all wore rough trail clothes, neckerchiefs, and woolly chaps. Their gloomy faces were still red from the ride in from the ranch, their hair matted to their heads. Their fur coats, gloves, hats, and mufflers were all piled on a nearby table.

The two men whose backs faced Colter were turned toward him now, their killers' eyes appraising him with the dullness of predatory animals, though beneath that dullness there lurked a cunning gleam, like the headlamp of a locomotive seen from a long ways away in the night.

They'd all been eating when Colter had walked in, cloth napkins tucked into their shirts. Now Garrett used his napkin to wipe his mouth and then said in a thundering voice that echoed inside the low-ceilinged, cavelike room, "I hear you got paid, Mr. Farrow. Decided to spend a little of my money on a good breakfast, did you?"

He smirked as he slid his eyes to the others.

Colter shrugged. "Sure. Why not?"

He walked to a near table, kicked the chair out, and sat down facing Garrett's men. Morgan was ahead on his right, sitting against that wall, about twelve feet away. Colter wanted to keep everyone else in the room in his vision field, in case it came to shooting, which he was pretty sure it would. Those fingers of apprehension were really raking him across the back of his neck, and he drew a long, deep breath to stay calm. Six against one were not good odds. Would Morgan pick a side? Colter doubted it. Morgan had a sickly, jaundiced pallor. Colter doubted he was even armed, but he had to assume Morgan was and that, despite what had happened out at his father's ranch, he'd take his father's side.

Seven against one were not good odds. Colter just hoped he could take Garrett out and at least two of the others before they all sent him down in a hail of lead.

Despite the tension, he still felt a few gnawing hunger pangs. That was good. If he was taken down, he wanted to die with a full belly. What's more, he didn't want Garrett to think he was one bit afraid of him.

There was a soft squawk, and Colter saw a stout, round-faced woman push through a swinging door at the back of the room. She was carrying a coffee-pot in one hand with a leather mitt and a small stone cream server in the other hand. Her powder pink muslin dress swished about her heavy legs. She glanced at Colter with quick, nervous eyes. As she saw her new customers, her eyes acquired an even sharper cast. She swept her glance to Morgan and then turned to Garrett's table.

When she'd refilled the cups of Garrett's men, she came over to Colter. A fine sheen of perspiration beaded her thin upper lip. "You're . . . here to eat?" She was a little out of breath.

"Yeah." Colter was perusing the menu card. "I'll have the ham and eggs. Do those come with pota-toes?"

"Yes, they come with potatoes."

"And buttered toast?"

"Of course," she said impatiently, turning with a breathy sigh and swishing on back down the room and through the swinging door.

Colter sat back in his chair, extending his feet out in front of him, beneath the table, and crossing his ankles. He hooked his thumbs behind his cartridge belt. Morgan cast him furtive glances while pretending to read the newspaper on the table before him, sipping his coffee.

Hawk's men were speaking now in low tones. Colter couldn't hear what they were saying, but their tones were furtive, mocking. Their knives and forks clinked against their plates as they ate. They sipped their coffee and set their cups back down on the table, wiped their mustache-mantled mouths with their napkins.

They cleared their throats, stifled belches, made their chairs creak as they shifted their weight around.

Meanwhile, the woman came through the swinging door again and brought a steaming platter of eggs and gravy-drenched biscuits and a slab of ham to Morgan. She refilled Morgan's coffee cup, swung around with another breathless sigh, and swished on back through the door.

Morgan set his paper aside and, sliding his eyes once toward his father's table, picked up his fork and knife and began cutting up his ham and his biscuits. Colter vaguely wondered if Hawk had even acknowledged the presence of his older boy, who had no doubt been here in the café before Hawk's men had arrived. Seeing them must have nearly given Morgan a heart stroke, Colter thought, feeling a smirk curl his upper lip.

The woman came with Colter's coffee, and as he

added cream and was stirring the brew with a spoon, Hawk Garrett shoved his empty plate away from him, wiped his mouth with his napkin, slid his chair back, and rose.

"Well, fellas," he said with a sigh, "I reckon we're burnin' daylight."

Colter watched the rancher and two of his other five hands toss their napkins down or take a last sip from the coffee mugs and rise from their chairs. Three of the others—two sitting with their backs to the wall, one facing the wall—remained in their chairs.

Colter was puzzled, though he tried hard to maintain a stony expression as he leaned carefully back in his chair, slowly sipping his coffee. Garrett and the two others walked over to the table on which they'd all piled their cold-weather gear, and slipped into their coats and gloves and donned their hats.

When they'd gathered up their rifles, Garrett plucked some coins out of his pants pocket and said with a mock air of disgust, "Well, since it don't look like Tatum's gonna buy, like he said he would, I reckon it's up to me to ante up!"

One of the men still sitting snorted and shook his head while the others chuckled.

Garrett adjusted his cream Stetson on his head, his long green muffler hanging straight down over his shoulders, and walked toward the door. Colter watched the man's rifle, which was angled toward the floor. Garrett held the weapon by the neck of its stock; he did not poke his gloved finger through the trigger guard.

Vaguely, while he waited and watched, hearing his heart beat slowly but commandingly, Colter wondered if Garrett and the two others were really going to leave. Or were they just trying to put Colter in a whipsaw?

Garrett swung toward Colter's table and stopped. He stared down at Colter. His eyes were like two chips of flint. Colter felt his insides clench when Hawk suddenly stuck out his right hand, holding it over the table, as though wanting to shake. Colter looked at the hand and then up into Garrett's face, the rancher's dark eyes mocking now, a mocking grin lifting his mouth corners and shoving his mustache up hard against his broad, pitted, bulb-tipped nose.

"What?" Garrett said with a wry chuckle. "You won't shake my hand?" He lowered his hand. "Why, you ugly, *insolent* little devil!"

The two other men stopped behind him, looking over their boss's shoulders at Colter and laughing. The sitting men laughed, too, their eyes flashing at Colter.

The redhead just stared up at Hawk Garrett, maintaining a bland expression but every muscle coiled and ready to spring into action. With half of his conscious mind, he imagined drilling one round through the center of the rancher's forehead, another through his belly button. And then he'd start in on the others, try to blow the wicks of as many of the five as he could.

"I just wanted to congratulate you on a job well done here in Justice City," Garrett told Colter, his eyes flashing mockingly, "and say that I hope you enjoy your breakfast." The rancher winked and pinched his hat brim. "Because it's the last god-damn meal you're ever gonna eat, amigo!"

He turned away from Colter. He did not so much as glance at Morgan, who sat tensely, a forkful of food held frozen in front of his mouth. Garrett's boots pounded the floor puncheons as he tramped toward the lobby door. The two men behind him glanced sneeringly down at Colter and then followed their boss out of the dining room.

Colter kept the dining room door in the periphery of his vision as he stared at the other three Garrett riders. One got up slowly, keeping his hands belly high, palms down, and then slowly turned toward Colter. His eyes, which reflected the light in the window behind Colter, were the blue of the spring's first lilac blossoms.

He backed around the far end of the table and sat down in the chair that Garrett had vacated. He stared at Colter with those eyes that set off the cold, hard planes of his face beneath a cap of coal black hair with a single streak of gray in it.

Through the window behind Colter came the clomps of Garrett and the other two men riding away down the street to the west. Heading off to find Dunbar, most likely. . . .

The thought caused anxious venom to spurt in Colter's veins.

With one of the three men before Colter having switched positions, the other two, separated by an empty chair between them, sat stiffly in their own chairs. The three stared at Colter. At the same time, Morgan was sitting tensely at his own table, before a plate of food he'd barely touched, sliding his gaze back and forth between Colter and his father's three ranch hands.

Or *were* they Hawk's ranch hands?

Colter felt a muscle twitch in his scarred cheek, under his left eye.

Had Garrett brought in professional killers?

Regulators? That would explain the five horses outside not wearing the Garrett brand.

All five of these men had the similar rangy,
whittled-down features and deep-set, cold, patho-
logical eyes of most of the cold-steel artists Colter
had known. They were not as weathered as most
range riders. And a couple wore cut-down holsters,
which made drawing pistols easier.

Colter would bet silver eagles against sourdough
biscuits that the guns in those holsters had had their
sights filed down.

Maybe that's what had taken Garrett so long to
make a move. He'd been waiting for the right men to
make it with—men he might have summoned from
the mining camps down the mountain. Maybe even
from Salt Lake City. That's why they'd split up just
now. Despite the reputation that Colter was sure had
made its way around the county by now, Garrett
was confident that these three regulators could take
care of Colter just fine.

That muscle twitched in Colter's cheek again.

Doubt raked at him. He hoped it didn't show in
his eyes.

He'd never faced men who looked this slick. This
coldly professional. Was Colter really as good as he
thought he was?

The blank stares of these men told him that he
was about to find out.

Chapter 29

Colter slowly uncrossed his ankles and sat up straighter in his chair. He slid his gaze across the three men staring back at him blankly and pulled his thumbs out from behind his cartridge belt.

The door to the kitchen swung open, and the plump woman entered the dining room with a platter in one hand, the coffeepot in the other hand. She stopped, looked at Colter and then at Garrett's men, closed her mouth, wheeled, and disappeared through the door to the kitchen.

The man with the lilac eyes glanced at the other two. The one nearest him dipped his chin slightly. A nod?

The man with the lilac eyes rose from his chair and, holding his hands purposefully above the grips of the two six-shooters holstered on his hips, grips forward, walked toward Colter. When he was four feet from Colter's table, he turned slightly to his right and began walking toward the door. His boots thumped and his spurs rattled.

"Hold it," Colter said softly.

The man with the lilac eyes stopped, frowned indignantly down at Colter. "You talkin' to me?"

"Where do you think you're goin'?" Colter asked him.

The man opened his mouth a little, as though flabbergasted to be asked such an impertinent question. Then the corners of his eyes crinkled as he smiled. "Wherever the hell I please, friend!"

Colter glanced at the man's guns. He'd unsnapped the keeper thongs over the hammers. The thongs hung down the sides of his soft brown leather holsters. Colter had no doubt that this man was intending to move to the dining room door to affect what Colter had suspected they'd try—to get him in a whipsaw. A cross fire.

Just because professional killers were good at killing did not necessarily mean they were brave men, or that they aimed to fight fair. Most whom Colter had met or heard intimate details about were cowards, and they'd ply any advantage, even an unfair advantage.

Colter narrowed an eye at the lilac-eyed man. "You ain't goin' nowhere."

The man with the lilac eyes stared shrewdly down at Colter. The other two sat in their chairs as stiffly as before.

Silence weighed heavy in the shadowy room. Morgan Garrett sat frozen, though Colter saw his throat work as he swallowed hard.

One of the men at the table slid his chair back abruptly and, keeping his cold, dark eyes on Colter, rose to his feet. The other man made the same move two seconds later. The man with the lilac eyes squared his shoulders at Colter and, holding his hands a few inches above the grips of his pistols, took two steps straight back from Colter's table.

The three were as tense as coiled rattlers, every muscle poised for striking.

Colter drew a deep breath through his nose. His heart tapped an insistent rhythm against his ribs. He drew another long, deep breath to calm it.

He'd just begun to slide his chair back when the man with the lilac eyes said, "No. You just sit right there, you ugly devil. You're gonna die sitting down!"

"Devil" had not finished sliding between his mustache-mantled lips before one of the men at the table—the man nearest the table's far end—jerked his hands toward his two, pearl-gripped .44s.

The man was fast. But he was too fast.

He fired so quickly that his slug screamed over Colter's right shoulder as the redhead threw that shoulder back, half turning to make himself as slender a target as possible, and his slug plunked through the dining room's front window. As Colter turned, his main gun in his left hand, his belly gun in his right hand, he shot the first shooter in the shoulder a quarter of an eyeblink before triggering his right-hand pistol at the second man at the table.

The second man fired his pistol into the top of the table before him as Colter's bullet plowed through the man's upper gun arm. The man howled and tried to raise the pistol again but merely fired into the table once more.

Meanwhile, the lilac-eyed man had been caught off guard. He got his own guns only half-raised before Colter swung his main Remington at him and fired.

The lilac-eyed hombre cursed shrilly as Colter's

bullet punched him back, but he got both his pistols raised. As he fired both guns and the other two regulators began shooting from cover behind the table, Colter pivoted, wheeling, and dove over a table behind him, sliding across its surface and taking the table and its white cloth with him as he hurled himself to the floor on the table's far side.

Four or five pistols set the room alive with tooth-gnashing thunder, several slugs hammering Colter's covering table and spitting wood slivers every which way. Colter rose to his knees and, wincing against the lead screeching around him and hammering the table, snaked both his Remingtons over the top of the table. Gritting his teeth, snarling like a bobcat, he sent his own lead storm back toward the shooters, punching the lilac-eyed man straight back into a table behind him with a grunt, blood flying out the exit wound in his back to paint the white cloth covering yet another table near the kitchen door.

Colter slid both Remingtons slightly right as the man who'd first fired lifted his head halfway above the rear right corner of the far table, near where Hawk Garrett had been sitting. Colter took an extra second to aim and was rewarded by seeing his .44 slug paint a purple hole in the man's pale forehead, an inch right of the bridge of his nose.

Colter winced as a slug from the other shooter's pistol tore flesh from the top of his right arm and jerked him slightly backward, causing his own return fire to blow up wood slivers and bits of white cloth from the top of the table from behind which the man was shooting.

The man fired two more rounds before both his hammers clicked on empty cylinders. His guns were empty.

Heart thudding eagerly, Colter threw himself over the top of his overturned table, hit the floor on his belly, and extended both his own Remingtons out before him and slightly up, toward the man he could see hunkered under the far table.

Colter gritted his teeth and squeezed his left-hand Remy.

Ping!

He squeezed his right-hand Remy.

Ping!

Colter said, "Shit!" and saw the man on the far side of the table show the white line of his teeth as he grinned and dropped one pistol to start reloading the other one.

Colter bolted to his knees as he dropped his second Remy and flicked open the loading gate on the main one. Quickly, casting anxious glances toward his adversary on the far side of the table, he shook out the spent cartridges. They rattled to the floor as he punched fresh from his cartridge belt, intending to fill all six chambers.

The other man settled with only two—Colter had been counting—before he flicked his loading gate closed. Still punching shells into his Remington's empty chambers, Colter hurled himself to his left, over the table that the lilac-eyed gent had overturned. As he did, the third shooter's two slugs blew up wood slivers just behind Colter's boot heels.

One slug spun the rowel of Colter's left spur.

As Colter hit the floor on the other side of the table, he rose to his knees, slipped the Remy's loading gate closed, and fired four quick rounds as the third shooter rose from behind his table, grunting and sighing fearfully, and went running toward the front of the room, apparently intending to hurl himself through the window.

He went through the window, all right—screaming, two of Colter's slugs in his back.

The window shattered with what sounded like the shrill screams of a dozen frightened little girls. The man thudded heavily onto the porch, causing the three horses tied to the hitch rack to whinny and pull back on their reins.

A shadow slid across a thick pool of blood in front of Colter and slightly left. In the crimson pool's reflection, Colter saw a figure move—a well-dressed man with an impeccably groomed beard. Morgan Garrett was rising to his feet behind Colter, and he was pulling something out of the inside of his coat.

Colter wheeled, raking his pistol's hammer back. As Morgan screamed, showing his teeth like an enraged cur, and extended a pearl-gripped Bisley revolver, Colter drilled a hole through the chest of the older son of Hawk Garrett. Morgan grunted as he triggered the fancy pistol into the floor between his brogans and, head flopping as though his neck were broken, fell back against the wall.

He slid down to the floor, dislodging an oil painting of a mountain meadow in springtime. He sat against the wall as he dipped his chin to look bewilderedly down at the blood pumping from the hole in the dead center of his chest, quickly staining his white cotton shirt. He lifted a heavy hand to the hole, touched his index finger to the blood gushing out of it. As if that had answered an important question for him, he gave a heavy sigh and his eyelids fluttered.

He slid sideways to the floor, where he lay shivering as though chilled to the bone.

Colter rose quickly and, looking around to see if there was any life in the men he'd shot, immediately began to reload his pistols. A heavy silence hung over the room. No sounds emanated from the kitchen. His empty cartridges pinged onto the floor as he loaded the first gun. As he slipped that pistol into its holster, he made his way to the front of the smoky room and looked out the broken window.

The man out there was crawling toward the porch steps. His bloody back was basted with blood. When Colter had finished loading his second pistol, he aimed through the broken window and finished the man with a round through the back of his head.

Then he replaced that spent cartridge, as well. He retrieved his hat from the floor, donned it, and headed outside, ignoring the burn in his upper right arm as he jogged in the direction of the Dunbar house from which he expected to hear shooting at any moment.

Chapter 30

Marshal Dunbar had just cracked a fourth egg into a hot iron skillet atop the range when he heard hooves thumping the cold ground outside his and Victoria's modest house on the north edge of Justice City. He reached for one of his pistols holstered on the outside of his blue-plaid bathrobe and swung toward the window over the table.

He left the iron leathered. Victoria put her blue roan gelding, named Old Matt after her father, up to the tie ring and swung down from the saddle. Watching her slip the bit from Old Matt's mouth, Dunbar chuckled.

She was wearing his old bear coat over a pair of baggy denim trousers, and her hair was invitingly disheveled. Victoria had gotten up before he had—which was usual for the dutiful child—and ridden over to the school to lay a fire in the potbelly stove and to tidy up a bit, which she did every morning an hour or so before class started.

Victoria unbuckled Old Matt's latigo, letting it hang from beneath the horse's belly, and then ran an affectionate hand down the roan's neck and withers speaking into the horse's ear, like a lover. Dunbar's eyes stung as he watched the beautiful girl, who looked so much like her mother at the same age that it made his old ticker ache.

As Victoria mounted the porch, he turned back to the eggs, sliding his spatula under them to keep them from sticking. They fried in the grease from Dunbar's usual six strips of bacon that remained in the hot pan.

"Oh, Pa, let me do that!" Victoria said as she closed the door and long-strode around the table to the range. "You know you always let the pan get too hot, and you never add water!"

As she lightly, half teasingly elbowed the big man aside, grabbing the spatula out of his hand and turning a shoulder to him, Dunbar grinned. He leaned his head toward the back of hers, drew a long, deep breath. Victoria smelled like cold air and wood smoke and that special scent that was all her own but that also smelled just how Dunbar remembered her mother smelling.

He touched his bear coat's heavy collar. "I thought you was a bear comin' in for me eggs, lil' gal. Almost hustled off to get my Henry!" He gave her a brusque peck on her cheek.

"With that wounded leg of yours, I don't think you'll be hustlin' anywhere for a while." She set the spatula down, picked up a fork, and poked the bacon around beside the sputtering eggs. "Go sit down at the table. If I can salvage anything here, I'll bring it over in a minute. How many times do I have to tell you that you have to add a drop of water to the eggs or they'll *burn?*"

"I'll never learn that one, me darlin'," Dunbar said as he eased his bulk into his usual chair at the end of the table. "It just ain't in me, I guess. Your mother tried. Oh, how she tried!"

"You're hopeless."

"Yes, I am. Hangin's too good for me."

"Don't give me any ideas, you old reprobate." Victoria brought the skillet over to the table, kissed her father's temple, and began filling his plate with the eggs and bacon.

"I would have fried you some, but I seen you already ate," Dunbar said, staring down at the eggs and bacon on his plate.

"Woke up hungry, I reckon." She went to the stove for the toast he'd nearly burned on the grate, buttered both pieces, set them on a small plate, and set the plate down by her father's right elbow. "I'll just have another cup of coffee before I get dressed. You haven't burned that, too, have you? I really wish you'd leave the cooking up to me, Papa."

"With all you got distractin' ya, a man would starve!"

"I don't have all that much distractin' me anymore," she said with her back to him as she used a mitt to lift the big, black coffeepot and fill a stone mug for herself.

Dunbar detected a sullen note of acrimony in her tone. He didn't blame her. The poor gal had lost her beau, and her old man hadn't even warned her what a slime Morgan was, for fear of hurting her feelings. Dunbar had been embarrassed for her, because nearly the entire town knew of Morgan Garrett's doings in the Blue Mountain Saloon. Dunbar hadn't wanted to tell her out of fear of humiliating her. The girl had her nose in the books so much that she rarely looked up to see what was really going on around her, and her father had liked that about her. For a time, it had protected her from the cruel, cold world of this Western frontier.

Dunbar didn't really know what he'd been thinking concerning his daughter and Morgan Garrett. Maybe he'd just hoped she'd eventually realize that Hawk Garrett's older son had been beneath her, that's all, and that she'd give him the cold shoulder soon and set her sights on someone better.

Victoria sagged down in a chair across from Dunbar, leaning forward, her hands wrapped around her stone mug. While she ate, she sipped the coffee slowly, thoughtfully, staring down into the mug as though she were reading tea leaves. She was still wearing Dunbar's bulky bear coat, which was about eight sizes too large for her. Unbuttoned, it sagged down her shoulders.

Dunbar liked it when she wore his coat. She'd always done that as a child, and the shaggy, overlarge garment made her appear as the child she would never be again.

She waited until he'd wolfed down over half his breakfast before she said, "I heard from Louis Blackleg that Cantwell offered to buy your badge back from you."

Blackleg was the half-breed Ute who supplied the school with split firewood. Victoria had spoken to her coffee, but now as Dunbar stopped chewing, she slid her faintly accusing blue eyes to him. "And that he offered to buy me out, as well. And he offered to buy the house from us for full market value." She shook her head slowly, turning her mouth corners down. "And you didn't take it."

"Aye." Dunbar sighed. "I didn't take it, me gal."

"And you didn't bother to discuss it with me before you turned it down. When you turned it *all* down." Victoria's eyes and voice were sharp. Dunbar steeled himself for a tantrum. As far as Scottish passions went in the Dunbar house, the apple hadn't fallen far from the tree. Victoria could make the glassware sing nearly as loudly as Dunbar.

He started to get riled now himself, remembering that day, those four fancy-Steves standing around him as if they owned the bloody porch he'd been standing on, and in a way he supposed they did. "They tried to pay me off right there on the street! Shoved an envelope full of money at me like I was one of George Atchison's cheapest percentage gals!"

Dunbar tossed his fork on his plate, sat back in his chair, and folded his arms across his broad, thick chest. "No, I couldn't do it. I shoulda discussed it with ya, me gal but I didn't. And then after it was too late, I was too much of a bloody coward to mention it. Afraid I'd get taken to the woodshed, I reckon."

He adjusted the eye patch over his empty socket and looked at her sheepishly from beneath his other brow. She sat staring at him obliquely, lips pursed. He couldn't tell what she was thinking, and he was thinking that he'd bet she could really make her students squirm. Especially the boys, who were all probably deeply in love with this rosy-cheeked Scottish filly.

"If you wanna leave your old dad, I could ask

Cantwell if that part of the offer still stands. The part about the school, I'm meanin'. I reckon it's about time you lit out on your own, made your own way without me weighin' ya down like a damn ship's anchor. I'd be bloody blubberin' in my beer about it, but I wouldn't blame you one bit, me gal. I'm a cursed old cuss!"

He waited. She didn't say anything. She was really making him squirm. Just like her mother. He was starting to set his jaw for a sudden torrential downpour of female ire when she spread her lips slightly, gave a slow blink. She slid one of her hands across the table and wrapped it affectionately around his forearm.

He looked at her long, pale hand with its one faint freckle between her index and middle finger knuckles. He squinted up at her. "You ain't just gonna warm me up for a good slap-down, now, are ya, Victoria?"

She squeezed him harder, chuckled. Her eyes glazed slightly. "Papa, I love you more than life. How could I ever leave you?" She rose from her chair and raised her voice with mock scolding. "Besides, you'd burn everything you tried to cook and starve to death!"

She kissed his forehead and then hauled his heavy coat up higher on her shoulders. "I'm going to go fetch wood for the box, or you'll freeze to death when I'm at school."

"I can fill the wood box. I ain't a bloody invalid!"

"You are a bloody invalid. Besides, I don't want you opening up those wounds again, so sit still and finish your breakfast."

Victoria grabbed his top hat off a peg by the front door and donned it. It nearly swallowed her head.

She tipped it off her forehead and laughed. "How do I look?"

"Like me!" Dunbar laughed. "You bloody look like me! Take it off before you scare Mrs. Franklin!" He laughed again.

Victoria laughed and, humming and throwing her arms out, weaving her hands through the air, danced to the back door and outside to the woodshed.

Dunbar watched her through the window left of the range and facing the backyard, the smile slow to leave his haggard face. When he saw her open the woodshed door and disappear inside, he hunkered back down over his eggs and bacon. He'd taken two bites when he saw something move quickly out the back window.

He turned his head, egg yolk dribbling over his lips.

His heart heaved when saw a man move out from behind the woodshed's far corner, moving stealthily, holding a Winchester carbine up high across his chest. Two more men came out from behind the same corner of the woodshed. The last man—with long gray hair hanging down from his cream Stetson to dangle over the collar of his wolf coat—was Hawk Garrett.

The three men—two of whom Dunbar had never seen before—formed a semicircle out in front of the woodshed, facing the closed door, and as Dunbar watched in shock, unable to move enough to even set his fork down, they raised their rifles to their shoulders. He could see their thumbs raking the hammers back.

They were waiting for Victoria to open the door wearing Dunbar's coat and his bloody hat!

Dunbar screamed like an animal and bounded up out of his chair, reaching for the two pistols on his hips. He'd moved too quickly on his bad leg, and as he slammed that leg against a leg of the table, he rapped his right hand against the table edge, dropping the pistol to the floor.

"Aw, bloody hell!" he screamed, dropping to one knee.

Beneath his own screams came the muffled roar of rifle fire.

"Vic-tor-iaahhhhh!" Dunbar screamed from his knees.

Colter ran up to a stout ponderosa pine at the edge of the Dunbar property. He leaned his shoulder against the tree, spread his boots, and raised both his Remingtons clicking the hammers back.

"Garrett!" he shouted.

At the same time, the woodshed door flew open and Dunbar stopped suddenly in the doorway, his arms filled with split stove wood. Only it wasn't Dunbar's craggy, one-eyed face beneath the thin brim of his top hat. It was Victoria's. The contrast couldn't have been starker.

Or more horrifying.

She opened her mouth to scream as all three rifles exploded, smoke and flames lapping toward the open door.

Victoria flew back inside the woodshed and out of sight as Hawk Garrett and the two professional gunmen wheeled, cocking their rifles, only to be blown straight back off their feet by Colter's roaring Remingtons. Colter screamed as he fired, gritting his teeth, punching bullet after bullet through the three men as they danced and pirouetted backward, throwing their rifles every which way as blood sprayed from their exit wounds to paint the sage-stippled ground and the woodshed's gray log wall.

Too late, the redhead thought. He'd gotten here half a second too late.

His guns clicked empty. The three gunmen lay spread-eagle on the ground before the woodshed. Two lay still. Garrett arched his back and lifted his butt with the heels of his boots, mewling as his life pumped out with his blood.

A great bellowing bear cry issued from the back door of the Dunbar house. *"Victoria!"*

Dunbar stumbled out the door as it slammed against the house's back wall. He staggered into the yard and dropped to his knees, sobbing. "Oh, Gawd— Victoria! Oh, bloody Christ!" He lifted his chin and wailed.

Colter stood frozen, guns hanging at his sides. He stared at the woodshed door that had closed when Victoria had flown back through the opening. His knees were mud. His heart beat slowly, heavily. It was as tender as a wound.

A leather hinge squeaked softly as the shed door opened. Victoria stepped through the dark opening. She was no longer wearing Dunbar's top hat. She stopped in front of the shed and stared in shock at the gunmen—all three now still and bloody in death, their half-open eyes staring skyward.

She glanced at Colter. And then she walked over to her father, who stared wide-eyed at her now, tears dribbling down his swollen, red cheeks. The old marshal climbed heavily to his feet, engulfed his daughter in his arms, and bawled as he held her, rocking her from side to side.

"It's all right, Papa," Colter heard her say as she wrapped her arms around her father's thick waist. "None of the bullets hit me."

Dunbar continued to rock her in his arms and bawl.

As he did, Victoria glanced at Colter. Her face was pale, blue eyes stricken, faintly incriminating.

Colter turned and, numbly reloading his pistols, headed for the livery barn. He crossed the main street and stuffed his second, freshly loaded pistol down behind his cartridge belt. As he turned down the side street, he saw Sarah standing out in front of the livery barn. She stared toward him, her wide eyes bright with fear. As Colter continued walking toward her, she sobbed in relief, her shoulders jerking, and she covered her mouth with her hand.

Colter stopped before her, looked into her eyes. She said nothing. There was nothing more for either one of them to say. Her lips quivered as she silently sobbed. Colter wrapped his arms around her, drawing her toward him, hugging her.

Sarah buried her face in his chest, hugging him back.

Colter pulled away from her, stepped around her, and walked into the barn. It took him only a few minutes to saddle Northwest. He swung into the saddle. Sarah stood in the open doorway, looking toward him. She'd stopped sobbing, but tears stained her flushed cheeks. Her eyes were pain-racked.

Colter rode Northwest up to her and stopped. "Good-bye, Sarah."

She sniffed, brushed her wrist across her left cheek. "You take care, Colter."

"You, too."

Feeling empty, he rode out of the barn, down the side street, and turned the corner, heading west. He'd have more men after him soon. Many more.

As Northwest's hooves clomped on the trail, Colter looked around. It was still early on a bright mountain morning. He could get a good ways down the trail by nightfall.

ABOUT THE AUTHOR

Peter Brandvold has penned more than seventy fast-action Westerns under his own name and his pen name, **Frank Leslie**. He is the author of the ever-popular .45-Caliber books featuring Cuno Massey as well as the Lou Prophet and Yakima Henry novels. Recently, Berkley published his horror/Western, *Dust of the Damned*, featuring ghoul hunter Uriah Zane. Head honcho at "Mean Pete Publishing," publisher of harrowing pulp Western and horror e-books, he lives with his dogs in Colorado.

CONNECT ONLINE

www.peterbrandvold.com
www.peterbrandvold.blogspot.com

Also available from

Frank Leslie

DEAD MAN'S TRAIL

When Yakima Henry is attacked by desperados, a mysterious gunman sends the thieves running. But when Yakima goes to thank his savior, he's found dead—with a large poke of gold amongst his gear.

THE BELLS OF EL DIABLO

A pair of Confederate soldiers go AWOL and head for Denver, where a tale of treasure in Mexico takes them on an adventure.

THE LAST RIDE OF JED STRANGE

Colter Farrow is forced to kill a soldier in self-defense, sending him to Mexico where he helps the wild Bethel Strange find her missing father. But there's an outlaw on their trail, and the next ones to go missing just might be them...

DEAD RIVER KILLER

Bad luck has driven Yakima Henry into the town of Dead River during a severe mountain winter—where Yakima must weather a killer who's hell-bent on making the town as dead as its name.

REVENGE AT HATCHET CREEK

Yakima Henry has been ambushed and badly injured. Luckily, Aubrey Coffin drags him to safety—but as he heals, lawless desperados circle closer to finish the job...

BULLET FOR A HALF-BREED

Yakima Henry won't tolerate incivility toward a lady, especially the former widow Beth Holgate. If her new husband won't stop giving her hell, Yakima may make her a widow all over again.

Available wherever books are sold or at
penguin.com

National Bestselling Author

RALPH COMPTON

THE BLOODY TRAIL
SHADOW OF THE GUN
DEATH OF A BAD MAN
RIDE THE HARD TRAIL
BLOOD ON THE GALLOWS
THE CONVICT TRAIL
RAWHIDE FLAT
THE BORDER EMPIRE
THE MAN FROM NOWHERE
SIXGUNS AND DOUBLE EAGLES
BOUNTY HUNTER
FATAL JUSTICE
STRYKER'S REVENGE
DEATH OF A HANGMAN
NORTH TO THE SALT FORK
DEATH RIDES A CHESTNUT MARE
RUSTED TIN
THE BURNING RANGE
WHISKEY RIVER
THE LAST MANHUNT
THE AMARILLO TRAIL
SKELETON LODE
STRANGER FROM ABILENE
THE SHADOW OF A NOOSE
THE GHOST OF APACHE CREEK
RIDERS OF JUDGMENT
SLAUGHTER CANYON
DEAD MAN'S RANCH
ONE MAN'S FIRE
THE OMAHA TRAIL
DOWN ON GILA RIVER
BRIMSTONE TRAIL

**Available wherever books are sold or at
penguin.com**